Dear Reader,

They say that people are the same all over. Whether it's a small village on the sea, a mining town nestled in the mountains, or a whistle-stop along the Western plains, we all share the same hopes and dreams. We work, we play, we laugh, we cry—and, of course, we fall in love . . .

It is this universal experience that we at Jove Books have tried to capture in a heartwarming series of novels. We've asked our most gifted authors to write their own story of American romance, set in a town as distinct and vivid as the people who live there. Each writer chose a special time and place close to their hearts. They filled the towns with charming, unforgettable characters—then added that spark of romance. We think you'll find the combination absolutely delightful.

You might even recognize *your* town. Because true love lives in *every* town . . .

Welcome to *Our Town*.

Sincerely,

Leslie Ge

Leslie Gelbma
Editor-in-Chie

OUR·TOWN

SUGAR AND SPICE

DeWanna Pace

J

JOVE BOOKS, NEW YORK

SUGAR AND SPICE

A Jove Book / published by arrangement with
the author

PRINTING HISTORY
Jove edition / November 1996

The Putnam Berkley World Wide Web site address is
http://www.berkley.com/berkley

ISBN: 0-515-11970-9

A JOVE BOOK®
Jove Books are published by The Berkley Publishing Group,
200 Madison Avenue, New York, New York 10016.
JOVE and the "J" design are trademarks
belonging to Jove Publications, Inc.

PRINTED IN THE UNITED STATES OF AMERICA

10 9 8 7 6 5 4 3 2 1

*This novel is dedicated to those wonderful
writers in my current critique group.*

*Jenny Archer, Kim Campbell, Joni Carlile, Susan Collier,
Bruce Edwards, Loretta Harrison, Bill Ice, Ed Jones,
Jodi Koumalats, Kate McHugh, Vera Sharp, Karen Smith,
Ronda Thompson, Pamela Waddell,
and Brendan Wimberly.*

*Secondly, to Jean Price, my agent. Thanks for
believing in me and being the most
author-friendly agent in the business.*

*To Gail Fortune, my editor.
Thanks for helping me hone my talent.*

And finally, to the Williams/Pace clans:

*Doris, Eddie, Karen,
Jimmy, Teresa, Tommy,
Roy, Dionne,
and myself.*

Survivors, one and all.

You're all the keeping kind.

❖ *Prologue* ❖

May 1886

RACHEL SLOAN HEARD the exasperated intake of breath above her. Just as she glanced up from the hemming to see if she had accidentally stuck her employer with a pin, the distressed woman thrust the letter she'd been reading aloud toward her. Rachel ducked so she wouldn't be hit.

"Will you look at this?" Joanna Tharp's cheeks paled from a slight shade of pink to death white. "He's coming here . . . to Richmond! He'll ruin everything!"

"Ben?" Anticipation filled Rachel as she rose from bent knees and read the rest of the letter. She carefully folded the pages and placed them in her skirt pocket, to save until a time when she would be alone and could treasure every word. It seemed she would finally get to meet the businessman who had written all those engaging missives and, unknowingly, shared his dreams with her.

"All that bending over has addled your brain, Rachel. Of course I mean Ben." Joanna took a position in front of the dresser and pinched her cheeks to help them regain their color. She turned this way and that, sucking in her stomach. "Who else but kind, hardworking, *persistent* Ben McGuire would wait until harvest is over, and the townspeople can catch their accounts up-to-date, before he'll do something for himself? He's such a . . . a . . . Samaritan.''

"Aren't you just a tiny bit thrilled he loves you enough to give up his *home* to be with you?'' Rachel stood behind her employer, readjusting the bow at the back of the red taffeta gown she'd been hemming most of the afternoon. The bow needed to be slightly larger to have the slimming effect she hoped would hide Joanna's recently expanding waistline. "Most men would have given up the courtship long ago.''

Rachel recalled every one of the letters Ben had written throughout the past seven years—years spent building the dreams he and Joanna had planned during their earlier court- ship . . . years spent loving the girl Joanna must have once been. Sympathy stirred Rachel's heart. The Ben McGuire she'd come to know through the strong, bold handwriting had a surprise in store for him if he believed Joanna Tharp was the same woman who had left Valiant, Texas, at age fifteen.

A smile curved Joanna's lips as she sighed. "There is something endearing about having a man who pines his life away for me.''

But the smile quickly faded and Joanna's dark brows veed as she glared at Rachel through the mirror. "Oh, now, see what you've got me doing? I should have never let you read those letters. You've been moonstruck over him ever since—''

"*Let* me?'' Rachel scolded gently as she remembered the circumstances that demanded she invade Ben's privacy, a decision that made her feel uneasy even now. She deliber- ately tied the bow tighter around Joanna's waist and made her suck in deeper. "I believe you *insisted* that I read them. . . . Remember? Back in February, when you thought Daniel might ask me to marry him.''

Joanna laughed and turned, her ebony ringlets bobbing as

she enthusiastically nodded. "You mean when I said if you didn't read them, I'd tell Daniel that you were my twin and that Sam was your son and not my own."

"Yes, then." Rachel busied herself with gathering her sewing instruments so she wouldn't have to look at the hauteur on her employer's face. Let the woman think her ploy had worked, because Rachel didn't want anyone believing she was an unmarried mother; Rachel knew the truth. She hadn't wanted Joanna's six-year-old son used as a threat. It seemed sad enough that the child was constantly sent away to boarding school to keep him from interfering with his mother's social life, much less be used in her latest mischief. She, personally, always enjoyed the brief moments Sam was at home.

"That's the whole point"—Joanna let the gown drop to her ankles—"you'll never be more than a seamstress if you don't learn how easy it is to keep a man willing to satisfy your every whim. I've told you before, that's the quickest way to move above your station."

Though her employer's reasoning was wrong, Rachel silently admitted she had actually gained by complying with Joanna's demands. She now possessed a deep, abiding respect for the man who wrote the letters. "I can hardly wait to meet him."

Green eyes focused on Rachel, examining her from head to hem. After an ensuing silence that became increasingly uncomfortable, Rachel discovered what was on Joanna's mind.

"You will meet him"—Joanna's hands raised Rachel's waist-length hair to her crown—"but on his own grounds. Cut a few inches off the back and sweep it up in curls and you'll look just like me. He'll never know the difference."

"No, no, no, no, no." Rachel moved away from Joanna,

suspecting she was about to become part of her employer's scheme of the week.

"But why not?" Joanna's balled fists rested at her hips. "I hired you because we look so much alike. Look at us"— she waited until Rachel stared in the mirror at the two of them—"same black hair, green eyes. Same height, and we're both slender."

I'm slimmer and younger than you, Rachel silently countered, though their similarities were disturbing. Being such a look-alike to Joanna had proven helpful when her employer tired of the endless fittings and hemmings necessary to keep her title as Richmond's best-dressed belle. Standing in for a dress fitting was one thing, but pretending she was Joanna was out of the question!

Realizing exactly *all* that her employer said, Rachel demanded, "What do you mean, *on his own grounds*? Why are you so afraid he'll move to Richmond?"

"I'm not afraid. I just regret giving him false hope through the years." Joanna opened her armoire and loudly searched through the dresses. "I really don't have time to spare. You know how busy my social calendar is this summer."

Rachel knew better. The woman had another reason for not wanting him there. Joanna had a nasty habit of tapping her foot when she lied, almost as if she were impatient for the listener to believe her.

Rachel moved alongside her and lifted out a crimson tea gown. "Here, your fan and brooch will look lovely with this, don't you think?"

Flashing her an appreciative smile, Joanna accepted the choice and allowed Rachel to help her into it. "You know me so well, Rachel."

"Well enough to realize you've got another reason for not wanting Ben to come to Richmond."

Surprisingly, Joanna turned and gently grabbed Rachel's wrist. "Can I confide in you?"

Rachel stared back at her, seeing scorn for the first time in her employer's eyes. "Only you can answer that, Joanna. It depends on whether or not you trust me."

"I have to trust you. You're my only hope." Joanna began to pace, as if searching for words. Finally she stopped and faced Rachel. "Ben McGuire knows something about me no one else does. If I make him angry, he might decide to tell someone I'd rather not know about this particular secret...."

Rachel wondered if the secret was what she'd always suspected but Joanna had never admitted to—that Sam was Ben's son. The boy was as good-natured as Ben seemed to be.

Joanna breathed a sigh of relief, as if she'd cleared up everything instead of being deliberately vague. "It doesn't matter who discovers this secret in Valiant; I don't have to live there anymore, and it would only hurt Ben. But *here* in Richmond, well, let's just say that *I* would suffer greatly. That's why you must go to Valiant in my stead, so Ben won't sell his general store and come here."

Joanna rushed over and opened her reticule, spilling its contents onto the top of the dresser. She lifted several bills. "Name your price. Or better yet, let me pay the ticket to Texas and give you enough funds to play the role extravagantly. You can have last year's wardrobe; I won't donate it to charity as I'd planned. And you can use our home. Tharp House is one of the finest in all Valiant. Ben has seen to its care since we left."

Her tone seduced, beguiled. "Harvest isn't until the end of August, possibly the first week of September, depending on the weather. Imagine having three months to be rich and pampered and courted. Your position here will be waiting for your return in September, just in time to get my new

Christmas wardrobe under way. All you'll have to do in exchange is stay for the summer, allow Ben to woo you, then break off the courtship gently so he won't be angry.''

It sounded so simple. Overwhelmed by the abundance of possibilities, Rachel contemplated all she'd been offered. An expense-paid journey. Clothes and money to play the part. But most important, a home of her own for three months. Temptation dangled in front of her like a piñata waiting to shower her with gifts. But her conscience crept in and burst the fantasy, reminding Rachel that if she accepted, she would not only get to meet Ben, but have to lie to him as well.

Rachel searched for an easy way out of the situation. "I don't think I can convince him I'm you. You're more''— she forced the words out, reminding herself they were for her own good—"beautiful than I.''

Motioning for Rachel to turn completely around so she could view her fully, Joanna announced, "Well, that may be true, but you're pretty in your own way. Besides, he'll hardly expect me to be the same person after seven years.''

"I can't.'' Rachel's chin rose in defiance. It was the first time she'd ever deliberately set herself against Joanna. "I won't.''

"*Won't* is such a final word, Miss Sloan.'' Joanna's eyes narrowed into emerald slits. "Perhaps you'd better think about this overnight. Mother and Father wield a lot of power here in Richmond—''

You mean you *do,* Rachel added silently.

"—and might make it difficult for one of their former employees to work anywhere in this city . . . no, in the *East* . . . ever again.''

You mean you'll *see to it I won't.*

"That is, if they thought that employee wouldn't do any-thing within her power to help the family during a crisis situation. And this is a crisis. They might even feel compelled to stretch the truth as to the reason the employee left their household.''

Which means you'll *tell everyone I stole from you or something far worse.* Having been on the ragged edge of hunger before and vowing never to be so again, Rachel dared not take Joanna's threat lightly. This wasn't the first time she'd angered a socialite and was forced to move on; it probably wouldn't be the last. But Richmond had its appeal and steady employment. The one obstacle standing in the way of enjoying the offer and appeasing her employer was that Ben didn't deserve what was being planned for him. He was guilty only of loving Joanna Tharp and, perhaps, being a dreamer. If only she *dared* meet him.

''Tell you what I'll do,'' Rachel finally relented, ''I'll think about it overnight and let you know in the morning. But I'm making no promises.''

Joanna's eyes widened as triumph filled their depths. ''I told Mother and Father you'd be loyal. Don't disappoint them.''

Rachel averted her attention from Joanna and stared at her own reflection in the mirror. ''It's me I'm afraid I'll disappoint.''

''You really think I should?'' Surprised, Rachel couldn't help but feel pleased by the young soldier's declaration.

He quit rocking the porch swing and turned toward her, his expression earnest. ''Everybody needs a home once in her life . . . even you, Rachel Sloan. Living with the Tharps can't be all that wonderful, can it?''

She peered at the amber glow radiating from the fine homes that lined Windsor Street and shook her head. ''It'll do until I can afford one of my own. And, at least, everything's clean and warm.''

Daniel took her hands and squeezed them gently. ''Look,

you know I'm here only for a few more days before I have to return to the capital. I'd like to know you're doing something exciting too. Why not pretend to be Joanna Tharp for a while and enjoy some of the privileges she mentioned?''

He offered a reassuring smile. ''This Ben fellow sounds like a decent sort and deserves a bit of time to court the woman he loves. You can waylay any advances and tell him you need time to get to know him again. At the end of summer, bid him farewell and tell him you can't marry him because you're in love with someone else. Then he'll be free to love another.''

The dark-haired soldier lifted her gloved hand to his lips and lightly brushed her knuckles with a kiss. ''You could always marry me, but then, we both know I'm married to the army. So why not do something noble for someone who deserves it. Make Ben happy for three months.''

Rachel heard the clearing of Thadeus Tharp's throat and recognized the signal that it was time she and Dan call it a night. ''Guess I'd better be going in now. Thanks for listening.''

Daniel leaned over and kissed her lightly on the cheek. ''I hope this is good-bye instead of just good night, Rachel.'' He yawned. ''Next time I see you, I want you to be able to sew buckskin and buffalo hide with the best of them.''

''Oh, Valiant's not one of those wild and woolly places. It's settled,'' Rachel informed him. ''Just like my decision.''

Her mind, indeed, had been made up from the moment Daniel had convinced her that Ben might actually benefit from, rather than be a victim of, the deception.

Now all she had to do was convince Ben McGuire she was Joanna.

◆ 1 ◆

THE EARLY JUNE evening offered a cool breeze to the crowd waiting at the depot for the 5:50 train. Speculation rippled through the group as many voiced their opinions on whether or not Stamp Kincaid could drive it in as early as he'd promised.

Just as Ben McGuire pulled out his timepiece and opened it to check the hour, the planked boards of the depot's landing quivered beneath his boots. He quickly snapped the cover shut and searched the quarter-mile of eastern track for sign of Jimmy. The thirteen-year-old raced into view, waving his hands and running toward town.

"Stampede's kept his word," a voice complimented.

"Ten minutes to spare," informed someone else.

A hand patted Ben's back, then another, and another. He nodded his thanks, half listening to the well-wishes from the townsfolk of Valiant. The string tie around his neck felt suddenly tighter as he swallowed hard to clear his throat. One boot top went to the back of his calf, then the other to make sure they were polished adequately. The white shirt and black trousers fit him perfectly, he'd seen to that, but there was nothing he could do about the seven years' difference in his face.

"There she blows!" Nash Turner hollered.

Just as Ben's eyes focused where the blacksmith's finger pointed, he saw the puffs of smoke and heard the incoming steam whistle that heralded the arrival of happiness into his life once more.

"Isn't it romantic?" a feminine voice broke with emotion beside him. "Oh, I promised myself I wouldn't do this. I'll stain my—"

"Allow me, Clementine." Ben pulled the freshly ironed handkerchief from his pocket and handed it to the dress-maker.

"Oh, you shouldn't, Ben." Though the freckle-faced woman protested, Clementine grabbed the offering and quickly dabbed her eyes. "*She* might need it."

"Joanna always carries one of her own," Ben assured her, removing his Stetson and dusting it against his thigh before settling the hat back on his fair hair.

The cowcatcher sped toward the depot, angling steam and dust behind it. Children squealed with delight as great billows of steam puffed and flushed them from the buffalo grass along either side of the tracks. The Ladies Temperance Band struck up a lively tune as the engine ground to a halt in a cacophony of slamming iron and hissing steam.

Ben unfastened two buttons on his double-breasted shirt and gently pulled out the lace handkerchief he'd kept next to his heart since waking that morning. Holding it up to his nose, he breathed in and believed he could almost smell the honeyed fragrance of Joanna. But, of course, he couldn't. He'd wiped away the tears that had stained them the night she left Valiant, then placed the handkerchief in his safe and dreamed of her ever since.

Stamp Kincaid stepped from the engine onto the platform and shouted to the exiting passengers, "Welcome to Valiant, biggest little settlement in the Texas Panhandle! West of

Wichita Falls, east of Albuquerque, north of El Paso, and south of Indian territory. Soon as we take on water at the Wild Horse, all aboard for Albuquerque.''

Ben searched each face that exited the train, impatient as a family of nine took their time setting baggage and belongings on the platform. When a lacy parasol came into view behind the family and opened, a collective hush fell over the crowd. The band stopped playing. Ben took a step forward. It seemed the whole crowd took it with him, and he could feel their curiosity as if it were a living current pushing him toward her.

Though lovely, the woman shaded beneath the parasol was fair-haired and blue-eyed . . . definitely not Joanna. A smile lifted her lips and her gaze settled on Ben in obvious approval. Disappointment filled him as he tipped his hat to bid her welcome, then quickly awaited the next passenger to disembark.

Immediately, his mood turned sour. Of all times for *Sterling* to come home. He watched as the bearded politician in the top hat and frock coat waved to the crowd like a returning hero. Though ten years Ben's senior, the gray-haired man still cut a dapper figure. A long-held grudge crept up to consume Ben as he wondered if Sterling Whipple and Joanna had traveled together purposely.

The temperance band struck up its tune once more, forcing Ben's attention away from Sterling and to the beautiful creature exiting behind him. *Joanna!*

Like a man too long without food, Ben feasted upon her loveliness. Though Joanna's dark, shiny hair was swept back in her favorite ringlets, she wore it longer than he remembered. Seven years and motherhood had better defined her comely figure and enhanced her beauty, giving character to a face he'd once thought delicate.

But when she turned and peered out into the crowd, Ben's

heart slammed against his chest. Never in all his dreams had
he remembered her eyes being such a deep shade of green—
as if a painter had added midnight to their depths.

God, how he wished he and Joanna were alone and
Sterling Whipple were miles away. Suddenly he felt tongue-
tied, afraid he might say the wrong thing and cause Joanna
to leave again, all the while wondering which words might
convince her to stay. All her telegram said was that she
planned to visit for a while. She'd made no promises to settle
here.

You're not seventeen anymore, Ben McGuire. He forced
himself to move toward her. *And you've got everything to
offer her this time except patience.*

"Joanna! Over here." When Ben waved to her, the band's
tune surged in volume and the crowd cheered.

Sterling Whipple lifted his hat and waved back, his face
beaming with pleasure. "My fellow constituents, what a
pleasant sur—"

"Excuse me, sir," Joanna shouted above the din, "but I
didn't want to hit you with this carpetbag and there doesn't
seem to be much room to get by. There's someone calling
for me. I'm sorry to trouble you."

The politician turned and looked at her, his eyes widening
into saucer-shaped obsidian. He backed against the railing as
if she were a red-hot coal too close for comfort, his face
draining of color. "No trouble at all, Miss Tharp. What a
p-pleasure it is to see you again."

Ben noticed Sterling's surprised expression and almost
laughed at the man's distress. They may have traveled on
the same train, but the lack of recognition in Joanna's eyes
revealed she barely remembered the politician. What a blow
that must be to the conceited man, and how ironic, since
Sterling was one of the reasons she'd left.

The crowd parted to allow Ben a direct path to the railing.

He reached out a hand to help her step off the car and onto the platform. "May I be of assistance?"

"Ben?"

The sound of his name upon her lips as those glorious green eyes looked up into his made Ben stare transfixed at the woman before him. Had it been so long, she'd forgotten him too? No . . . the smile of welcome as she returned his stare said she was glad to see him. After he took her carpetbag and set it down, he became aware that she'd said something else. "I'm sorry"—Ben blinked away the hundred memories she conjured and concentrated on the reality in front of him—"I didn't hear you."

He pointed toward the band and blamed his lack of concentration on the exuberance of the temperance ladies. "The noise."

Joanna held out her hand, her lashes brushing against her cheeks as she shouted back, "I said, thank you. I'd be honored."

Their fingers threaded, then locked. She easily followed his lead and stepped clear of the train. The momentum brought them face-to-face, their bodies almost touching. Ben knew propriety required that he move back and give her more room, but for just this one moment, propriety be damned!

He took off his Stetson and allowed his gaze to sweep her from the ostrich-feathered bonnet, past the becoming flare of her serge travel suit, to the impracticality of her Moroccan slippers. A jolt of attraction blazed through him, so strong his boots rocked backward and he had to widen his stance to rebalance himself.

She was everything he'd dreamed of, yet somehow different . . . magnificently more.

Had he noticed the difference? Rachel wondered, reeling under the sensations ignited by his close examination. She thought for a moment she wouldn't be able to breathe if he didn't let go of her hand and step back, giving her room to regain her equilibrium. But to her dismay, he didn't move, and she found herself looking up into a rugged handsomeness that surprised her. For some reason, she imagined anyone that kind and good had to be uglier than sin, or else why would Joanna leave him?

But this was an easy-to-look-at face, full of adoration, kindness . . . and trust. Guilt twisted inside her.

Though he only stared, Ben's gaze left a heated backtrail everywhere it surveyed. The approval shining in the morning-glory-blue of his eyes forced a shiver down from the top of Rachel's head to pool into a thousand tingles at the base of her spine.

Six feet two inches of solid muscle was a far cry from the "boy" Joanna had described. Blond-headed Ben McGuire had become a man of immense shoulder span that veed sharply to a slender waist, then flared to work-hardened thighs. Power exuded from him like a natural perfume, tempting her to reach out and test its ripple beneath her touch. Rachel knew beyond a shadow of a doubt she'd gotten herself into major trouble this time. He was handsome to a fault.

She was so fascinated by the man's mere presence, Rachel realized too late his face was bending toward hers. He was going to kiss her! For the hundredth time since leaving Richmond, she wished Joanna hadn't been so vague about the intimacy of her and Ben's courtship.

Ben's face went right on by as he stooped to pick up Rachel's carpetbag. "I'll grab this one, and Jimmy can get any others you have."

Rachel's heartbeat pulsed in her throat. She was relieved yet strangely disappointed. Disappointed that she'd wondered what it would be like to kiss him. Disappointed that he hadn't defied propriety and kissed her in front of everyone!

A gangly, brown-eyed boy leapt onto the platform, all out of breath. "Got any baggage, lady?"

"Forget something, Jim?" Ben reminded the boy softly, thumbing the air above his head. "And her name is Miss Tharp."

Jimmy grabbed his slouch hat and swiftly let it slide off into his fist. He slung his brown hair to one side to get it out of his eyes. "Ben's trying to teach me manners, ma'am. I ain't had much before, so they don't come easy for me like most other folks."

"This is my thirteen-year-old son, Jimmy Don," Ben said by way of introduction. "I hope you two will spend some time getting to know one another."

"His newly *adopted* son," Jimmy corrected Ben in a sullen tone. "Guess your belongings are still aboard?"

Sam has a brother. He'll be excited. Rachel almost spoke the words aloud, then realized Ben had kept Jimmy a secret from Joanna. "Adopted?"

"He's a McGuire now."

What wasn't being said was as powerful as what had been. Ben would treat him no less than a blood son, but Rachel suspected that meant something different to the two of them. Feeling the tension between the pair, she decided to ask more about the adoption later. Rachel informed them that the trunks were in the baggage car, marked with her name.

"Take them to Tharp House, will you, Jim?" Ben lifted a key from his pocket and handed it to the boy. "And remember to lock up after you leave. You never know what kind of scavenger might wander in."

Father's and son's gazes locked for only an instant, but an instant that made Rachel wonder what hidden message had passed between them.

A bald man moved up through the crowd, followed closely by a full-figured woman dressed in white from her high-necked collar to the lace-bordering hem. Though she used a cane, no disability hindered her movements. With a wave of the ivory-handled walking stick, the band ceased playing and the crowd quieted.

The man offered his hand to Rachel. She wasn't sure of the proper etiquette, but he quickly relieved her of the decision. The stranger lifted Rachel's hand and gently brushed a light kiss over her gloved knuckles. His hazel eyes offered a welcome as genuine as his words.

"Pleased to have you here in Valiant, Miss Tharp. My name's Nash Turner, and I'm the local smithy most days. Undertaker, occasionally. You probably won't be needing my services—shoeing and nailing, I mean—'cause Ben here has pretty much kept your place in top form."

"A pleasure to meet you, Mr. Turner." Rachel nodded a greeting, then became aware of a set of yellow-gray eyes staring holes through her. Pure malevolence radiated from the woman in white who had silenced the crowd and now glared at Rachel's hand, her painted lips pursed into a grim line.

Realizing the woman must lay claim to the man in some manner, Rachel quickly freed her hand, letting it fall to one side. The last thing she needed was for someone to think Joanna was there to steal anyone's heart but Ben's! If looks could melt, her kid glove would have been a leather puddle.

"You remember Ophelia"—Ben tried to ward off the animosity—"Miss Finck now owns the Lazy Lady Saloon."

Nash stepped out of the way so Ophelia could move forward.

"Thank you, Nash." The saloonkeeper eyed the smithy, then focused her regard on Rachel. "Of course Miss Tharp remembers me. We know each other almost too well . . . don't we, dear?"

The underlying threat in the woman's tone was clear. Apparently, there was no love lost between Ophelia Finck and Joanna Tharp, and lots of history. Rachel made a mental note to stay as far away from this woman as possible or to somehow mend the fence that separated them. "I'm looking forward to getting reacquainted, Miss Finck. I remember so little about Valiant." Though she knew better, something inside Rachel couldn't let the challenge go unanswered. She wouldn't be bullied no matter what her identity was for the summer. "Or about you."

Nash spoke up, "Oh, anything you want to know, just ask Ophel—"

His mouth clamped shut, and he looked as if he'd swallowed something sour.

"What Mr. Turner means to say is that I make it my business to stay informed about all that goes on in Valiant, and have for several years." Ophelia eyed Sterling Whipple with obvious disapproval. "*Somebody* around here has to keep an eye on the pulse of the populace." She aimed her wolf-colored gaze at Rachel and announced, "Anything you find difficult to recall, just ask. I'm sure between the two of us, we'll be able to restore your *memory* . . . if nothing else."

"Feels a bit chilly, wouldn't you say?" Ben whispered at Rachel's side.

"Blue norther might describe it adequately," Rachel replied, despite the warm wind wafting through the depot's gabled porch. So, Ophelia's icy regard wasn't her imagination, after all. Ben felt it too. Rachel eyed the crowd, aware that several people leaned over others to hear the conversation between her and Ophelia.

"All aboard for Albuquerque!" the conductor yelled.

A collective gasp rippled over the startled gathering. Rachel thought she sucked in at least a gallon of steam. Her heart hammered in her chest and she was forced to grab Ben for support.

"Are you all right?" Concern filled his face as his hand reached out to steady her.

It was a bronze face, with a strong jaw, prominent cheekbones, and a wide, firm mouth. Laugh lines bracketed his mouth, indicating he was a man who laughed and smiled often. His sandy brows grew in an inverted V, giving his face an amused expression that added character to the image she'd drawn from his letters. An older version of Sam?

Though meant as a kindness, his touch sent waves of warmth radiating through Rachel. She fought the impulse to throw her arms around his neck and explore the pleasant sensations further, but decided that wouldn't be the best of ideas. Whatever Joanna's reputation in this town, Rachel doubted it needed any more tarnishing.

Everything started to close in on her—the heat, the people, Ben's nearness. She felt trapped, as if she were a cherished bird in a gilded cage. "Could we be going now? I'm afraid the heat is a bit much after the long ride."

Ben urged her away from the engine that was building a full head of steam. "Of course. Would you prefer to ride or walk?"

Before she had time to think, Rachel asked, "You mean it's close enough that we can walk?"

Puzzlement filled his blue eyes. "It *has* been too long, Joanna. Your home is a street away from Main. Near the Whipples and the Harringtons. I thought you might enjoy the walk since you'd been riding so long."

Rachel tried to hide her blunder. "Walking will be fine." The jaunt would allow her to become familiar with the town's layout, give her time to resist the impulse to hop the next train back to Virginia, and hopefully work off a little of the steam Ben had created within her.

❖ 2 ❖

THOUGH THE TEXAS sun was warm, promising an even hotter summer than Joanna had predicted, Rachel's spirits lifted as Ben escorted her up Main Street. She'd expected the same arid plains and mesquite, dotted with ocotilla and prickly pear, that filled most of the Texas High Plains. Instead, gentle sloping hills banked the west side of town and rose fertile and green near the lake the conductor had called Wild Horse.

"A lot of our businesses are bricked," Ben said, motioning as they passed several that had raised and planked sidewalks as well.

"It's all so lovely." She strained one way and then another for fear she'd miss seeing something. Valiant had most of the businesses any good-sized settlement offered: hotel, restaurants, livery, boarding- and bathhouses, telegraph office. "Why, you even have an opera house!" she exclaimed.

The town was living up to its name . . . making a valiant effort to bring civilization to the Texas Panhandle.

Murmurs swept through the crowd that followed behind them, drawing her attention away from the multitude of businesses to the strange procession.

"Does every newcomer who comes to Valiant get met at

the train by everyone in town?'' She felt like a mother goose leading a gaggle of ducklings.

Ben laughed, the lines around his eyes crinkling. ''No, only the founder's daughter.''

''Oh.'' That's just great. Now she had to be not only Joanna but civic-minded as well. ''Are they always this easily led?''

Ben leaned closer. ''No. Come Saturday night, it'll be like the parting of the Red Sea. Half are willing sinners, the other self-professed saints. The one thing that binds them is curiosity. But you know that. Nothing's changed since you left except we've spit-polished our businesses and homes a bit. You can thank your Mr. Whipple for that. He's head of the 'beautify Valiant' committee.''

My Mr. Whipple? Better make a point of finding out who this fellow is and why Ben dislikes him so. That was the second time Ben had mentioned the man's name, and with bitter control.

''Which are you, Ben?'' She changed the subject for fear he might ask her something about this Whipple acquaintance. ''Sinner or saint?''

''Guess I've had my stint at being a saint. I might just try the alternative for a while. Which do you prefer now, Joanna? Demon or deacon?''

''I think''—she glanced down one of the side streets at the picket fences and comfortable-looking cottages, elegant residences that would rival anything in Virginia—''that maybe you feel a bit of animosity toward me.''

''Nothing that can't be forgotten given certain circumstances.''

Tinny music echoed from the saloon, and a freight wagon filled with supplies was hitched in front of an overland freight company storefront. Rachel tried to focus on the vibrant purples of Indian paintbrush and sage, sunflowers and red firewheels that filled the yards and window boxes with kaleidoscopes of color. But it was the morning-glory blue of Ben's eyes that demanded her rapt attention.

"What circumstances?" she asked. But the answer was written in his eyes . . . he loved her.

"Remember the cellar of the First Baptist?"

They were approaching a solid white frame church at the end of Main Street.

Rachel didn't know what to say, so she stared at the cottonwood trees flickering in the wind, their greenish-silver leaves offering shade to cool the fierce Texas sun. Maybe he would think she was recalling memories and wouldn't ask her to supply them. But no such luck. He stared at her intently, unnerving her. *Think fast, Rachel,* she told herself. Relief filled her as she decided upon answering his question with one of her own: "Which time are you thinking of?"

Ben chuckled. "You always were evasive. I see some things are the same." His tone became a whisper. "I'll give you a hint. It had to do with our first kiss."

They'd kissed in church? Rachel's heart fluttered as if it had taken on wings. "How could I ever forget?"

"You don't remember, do you?"

Though his tone teased, she saw hurt in his eyes. "Of course I remember," she lied softly, unwilling to further harm the man Joanna had discarded so carelessly.

"Good," he said earnestly. "Because at some point during your visit, I plan to repeat it."

It wasn't a threat, nor even a challenge, but a stated fact. Ben McGuire, she'd learned through his letters, accomplished anything he set his mind to, and there was no doubt in Rachel's mind that he would see the kissing was done and done well.

Feeling herself sinking into deeper trouble with each step closer to Tharp House, Rachel wondered if pretending to be Joanna was such a wise decision no matter how honorable her motivations. After all, it would have to be an extremely beautiful home to be worth all this trouble.

Just as the thought entered her mind, they turned the corner and came to a halt in front of a wide-verandaed house whose columns rose to its second story.

"There it is. Seven years older, but no worse for the wear."

Rainbow rows of flowers and shrubbery grew in front of the house, along the picket fence that surrounded the front-yard, and in the garden that grew on one side. As they reached the gate emblazoned with an elaborate old English T and H design, Ben swung it open.

Jimmy waited on the steps, sitting next to a dog that looked half wolf, half hound. When Rachel followed Ben, both boy and dog looked up. Jimmy scowled and the mutt growled.

"Quiet, Bowie"—Ben patted his leg and gave the dog a low whistle—"this is a friend."

Jimmy rose, wiping his grubby hands on the seat of his overalls, and came toward them. "Locked up, but thought I'd better stay close so you two could get in." He dug into his pocket and offered Rachel the key.

Weary, Rachel couldn't wait to be alone as quickly as possible. She needed a reprieve from having people breathe down her neck, their curiosity as stifling as the heat. Nor did she care at that moment why Ben and his son were so uneasy in each other's company. But the one thing she did not want was to make contact with the young man's dirty hand that was reaching toward the only clean white kid gloves she possessed. What had he been doing to get them so filthy?

She stripped off one glove and accepted the key, offering the boy a smile. "Thanks for your trouble, Jimmy. And to you, Ben." She reached out and gently tugged her carpetbag from his grasp. "If you'll forgive me, I think I'll go in and get settled. Perhaps tomorrow I'll be refreshed enough to thank you all properly.''

The crowd began to disperse, wishing her well. Several issued offers to tea and the Ladies' Aid Society. A quilting bee would take place in a few days, and her hands would be appreciated in the undertaking.

Ben waited until all but he and Jimmy remained. "I'll see you in about an hour and a half, Joanna. Then I'll take you to supper at Delaney's.''

Her protest met with no success.

"You shouldn't have to fend for yourself on your first night. There's a bath waiting for you. Jim kept the water hot until it was time to watch for your five-fifty train. It's probably had enough time to cool off."

"It seems I owe you several kindnesses, Jimmy." Rachel walked up the steps before she realized Bowie was the meanest-looking creature this side of the Mason-Dixon line, and he definitely didn't approve of her yet. He barked sharply, and she backed hastily down the steps, looking at the brown-eyed boy for help.

Jimmy addressed the wolf-dog in prompt and strong tones. "Bowie, old fella. I toldja she ain't no enemy. Now, you lie down there and swallow your temper, or she's gonna kick you offa your favorite porch."

Bowie grumbled in his throat, cast Rachel an estimating look, then finally lay down directly in her path. She would have laughed and tiptoed around him cautiously if he didn't look so determined to have his way.

"He won't hurt you." Ben bent and lifted the stubborn hound as if he were a mere sack of beans. "He likes everyone to think he's touchy as an old cob, don't you, boy?" When Ben scratched the beast's ears, the dog snuggled and wagged his tail.

Rachel mumbled another thank-you with one eye focused

on the dog, but Bowie only slanted his attention from Ben to Rachel as he watched her go by. She worked the key into the lock, said a quick good-bye, then let herself in.

Dropping the carpetbag onto the polished floor, she shut the door behind her and leaned backward against the oak panel. At last, she thought, breathing a sigh of relief that expelled the tension that prying eyes had stirred within her. Her own eyes remained closed as she allowed the silence to envelop her.

The smell of money filled her senses. Though this Tharp House could never compare to the more luxurious one in Richmond, no dusty cracks and crevices, no stale or mildewed carpets and curtains marred this home. Clean, fresh, rich fragrances of polished furniture made of cedar and rosewood revealed that the Tharps had never been destitute and meant to preserve their wealth wherever life took them.

Rachel assumed that when Joanna's parents moved to Richmond to oversee their newly burgeoning tobacco production, the home left behind in Valiant had been like most of those on the frontier—soddy, or clapboard at best. She'd been wrong. This family home would indeed serve the Tharps well if they ever lost their fortune back east. Precaution was the foundation of wisdom according to Thadeus.

Meeting Ben stirred old speculation within Rachel. Had the Tharps actually moved to protect the family name from gossip? Sam's birth had come surprisingly soon after they left Valiant.

Even as her senses reeled with the luxury of the home now miraculously at her disposal, an equal sense of loneliness and strangeness enveloped Rachel. There was no one to share this happiness with, no family to fill its walls. The impulse to run back to the love and safety of her childhood overwhelmed her.

But, of course, there was nothing to run back to. She could

only go ahead. Rachel blinked moisture from her eyes and crossed the hallway to the stairs rising to one side. At her left a huge parlor, ornamental and frivolous, lay in wait for her inspection. Upon further survey she discovered a library and kitchen, which she promised to explore later, when there was more time.

Rachel mounted the stairs, grateful that despite the heat outside, the house was wonderfully cool. She went past two closed doors, then spotted vapor drifting around and beneath another door. *The bath.*

The steam from the enclosed bath rushed against her face, tightening her cheeks in response as her eyes narrowed to peer into what looked like a sitting room. A tub of water sat in its center. Dipping a finger into the inviting pool, she pulled the digit out quickly, deciding that the bathwater would be perfect in a few more minutes. Hot enough to clean off the travel dust and to scrub her hair until it shone.

A search for fresh towels yielded another surprise. A piece of parchment lay atop the towels folded on the dressing table near the tub and was marked simply *Joanna.*

Rachel folded the note into her pocket for the time being and carried her carpetbag into the adjoining bedroom. Done in off-white and soft blues, the spacious boudoir offered a sense of restfulness.

Her trunks were not anywhere to be seen, so she could only assume this wasn't Joanna's bedroom. Strolling to the window facing west, Rachel looked out over the veranda roof that sloped beneath the window. She could see Ben, his son, and the dog walking up Main Street. The two-storied home gave ample view of one side of the business district . . . and if she were guessing by the way Ben worked with the door of the establishment, direct view of the general store. How convenient.

Feeling as if she were prying, Rachel turned from the sight

and noticed a small rocker with a blue cushion. It beckoned to her, invited her to rock away the tension of meeting Ben.

As she sat, the parchment in her pocket made a crinkling sound. The water needed to cool a bit more, so she decided to read the note while she waited.

Joanna,
What other little surprises do you have in store?
Don't think that being here in Valiant changes any-
thing. I'll deny the truth if anyone ever learns it.
You've become quite an actress since I saw you last.
Even I was convinced you didn't remember much. You
fooled them all. Bravo.
Remember who you're dealing with, and you'll stay
alive.

The ormolu clock sitting on the dresser chimed, nearly scaring Rachel out of her wits. She read the note a second time and then a third. The lack of signature made it all the more threatening. Whoever had written the words believed she knew who made the threat.

Though the handwriting didn't look familiar, anyone could disguise their script if they really wanted to. So any number of Joanna haters could be the culprit.

The question was how many people other than Ben and Jimmy McGuire had a key to this house?

❖ 3 ❖

ONE OF THE first things Rachel learned about Ben McGuire that she didn't already know through his letters was that he was prompt. At exactly seven-fifteen he knocked on the front door, the thirteen-year-old in tow.

"Don't you have a key?" Rachel let them in.

Puzzlement creased Ben's brow. "No, I gave it to Jim, then I saw him hand it to you earlier."

"I did give it to her," Jimmy insisted as the wolf-dog followed his master inside and heeled beside him, his tail thumping the floor. Bowie snuffled and drooled a little.

"Sure you did. I just wondered if I had the only one. I have a knack for misplacing things." She eyed the dog, deciding he would provide a way for her to guide the conversation back onto safer ground. "You did say only *three* of us were dining together?"

Ben laughed. "He'll probably eat better than the rest of us. Delaney's bulldog has her eye on Bowie, and he's just cad enough to court her for her status—lots of leftovers. Oh, I forget. You haven't met Delaney yet. He bought out the hotel and restaurant last year."

It may not have dawned on Ben what he'd said, but Rachel

found herself wondering if he had courted Joanna for *her* status.

The letters filled Rachel's mind, and she knew without asking that no man who had spent years building the life he and Joanna planned together would have continued to court her from a distance but for one reason—love. This man did not write the note she had stored away in her reticule.

She suddenly felt stifled by the house and the possibility that someone else might have access to it. "Shall we go? I'm starving."

Boy and dog jumped up together. "We were ready an hour ago."

Ben glanced at her chignon. "Your hair's still wet, and you've probably forgotten how cool our Texas nights get. You might want to wear a bonnet or a scarf."

"Right." Rachel was halfway up the stairs before remembering that she hadn't wanted to undress completely for fear whoever had written the note might be lying in wait for her in a closet or behind one of the doors.

Hence, she still wore the serge travel suit she'd changed into at Wichita Falls. The steam in the sitting room had allowed her to easily brush it clean. "Come to think of it, my hair will dry quicker if I don't wrap it up. That way I won't have to go to sleep with it wet."

Jimmy fidgeted, arching one sole like a horse with a sore shoe, and sighed elaborately.

"You'll have to excuse my son, Joanna." Ben shot the boy a stern expression. "Patience is not one of his better talents."

Bowie barked.

"Who asked you?" Jimmy snarled back.

Bowie sighed too. Ben laughed, and Rachel joined him, needing the laughter to hide her growing discomfort.

* * *

"Why is everyone looking at me?" Rachel eyed Ben over her water goblet. "Especially the women?"

Ben dabbed his mouth with a linen kerchief and placed it next to his plate. "They want to know if we're going to resume our courtship."

"Yeah, 'cause they all got their pantaloons twisted up in knots over Ben, and he won't have a thing to do with none of them," Jim informed Rachel around a mouthful of sourdough biscuit. " 'Cause of you."

Still on edge since reading the note, Rachel nearly dropped her water glass.

"James Donald McGuire. Watch your overactive imagination around the ladies." Ben admonished his son's brash explanation. "Some of the local women are marriage-minded, and rightly so. I'd just prefer they targeted their arrows at somebody else."

"Then you're not wanting to marry?" Excitement filled her at the thought that she would be spared the awkward task of declining his proposal at the end of summer. She lay her fork on her plate and searched his face.

"Are you?" A knowing smile lifted his lips.

She realized what he'd done. Ben used her own ploy of answering a question with a question, so he could evade the truth. Clever, but curious nonetheless.

A throat cleared above and to one side of Rachel. She glanced up to see a freckle-faced woman about her own age waiting impatiently to interrupt their conversation. The woman half curtsied, making her red hair teeter on its elaborate perch atop her head.

"How do you do, Miss Tharp." The redhead offered Rachel a card. "My name is Clementine Crawford . . . of the Fort Worth Crawfords. Of course, my mother is a Maynard from Harrisburg, Pennsylvania, and she—"

"Clementine is our local dressmaker," Ben interjected.

"She owns the shop just east of Doc's office. You'll be glad to know that she studied abroad and knows all the latest Paris designs."

He sounded as if he were trying to convince her of something. Possibly to remind her that Valiant was a modern settlement equipped with every convenience a woman of Joanna's social standing preferred. *Don't try so hard, Ben*, Rachel secretly reassured him.

"Not *all* of them," Clementine gushed, her adoration for Ben etched in her every blushing feature. "But most."

"Do introduce us, Clemmy dear." A dark-haired vixen rose from her table, adjacent to theirs, and moved directly behind Ben. "I'm dying to meet the Joanna Tharp I've heard so much about. I already know you have wonderful taste in men. Now, I'd like to hear all the wicked gossip about what's happening in Richmond."

"Gwenella, this is Joanna Tharp." Clementine pointed her ivory-handled fan toward the eavesdropper. "Joanna, this is Gwenella Duncan."

One introduction led to another and another, until it seemed every eligible woman in the restaurant hovered beside the McGuire party like buzzards waiting to swoop down and attack Rachel. Any one of them could have written the note.

"Ain't you bone pickers got nothin' better to do than keep a poor man and his gal away from their vittles?"

The women scattered like tumbleweeds in a fierce wind as the buckskin-clad stranger turned a chair backward and straddled it as if he were mounting up. He grabbed a drumstick from Jimmy's plate.

"You wasn't gonna eat this one, was you, Jim?" The stranger, not waiting for the lad's answer, bit a healthy hunk out of the meat and started chewing.

Rachel could only gawk at the wiry hank of salt and pepper hair and bronze skin. Eyes the color of harvest wheat stared back at her. She'd seen a tiger once being off-loaded from a barge in Atlanta and thought it had the most unforgettable eyes she'd ever seen, but she'd been wrong. The gold of the stranger's eyes beat the tiger's by nuggets.

"What you looking at, lady? Ain't you never seen a fella eat before?"

"Then you *are* a man?" she asked softly, aware that the cleavage revealed by his buckskin shirt made her think he was a she.

"You trying to pick a fight after I scattered them quail for ya?" The man-woman stood and glared fiercely at Rachel.

"Sit down, A. J." Ben also aimed his demand at Jim. "And you quit laughing. There's nothing humorous about this at all. Joanna's new around here, or at least hasn't been back long enough to know she's not supposed to concern herself with the way you wear your pants."

"Oh, well, since you put it that way." A. J. sank into the chair once again and finished off the chicken leg. "Alewine Jones is the name on the deed. Horse trader. Freighter. You name it, I'll tame it." She laughed at her own joke. "A. J.'s what ever'body 'round here calls me. Proud to meetcha, ma'am."

"Ra—Joanna Tharp." Rachel caught her near blunder in time.

"*The* Joanna Tharp?"

"Has there been more than one?" Sarcasm edged her tone, until she realized she was being unfair. The stranger had no way of knowing the concern that filled her.

"You want your butt-kickin' now or after you finish your meal? Makes me no mind whatsoever."

"All right! A fight!" Jimmy started stuffing food into his mouth as if he were afraid he'd miss something.

Rachel picked up her fork—small consolation against the

huge knife the frontierswoman wore nestled in the buckskin's waistband. Was this woman the writer of the note? "Why on God's earth do you want to fight me?"

"Don't play innocent with me, Little Miss Runaway." A. J. grabbed Jimmy's fork to even the challenge. "You know you left a good man high and dry-gulched. And what for? Some sorry, no good sonofa—"

"Alewine."

"—seabiscuit eater." A. J.'s mouth clamped shut when Ben's tone brooked no argument.

"Now is not the time to air old grievances. What's done is done. Joanna came home. Whether it's to stay or only visit, that's up to her. But just like you don't want anyone minding your business, then I'll ask you to stay out of mine."

"But, Ben—"

"Aly."

"Aw, shoot, Ben. Don't say that. You know I can't say no when you call me that."

"Promise me, Aly. Drop the subject."

"I'd rather dropkick—"

"Aly."

"Oh, turkey puke! Alllrright!" A. J. tossed the drumstick bone onto Jimmy's plate. "But that don't mean I have to like her, now, does it? That's plain asking a fellow too much." She rumpled the boy's hair, wiping grease off her hands. "You and me going fishing, boy?"

Jimmy nodded.

"Dawn, then. At the Wild Horse. West bank."

"Chores first," Ben reminded. "Gotta feed them chickens."

"You have live chickens at your store?" Rachel couldn't contain her surprise.

"Sometimes in my storage room, but you know I own a ranch just outside of town. That's where Jim and I live. We raise a few crops and beef," he said offhandedly. "Keeps me busy."

"Me too," Jim complained, grumbling about the chores.

"Mind your pa," A. J. said. "They'll bite till the dew dries. Got plenty of time. See ya, scamp. And tell that no-good, mangy stinkbait you call a dog to keep his yap shut when he comes loping up to the crick. Gives my grubworms the vapors chasing and slobbering all over 'em like 'at."

"Why don't you go with Aly, Jim, since you gotta get up so early?"

As the door to the restaurant banged shut behind the fishing partners, feminine sighs of relief blended together and the room felt considerably more empty.

Rachel faced Ben. "What was that all about? I thought she might scalp me with that fork."

Something dangerous narrowed Ben's eyes. "As if you didn't know"—his accusal was low and soft—"and there's nothing Alewine won't do to protect a friend."

Rachel rose from her chair. "I think it's best I go home now, Mr. McGuire." And she meant more than the few streets to Tharp House. She wanted to go all the way back to Richmond. This was a huge, horrible mistake, thinking she could fool Ben into believing she was Joanna, much less convincing an entire town. How many more Ophelia Fincks and Alewine Joneses awaited her? At least they were openly hostile. She also had the secret letter-writer to worry about.

Though everything she ever owned and achieved had been hard-won, Rachel hated the idea of defending herself against people who were obviously in the right and had every reason to despise Joanna. Her employer had treated Ben shabbily and discarded him like last year's wardrobe.

The dress Rachel wore felt as if it were a hair shirt burning into her skin. She had to get out of Joanna's clothes and into something of her own. She might have to play Joanna by day, but at night, for as long as she remained in Valiant, she would be Rachel Sloan. "I'm very tired and don't think I can eat any more."

"I'll settle up with Delaney, then we'll be on our way."

The anger in Ben's voice was gone, and now she sensed she'd hurt his feelings by ending the evening early. Too late she realized he may have sent the boy home for other reasons than getting enough sleep for early fishing. Had Ben planned to kiss her?

Strolling home in the dark with him, holding his hand and feeling him next to her, made Rachel even more determined that something must be done. She had to find a way to ease the inevitable parting with him after summer and assure the moonstruck ladies in love with Ben to quit considering her a threat. If she could only think of something, then she wouldn't have to give up Tharp House so soon, and she might find out who else had access to it.

Whoever it was didn't know who they were up against.

Searching her past experience for a logical answer to her dilemma, possibilities evaded Rachel. Besides, what did she know except sewing?

Sewing? An idea took shape. Why not do what she always did when she made a mistake on a garment—match cloth to repair it? Couldn't that also apply to people?

A list of possible brides most suitable to replace Joanna ran through Rachel's head as she recalled each of the eligible women she'd met so far. "Ben, what do you like best in a woman?" she asked, eager to put her plan into action.

He opened the gate for her and guided her toward the porch. "Best? I don't know for sure. Perhaps the willingness to let a man walk her home and kiss her good night . . . especially when the look in her eyes all evening says she wants him to."

"Eyes can be deceiving," Rachel confessed as she unlocked the door and searched the darkened interior cautiously before turning around. Ben stood achingly close. She found his nearness far more distressing than the possibility of an intruder lurking somewhere within Tharp House. "Do you always trust what you see?"

He lifted her hand gently, bringing it to his lips and brushing a whisper-soft confession against its surface. "Only if my heart says I should."

His eyes enchanted her, weaving a spell so binding that she was lost in the magic of the man, the intensity of the love staring back at her, and the cauldron of sensations he stirred within her.

"I want to kiss you, Joanna. I've missed you so."

Like a burst of winter air that chilled a heated room, the mention of her employer's name swept through Rachel and cooled the desire he had stoked so easily inside her. Rachel's hand slipped from his grasp and quickly reached to straighten nonexistent problems with the chignon at the top of her head.

"N-not until you've had time to know the real me," she stammered, aware of the strange huskiness that filled her tone. "I'm not the same woman you once loved."

❖ 4 ❖

YOU'RE DOING THE right thing, Rachel, she told herself as she stood in front of the batwing doors that led into the Lazy Lady saloon. Tinny music being banged out on the piano jarred her senses, causing her pulse to race faster and take on the jaunty rhythm. Resisting Ben's kiss on the porch the night before had been difficult enough, but mustering the courage to ask for Ophelia Finck's help seemed impossible.

You've never run coward in your life. She swallowed back the nervousness that threatened to tighten her throat and tested every button that fastened the collar of her shirtwaist and sleeves. Rachel took a deep breath, then pushed open one of the doors. For the first time in her life, she stepped inside a saloon.

Smoke and cheap perfume assailed her, layering the air with hazy images and a combination of odors she wouldn't long forget. Sawdust blanketed the floor despite the wooden planking beneath her feet. Rachel supposed it had been added to make dancing more brisk. But, from a stain near one of the spittoons at the end of the bar, she suspected it might really be a protection from spills.

A dozen pairs of eyes focused on her at once, their intense regard heating her skin in a blush that surely matched the color of her dress—a color she wished Joanna favored less.

The music stopped. Men looked up from their poker and faro games. The gaily dressed women frankly appraised her, then tightened their embraces around their current benefactors. A handsome man, dark-eyed and raven-haired, turned his cards over and raked in his chips.

"I'm calling it a night, boys," he announced, tipping his hat toward Rachel, "or, better yet, a day. Just take a look at what your glorious Texas dawn brought my way this morning." He stood and sauntered over to Rachel. "You look like Lady Luck in the finest flesh and, might I say, beautiful set of bones."

"You have me mixed up with someone else, sir—"

"Not *sir*. Nicodemus Turner. Gambler"—he half bowed—"and exceptional lover."

"Rogue," Rachel countered, resisting the urge to slap him. Instead, she clutched her handbag tightly and searched the room for a sign of the saloon's proprietor. Though the world she'd stepped into should have been foreign to her, Rachel recognized the expression staring back from each spectator. It was a craving to experience something more, a hunger for life better than that which had been dealt them, a ravenous search for satisfaction. She knew the look well, for it had stared back at her from a mirror ever since she'd left her parents' home.

"Rogue . . . rascal . . . I've answered to both," the gambler admitted. His gaze swept to her hands, then focused unrelentingly on her face. Dimples bracketed his lips, making the smile that blazed across his mouth even more disarming.

"Better sip on something from the local brand, Nicky dear," a woman's voice taunted above them. "That one is Ben McGuire's private stock."

"*She's* Joanna?"

Though equally curious to see why Nicodemus Turner

sounded so surprised, Rachel's attention followed its first impulse and found Ophelia Finck on the second-floor landing.
The saloonkeeper moved from the doorway marked Office
to the top of the stairway that led down to the main floor.
Dressed in an almond-colored blouse and skirt, only a black
string tie at her collar offset the starkness of Ophelia's clothing. Rachel found neither disapproval nor welcome in the
woman's face.

"Why are you here?" Ophelia demanded as she walked
down the stairs like a queen gracing her subjects with her
presence. Her cane seemed more scepter than crutch.
"Women like you don't generally dirty their shoes with my
sawdust."

Several of the men moved toward her, jockeying for the
right to help her down the last few steps.

"I rather hoped we could talk in private, Miss Finck." A
glance at the gambler made Rachel realize he had no incli-
nation to move away from her and every intention of eavesdropping on the rest of her conversation. The man had no
manners! She deliberately turned her back to him before ad-
dressing Ophelia again. "I have some business to discuss
with you . . . privately."

"Business, you say?" Ophelia eyed Rachel from shirtwaist to skirt hem. "The color's right, hon, but you've got
to give the boys a bit more show if you want to earn top
pay."

The woman's insinuation brought heat to Rachel's cheeks.
"Oh, I don't want employment, Miss Finck. I was hoping
you would do a little work for *me*."

Ophelia tapped her cane against the floor, stirring the sawdust at her feet. "So, life is fair after all. This time you need
me. Do I invite you to my office and listen, or"—her voice
boomed with mockery—"do I simply tell you to do what

you told me to do a long time ago? Do it your own damned self.''

Whatever had initiated the bad blood between the two women must have been something terrible, since the emotion still raged strongly within the saloonkeeper, but Rachel refused to let the woman simply ride herd over her. If she did, the days she remained in Valiant would be miserable.

''I'm certainly capable of 'doing it my own self,' as you say, but I thought it might go a little faster if the two of us worked together. I thought you might help me spread some news.''

Interest flared in the woman's wolf-gray eyes. ''Upstairs. My office. You've got five minutes of my time, Joanna.''

Rachel's back suddenly beaded from a chill that swept up her skin and ended in a shudder at the base of her skull. Her teeth gritted in response as the crowd's icy regard followed her up each step and lingered long after Ophelia closed the office door.

After seating herself in one of the chairs, Rachel admired the cushioned Belter furniture that filled the office space with white and green floral designs. Though the style would be considered out of fashion among the wealthy of Richmond, the high polish of pinion oil helped the rosewood wear its age well. Ophelia's office bore a look of elegance and success.

The saloonkeeper took a seat on the davenport adjacent to Rachel's chair. She'd expected the woman to sit at the large desk that filled one corner and supported bookshelves lined with ledgers. Rachel's pulse beat noticeably stronger in her throat, and she attempted to swallow back the nervousness. With a lift of her chin, she plunged in with her request. ''I appreciate you giving me your—''

''Cut the cordialities, Joanna''—Ophelia opened the ivory fan threaded over her wrist and began to stir away the morning heat—"there's no one to impress, so it's wasted effort. All I want to know is what news you expect me to spread."

Rachel ran through her plan mentally, making certain it was well thought out. Carelessness would arouse Ophelia's curiosity. "I'm interested in reacquainting myself with old friends and eager to meet new ones. Perhaps have a tea or two at the Thar—at my home. I thought you might spread the word."

"What's the hurry?" Ophelia closed the fan and tapped it against her thigh. "Afraid Valiant won't provide enough social life to suit your Richmond tastes?"

Let her think what she would, Rachel knew the sooner she started the matchmaking, the sooner she would arrive at the best likely prospect to marry Ben, and the sooner she could rid herself of any guilt where he was concerned. "Let's just say I'm used to nightly entertainment and would rather not wait until the weekend to see how Valiant amuses itself. Do you think you could possibly let everyone know I'll have tea and cookies every afternoon for a while?"

"Have anyone in particular in mind?"

The dark-haired socialite she'd met at Delaney's last evening rose instantly in Rachel's thoughts. "Well, you could tell that nice young woman, Gwenella Duncan, and her social group."

"You mean the Tight-Shoe Troupe?" Disdain filled Ophelia's tone. "That'll take about two hours to get the word around, depending on whether the little darlings have gotten out of bed yet."

"The Tight-Shoe Troupe?" Rachel bit at Ophelia's bait. "Why do you call them that?"

Ophelia stood and walked over to the window, pulling back the white damask curtain and peering outside. "I'd call them much worse, but I'm trying to improve my vocabulary. The troupe are the pampered daughters of Valiant's wealthier citizens. The tight-shoe handle was hung on them one day when they all went shopping at Clementine's for shoes. Every one of them didn't want the other to know her true shoe size, so they all bought a size too small.''

The woman threw her head back and laughed. "For a full season, they couldn't last through an entire barn dancing without complaining their feet hurt something fierce. Served them all right for being so vain.''

The Tight-Shoe Troupe sounded just like Joanna Tharp— the kind of woman who obviously interested Ben and, therefore, now interested Rachel. "Perfect . . . I mean . . . they sound like people I should meet.''

"What's in this for me?''

Rachel expected the woman would want payment or a trade of some kind; she disliked Joanna too openly to do anything out of sheer kindness. "What do you think is a fair tradeoff?''

"Do you intend to invite *every* lady in town to these teas?''

"Everyone who's willing to pay a visit.''

For the first time since Rachel met the woman, Ophelia Finck looked slightly nervous, almost vulnerable. The woman's hand twisted the velvet cord that held the fan to her wrist.

"If I pass the word, then I want a written invitation to the . . . let's say . . . *third* tea party.''

"Consider yourself invi—''

"I want it *written*. That way there won't be any discussion over my right to be there.''

Understanding swept through Rachel, and her opinion of the woman altered. She'd been snubbed enough in her own life to know what motivated Ophelia's need for an official invitation. The saloonkeeper had probably never been allowed to attend a tea because of her social standing. Pretending to be Joanna just might have its advantages—one of which she would use to the fullest the day Ophelia came to call.

"You just let everyone know what I have planned"— Rachel stood and offered her hand—"then I'll go ahead and start baking cookies and preparing the tea for this afternoon."

Ophelia's yellow-gray eyes narrowed suspiciously as she stood and shook Rachel's hand to seal their pact. "*You're* going to bake cookies by yourself?"

Uh-oh. Rachel couldn't recall Joanna having cooked *anything* in Richmond. How was she going to get past this definite blunder? She must be more careful if she intended to fool *this* woman. Rachel eyed Ophelia directly and strengthened her grip. Why not simply tell the saloonkeeper the truth, rather than leave herself open to tripping up again? "You're going to discover that seven years has made a great difference in the woman who left here and the one who returned, Ophelia."

❖ 5 ❖

"DID I FORGET somebody's birthday?" Ben placed his bookkeeping ledger on the shelf beneath his work counter. Though larger than most general stores in other Texas settlements, his looked crowded today . . . with women. "Or is everyone in just a particularly good spending mood?"

"No birthday." Ophelia fingered the bolt of white silk that had been brought in from Fort Worth on the previous day's train. Seven daughters of Valiant's finest were crowded together in a heated discussion at the end of the counter, where various colored silks, satins, and velvets lay in bolts. "Let me have eight yards of this too. We'll see what Clem can string together in a couple of days."

"You might as well plan on a few weeks, Miss Finck," the tallest of the women informed Ophelia, turning away from the argument arising over the violet-hued silk. "Miss Crawford's time has already been engaged. I'm afraid she'll be too busy sewing *my* gown to be distracted with anyone else's."

Ben saw the fleeting look of disappointment that crossed Ophelia's face before she quickly masked it behind a seemingly offhand remark that she was in no hurry and could wait. He searched Gwenella's sharp-angled face and wondered why the men of Valiant found her so attractive. The downward curve of her lips seldom rose in friendliness to anyone.

The banker's daughter took too much pleasure in boasting about her promptness with the dressmaker—a trait that would have kept Ben from accepting any of the advances Gwenella had made in the past, even if he wasn't in love with someone else.

Unwilling to let Ophelia feel another moment's discomfort, Ben stepped in and attempted to cheer her. "You know, Ophelia, I can't remember if I ever told you, but that dress you wore for Easter Sunday was the prettiest thing I've seen in a long time. Seems to me it had tiny yellow rosebuds around the edge of the collar and sleeves. Maybe even around the hem. Frankly, I was too caught up in watching how it brought out the color of your eyes to notice anything else well enough."

"You know which one he's talking about, Miss Finck," prompted Alizabeth Bentley, the willowy blonde whose lashes fluttered open and closed so frequently, it seemed she must have sand in her eyes. "The one you wore the day I wore my Paris gown. The velvet sapphire that you and, I might say, several others said matched *my* eyes perfectly?"

Though the young woman's words were directed to Ophelia, Alizabeth's gaze demanded Ben's attention. He tried to keep his own eyes from responding to hers, but didn't quite succeed. Why was she staring at him so? Finally realization dawned. She expected him to remember her gown as well.

Try as he might, he honestly couldn't recall seeing Miss Bentley at that particular church service. His mind had been on the letter he'd written to Joanna that day. The letter that said he intended to sell out and move to Richmond to be near her. Ben didn't believe in lying, but he wanted to spare

Alizabeth's feelings. "Perhaps you'll wear it again soon, Miss Bentley, so I can get a better look."

"I'll do that, Ben."

"If your father hears how your voice gets all soft and low when you say Ben's name like that, he'll tan your hide," the redhead warned, poking the offender in the side.

"I said it the same as I always do," Alizabeth said, defending herself and fluttering her lashes even more extravagantly. "You're just jealous because he didn't say anything to you."

"That's because I didn't try to interrupt him when he was talking to Miss Finck and force him to talk to me!"

"I didn't force Ben to do anything, Penelope Walters, so you can just mind your own—"

"Girls"—the sternness of Ophelia's tone hushed the argument—"or should I say *young ladies?* This is no place to argue. Why don't we make our purchases and let Mr. McGuire conduct his business? Alizabeth, gal, you best do something about all that blinking. Makes someone wanta take a washcloth to your face."

Alizabeth's lids halted in mid-blink. The other women had the good manners to keep silent. Ophelia motioned toward the white silk. "I believe I'll still buy that and just save it for another day. Thanks for reminding me about the dress, Ben. I packed it away for special occasions, and it *would* be just perfect for this one."

Pleasure colored Ophelia's cheeks a becoming red, but the crmson hue that stained Gwenella's face looked almost painful.

"I wonder if anyone's offered to help Miss Tharp with her list of invitations?" Gwenella asked. "Someone should. After all, Joanna's been gone so long, she might need a bit of advice concerning who's the most beneficial to meet at her teas." Gwenella glanced at her cohorts, then back at Ben, deliberately ignoring direct eye contact with Ophelia. "She might open herself to all sorts of undesirables."

"Gwenella Duncan, if you think your highfalutin side-of-the-mouth double-talk is above my understanding, you best tie that bonnet a little tighter around those dyed roots, or I'm gonna pull out every strand of them . . . no matter *who* your daddy is."

In the time it took the others to snicker, Ophelia had crossed the distance that separated her from the group of young women. Her cheeks puffed as hardy as the blacksmith's bellows did when filling a past-due order.

Gwenella backed up, her complexion now ghostly white against the Marion bandelette of pin curls that waved darkly over her forehead and on each side of her sharp-boned cheeks. Her eyes looked like tin plates doubled in size as she held up her palms to ward off any physical threat the saloonkeeper intended.

"N-now, Miss Finck, I don't know why you took that so p-personally," Gwenella stammered. "I meant no disrespect whatsoever."

"Yeah, and I meant to pay your mother and father a little visit about those temperance meetings you've said you were attending on Tuesday nights in May, yet didn't. But don't take it personal. I thought they might want to know you'd . . . shall we say . . . opened yourself up to *desirable* elements."

"Gwennelllaaa"—a plump, brown-haired girl moved to the front of the group—"who's been courting ye? We tell ye everything. Just *everything*."

"Oh, do quit your whining, Belle. I'm not courting anyone. I just wanted to be alone for a while, so I told Mother and Father I went to the meetings. Is it a sin to want some time alone, for goodness' sakes?" She attempted to move past the saloonkeeper, but Ophelia refused to give way.

"Are you calling me a liar?" Ophelia's eyes narrowed.

"Ladies, *Ophelia,* as you said before, isn't this better set-tled somewhere else, where the *two* of you can talk this out privately?" Ben moved from around the counter and delib-erately took up a position between the two women.

"I'm willing," Ophelia said, shrugging, "but I'm not sure Miss Duncan has enough starch in her to do the same."

"Phele, you know that's not what I meant." Ben placed an encouraging hand on her shoulder. "I hoped you two could work out a way to be friends."

Taking advantage of Ben's voice of reason, Gwenella rushed around him and buried herself in the midst of her circle of friends. With a tilt of her chin, false courage glared back at him.

"That will never happen." Gwenella finally met Ophelia eye to eye, now that she had the strength of numbers to fuel her bravado. "If that woman is ever in this store before I am again, I want to know the moment I walk in so I can turn around and come back another time."

"Now, Gwenella—"

"No, Ben. That's how I feel. I understand that we're two of your best customers and that it's unfair to ask you not to sell to one or the other of us. But I don't have to do my purchasing at the same time."

"Considerate little witch, aren't you?"

All eyes focused on Ophelia's murderous expression.

Tension raised the fine hair on the back of Ben's neck as he waited to see what his longtime friend would do to her snobbish opponent. Though he didn't approve of Gwenella's prejudice for people less financially secure than the Duncans, neither did he want a cat fight there in the store.

Ophelia lurched forward, splaying her fingers like a cougar ready to sink claws into its prey. "Gotcha!"

Gwenella squealed, stumbled backward, and broke her fall by bumping into Penelope. "N-never speak to me again,

Ophelia Finck,'' she shrieked as Ophelia hooted with laughter. ''I don't have to listen to anything you say . . . no matter if we're in a crowd or alone. And my parents *will* hear of this, I promise you that. So gossip all you want. A lot of good it'll do you. They'll never believe your word over mine.''

She whirled, hurried past a woman who'd just opened the door, then called over her shoulder, ''And, Ben, I do *not* dye my hair!'' Gwenella pushed the woman aside without even looking at whom she bullied. ''Get out of my way!''

Ophelia tapped her chin with a gloved finger. ''Couldn't call that exactly starch, but that last denial had a little bit of gumption in it, bygawd!''

''Excuse me!'' The new customer sidestepped the fury as powerful as the wind that drove her inside the store.

A sudden glare of sunlight defined only the silhouette of the person who suffered the misfortune of blocking Gwenella's escape route. Yet Ben would know that shape even if he were nearly blind. ''Joanna! I'd hoped to see you today.''

Like railroad cars being whiplashed behind a runaway engine, Alizabeth, Penelope, and the other women raced out the door. Rachel couldn't help but stare at the exiting horde, for the air was still charged with a tension she could almost hear. She'd never seen chins tilted so high, nor spines so ramrod straight and in such formation! ''What is that all about?''

As the door slammed shut, Ophelia's laughter became girlish giggles and snorts.

''Yes, Ophelia, what *is* that all about?'' Ben handed Rachel a basket, though his attention remained on the saloonkeeper. ''Put your smaller purchases in there.''

Ophelia flicked an ermine-colored ringlet away from her neck, tilting her chin so high that the second one, which had begun to form in the past year, now disappeared. Try as they might, her lips refused to straighten into any semblance of seriousness. "Well, you might say it has something to do with tight shoes and tea."

Rachel motioned with the basket in the direction Gwenella and the others had taken. "That was the troupe?"

"Umm-hmm. All seven of them." Ophelia hiccuped, she was giggling so hard. "P-pardon me."

The two women exchanged glances.

"Why is it that I feel like I'm being left out of a very private joke?" Ben wrapped the bolt of white silk in a clean piece of calico to protect it from being stained. "Just what do tight shoes, tea, and a troop have to do with one another?"

"He really ought to know, since it'll be taking your afternoons away from him for a while." Ophelia took a jar of cinnamon from the shelf. "You'll need that. The troupe likes cinnamon."

Ben tied a ribbon around the purchase and laid it on the counter. Something more than disappointment raced through him at the prospect of not getting to visit Joanna during the few hours he could spare. Having a son, a home, and a store to take care of left little time for his own pleasure. "By all means, tell me. I'd like to know what will cut into my time with you."

Rachel turned her back to him, an act that in itself said she might be trying to avoid him. But why?

"I'm serving tea and cookies every afternoon for a while at the house. To get acquainted . . . or reacquainted, in some cases."

"Okay, so I'll come help serve refreshments. I'm not averse to putting on an apron, as you can see."

"No!"

She swung around with the force of her refusal, then

quickly turned back and seemed to study the labels on the jars of spices that lined the shelves in front of her.

"Usually only ladies attend formal teas," she hedged.

"I've always been considered unusual—particularly where you're concerned."

"We won't talk about subjects men tend to discuss."

"Ninety percent of my customers are women. I enjoy being around them and talking to them about anything they prefer."

"And believe me, they enjoy being with him"—Ophelia offered Ben an appreciative glance—"and talking to him. But a lot of good that does. Do you think he ever notices?"

"Do you notice, Ben?"

The earnestness in Rachel's eyes as she finally gave him her full attention made his heart thump a new rhythm. Something in her tone matched a need radiating from those emerald depths—a need that rushed over Ben like the first breeze of spring after a long, bitter winter.

A seed of caring somehow survived the seven years their love had lain fallow and possibly took firmer root through all the letters he'd written. Now he sensed that seed might thrive if he cultivated it patiently and with truth.

"I'm flesh and blood and nobody's saint, by any means. But as I stand here before you, Joanna, I swear I've given my heart to no other woman before, or since, you left Valiant."

"I see."

Their gazes locked, and it was as if he could feel the moment hers began to trace a tantalizing, intangible trail from the top of his head, lingering at his eyes and mouth, to the jut of his chin, and finally encompassing the width of his shoulders. The approval darkening the green to smoky-emerald sent desire surging through him, alerting every dormant sense within Ben to rouse him from his imposed celibacy. As her examination continued its sensuous search, he thought he might die from the pure pleasure of knowing he could still stir lust within Joanna, if not love.

A clearing of a feminine throat reminded Ben he and Joanna were not alone. Ben willed Ophelia away, knowing that if he and Joanna could have privacy, he would seek the kiss she'd denied him the night before. Maybe even more.

"I see too." Ophelia's eyes slanted downward to focus on the burgeoning proof of Ben's own desire.

Ben moved behind a shelf so his lower body would not be visible. Would Joanna think that his control over his passion for her now was no better than it had been in his bumbling youth? He yearned for more than her beauty, needed far more than her respect. Ben wanted Joanna to love him with all her heart.

"I think it's best that I mosey on back to the Lazy Lady." Ophelia picked up the bolt of silk and nodded politely to Rachel. "Joanna, to deny I'm envious would be harder'n getting a church pew with my name painted on it. And I sure as sin never thought I'd take sides with you on anything, but, lady, if you don't latch on to that long drink of water standing there pretty quick, some fine petticoat's gonna shanghai him right from under your bonnet and find herself a preacher."

Did he hear Joanna correctly? No . . . that was probably just the gust of wind that swept through the room as Ophelia left.

Still, he could have sworn the love of his life had said . . . she sure hoped so.

❖ 6 ❖

RACHEL WORKED HARDER than she'd ever worked in her life. By the time she learned where everything was stored and got accustomed to the Tharp cookstove, she had burned several batches of cookies. Uncertain how successful Ophelia was in spreading the news, she had no idea how many visitors to expect. She didn't dare fall short of offerings. Joanna was the sort of person who would have too many delicacies rather than not enough, and those who knew her before would think it odd if Rachel scrimped.

Despite the awkwardness of being in an unfamiliar kitchen and having to cook for an uncertain number of people, it felt good to have labored so hard when the work was for herself and not someone else. Imagine, having her first tea—the first party she'd ever given.

A glance at the assortment of cookies gracing the silver platter on the dining table urged her to untie the apron from around her waist. She deposited it on one of the pegs that hung next to the china hutch.

"What time is it?" she muttered, searching for the clock she'd seen earlier. A quick trip into the drawing room revealed she had just enough time to pay a last-minute visit to

Ben's store. If she hurried, she'd still have time to get her bath and prepare another batch of cookies.

Checking her clothes for signs of flour, she found none and decided she still looked presentable enough not to have to change before she went out—she didn't have time. She grabbed her reticule and headed outside.

The high wind felt good on her skin, cooling off the long afternoon of baking she'd endured. The Texas sun still beat a heated path beyond Tharp House's well-kept yard, but above the canopy of shade trees, everything looked a yellowish-gray. Clouds climbed high into the sky, like gigantic curling waves of wind. Though full of the scent of mesquite and wildflowers, the air felt somehow heavier, making it more cumbersome to move.

You're just tired, she told herself. Once she had her bath, she'd feel better. Purposefully livening her steps, she went through the gate and headed in the same direction Ben had taken her last night. As Rachel turned the corner onto Main Street, she noticed a lone man standing in the shade near the church, watching her. For a moment, alarm washed away her exhaustion. Could he be the author of the note?

Unwilling to be ruled by fear, she took her courage in hand and waved, making sure whoever he was knew with all certainty she had seen him. ''Hello there. Good to see you!''

He waved back, but didn't say anything. Instantly he moved from where he leaned against a tree near the church and hurried inside. The only thing noticeable about him from that distance was his salt and pepper hair.

''Probably just curious,'' she decided aloud, needing to hear the sound of her own voice to calm the rapid rhythm her pulse had taken. Can't blame him. *I'd* like to know a whole lot more about Joanna Tharp myself. Rachel took a deep breath and hurried about her business. Perhaps some of her curiosity would be satisfied that afternoon at the tea, and she would learn some of her employer's past from people who knew her then.

"Forget something?" Ben asked as the fierce wind drove her inside his store.

Pushing the hair out of her eyes, she noticed Jimmy was sweeping the floor while Ben wiped the counter clean. "Yes. Enough cinnamon and flour to replace the cookies I burned. I'm not sure I made enough."

"Here, Jim. Why don't you finish up so I can help Miss Tharp get what she needs? Mind the store for me while I walk her home."

"Yessir."

"Oh, that's unnecessary," Rachel said, anchoring a lock of hair behind her ear, realizing she must look a sight, "and I best hurry before my guests arrive."

"I was wondering if you might have the time to talk to me on the way. I've waited a long time to have the pleasure of your company, you know."

What could she say but yes? Her heart certainly didn't want her to deny him, for it pounded a steady "let him, let him, let him." How many times while reading his letters to Joanna had she dreamed of Ben actually saying those words to *her*? Of hearing the tone that filled the words with meaning greater than any written script could impart? Of strolling hand in hand with a man whose dreams had been built around his love for her?

Rachel accepted his invitation, unwilling to throw away her last chance to enjoy Ben's company alone before matching him up with one of the townswomen. "I'll talk with you only as far as my porch swing. I haven't much time before guests start arriving."

Ben nodded and removed his apron. When he handed her a basket to hold her purchases, his fingers lightly touched her own. Heat skimmed the surface of her hands as flesh brushed against flesh.

Startled by the sensation his touch aroused within her, Rachel discovered that her body refused to obey her mind. Her mind warned her to move far away from the next possible touch and get busy filling the basket with the needed items. Her body stayed rooted to the spot while her eyes stared into morning-glory blue that would forever alter the way she described her favorite color.

"Need anything in particular?" Ben stood only inches away from her.

You, she answered silently, but attempted to blink herself into full concentration. Why did his eyes start blinking too? "Two ounces of cinnamon and a pound of flour."

"Anything sweet?"

She sighed. *I think I am on you,* she wanted to say, but resisted the impulse. "Maple syrup. I like it better than sugar in cookies."

Rachel watched him gather the requested dry goods and the jar of syrup, admiring the way his fluid movements showed he was a man of fine form and work-hardened muscles. Though he spent much of his time clerking in the store, from his letters she knew he spent almost an equal amount outdoors building and ranching.

"How much do I owe you?" She dug into her handbag to pay him.

"I'll just put it on your account. You can settle with me at the end of summer if you like. Besides, you're in a hurry." He took the basket and offered her the bend of his arm. "Let me carry that for you."

"Good afternoon, Jim." She noticed the boy didn't look altogether pleased that he was left alone with the running of the store. Perhaps she could appease him. "Come by later or in the morning and I'll have some cookies you and your father can share." That is, if she managed to get more made in time.

"I might," Jimmy said noncommittally, but at least he glanced up from his chore. With a look from Ben, he slung the hair out of his eyes. "But thank you for offering, Miss Tharp."

"You're welcome."

They left the building in silence. The midday sky had taken on an unhealthy amber glow. Tiny splatters of rain warned that the swollen clouds intended to release their burden. Lightning ripped the skyline horizontally and vertically. Wind-driven sand stung Rachel's face and hands.

"Looks like we're in for a storm," Ben warned. "You might want to call off the tea. If it's bad out, the women won't chance it. Especially those driving in from their homesteads. Then again, with a new woman in town, they just might."

So intent on protecting her eyes from the stinging sand, Rachel missed a step coming off the sidewalk. Ben's fingers tightened over her hand, protecting her from injury and guiding her back to safety at his side.

They managed to make it as far as the end of Main Street before rain began to pelt them and form balls of ice.

"Gotta get to shelter!" Ben shouted through the deluge. "Head for the church!"

He handed her the basket and pulled her closer to him to protect her from the hail's icy sting. Rachel held on to him tightly, too busy running and trying not to slip to think about the storm of sensations raging through her by his nearness.

"We made it!"

The declaration rumbled against her cheek, and she found it pleasant to feel the vibration of his words as he spoke.

"Good thing Brother Ethan keeps the door unlocked. He says what a sinner might taketh away, the Lord giveth back."

"Sounds like an optimist to me." Rachel felt a moment of remorse when he left her and held the door open.

"He's new in town, but you'll like him."

Ben's warm breath rushing over her head as she passed him sent a chill down her spine that had nothing to do with the cold rain. She shivered.

"Cold?" He started to pull off his shirt, then chuckled. "I'd offer you my shirt, but I believe it wouldn't be any drier than what you're already wearing. And if Brother Ethan's about, he might not approve of me visiting the house of the Lord bare-chested."

"That's all right. I'll just sit here in one of the pews and rub my arms. That'll stir up some heat."

For the first time since entering the sanctuary, she wondered if the man she'd seen earlier was still inside. A glance at the rows of pews and the altar assured her they were alone. Ben moved to a nearby closet and disappeared, only to come out again, shaking his head.

"No luck. Thought there would be a baptismal robe or two hanging in there, but Ethan must have taken them out to launder. Guess we'll just have to dry off the best we can. Hope that rain lets up soon, so you don't catch a cold from the dampness."

"And so I can be home when guests arrive," she reminded Ben, taking a seat in the last pew.

"Well, where would you like to start? As you know, I can write a bucketful of letters, but when it comes to face-to-face talking with you after all this time, I feel like I'm a tongue-tied tadpole again."

Rachel laughed, relaxing a little. "Say that again several times and that'll loosen you up."

"How's everything at the house?"

Despite the voice of reason that said the note had not been

written by Ben, suspicion filled her tone. "What do you mean?"

He took a seat beside her. "Just wanted to know if everything was to your liking, and whether there was anything else I can do to make your stay more pleasant"—he placed a hand over hers—"and longer."

She allowed his hand to remain. He was the one person whom she could trust not to want her to leave. That was apparent in the way he looked at her now. "You've been too kind already, Ben."

"I'd like to be more."

An awkward moment ensued. She didn't dare speak first. Her heart was creating a list of questions that were inappropriate to ask while waiting out a storm. Her pulse beat rapidly beneath the palm that encompassed her hand.

"Why did you—" They spoke in unison, then chuckled with embarrassment.

"You first," Rachel insisted.

"It's your turn. I've already asked one."

"Well, I was wondering why a twenty-four-year-old man adopted a thirteen-year-old boy."

Ben let go of her hand and leaned forward, resting his elbows on the next pew. She followed his gaze and wondered if he was staring at the large crucifix that graced the center of the back wall.

"Because Jim needed a home."

His answer was so casual, Rachel didn't react at once. He hadn't said "Because I needed a helping hand" or "Because it was the Christian thing to do." He'd stated a reason that had nothing to do with his own needs but everything to do with the boy's.

Suddenly admiration rose from the deepest part of Rachel. If the words Ben McGuire had written Joanna were any indication of his true character, he was already a finer man than most she had ever met. But being willing to give an orphan a home, to protect Jimmy from the ordeal of making a living on the streets, well, Ben had just moved into near sainthood in her book. The stone wall of indifference she'd built around her heart since being kicked out of her parents' home cracked open and made Rachel wonder if maybe there wasn't at least one true hero left in this world.

She leaned forward and placed her elbows on the next pew just as he had. "If you don't mind, I think I'll accept that dare now," she whispered. The admiration she felt for him warmed to something more adventurous.

"Dare?" He turned and stared at her, puzzlement creasing his brow.

He was so close, she could feel his breath brush the top of her nose. He smelled of soap and cinnamon. She couldn't remember ever feeling a grain of the same attraction for Daniel that blazed inside her now for Ben. "Ben," she whispered, and saw the question in his blue eyes. "We're in *church*. The first place you ever kissed J—me. You said you would again before I left Valiant."

Knowing that having been an urchin of the streets would make people think the worst of her, Rachel had held on to her virtue like a prized gift. Only once in her life had she allowed a man to seduce her to the point of loosening the ribbons of her desire. But he'd betrayed her, and only sheer luck had prevented her from offering the gift of her love completely.

Kissing was a prerequisite to the temptations that led to losing one's virtue, according to Joanna, and Rachel's own encounter had taught her that too. But Rachel was drowning in passion as potent as hundred-year-old whiskey. Before she could deny herself just a taste, before she could remember that this very evening she would deliberately select a woman to court him, Rachel went gladly into Ben's arms.

She had dreamed of his kiss, longed for it every night since reading that first letter. But the perfection of his lips blazed a welcome path at her temple, against her cheek, the bridge of her nose, driving reason to the forefront of her whirling thoughts. He paused only an inch from her lips, as if enthralled. She knew if she allowed the kiss to continue, her heart would never be her own again.

Bands of iron encircled her slender waist as he stood, pulling her up and closer so their bodies would meld together. He felt so good against her, thigh to thigh, breast to chest. Rachel fought the urge to tear open the buttons of his shirt and follow the impulse to press her lips against the heat radiating from beneath his clothing. Instead, she took a step backward.

"Relax, Joanna," he whispered, tracing the outline of her bottom lip with his fingertip. "You won't find me the awkward kisser I used to be."

"Please stop."

Ben let go, staring down at her. "But you're the one who wanted me to follow through with the dare." Anger and disappointment battled for a moment before leaving him with a wounded expression. "Hell, Joanna, I thought you asked to be kissed. Now you look at me like I was taking unwanted liberties."

She couldn't explain what she felt. She'd wanted him to press his mouth hard and demanding against her own all right, but knew that could never be. The passion she would taste upon his lips would be meant for another woman. For the real Joanna.

Rachel grabbed the basket and moved around him into the aisle. "The rain's stopped. Brother Ethan might walk in, or that other man. We wouldn't want them to find us kissing in church. I—I don't know what I was thinking when I accepted the dare. Besides, I'll never get the cookies done in time now.''

''What other man are you talking about?''

''The one who watched me from the time I left the house until I waved at him.'' She explained what had happened earlier, but left out the circumstances about the note.

''And you say all you saw was his hair?''

She nodded, grateful that this new subject was giving her time to regain her composure.

''Just be careful, Joanna. Valiant's a safe place for the most part, but I'll find out who it was.''

He offered his arm and she accepted it awkwardly this time. The walk home ached with the uncomfortable silence that had risen between them.

Ben bid her good afternoon, planting a kiss on her forehead before she could object. ''That's for letting me walk you home. You go on in. I'll take a look around and see if I can spot that suspicious-looking character. Just remember, Jo, you can't dare most men and expect them to honor your wishes when you change your mind.'' He gently cupped her chin with his hand. ''But then, I thought you had learned that seven years ago.''

❖ 7 ❖

Rachel's mouth ached from forcing a smile and her head hurt from nodding too often as she pretended she was actually listening to the gossip being shared by several of her visitors. If Ophelia Finck truly did everything the troupe accused her of, the woman ought to have a book written about her. Rachel offered the platter of refreshments to Gwenella Duncan. "More cookies? Tea?"

"I believe I've had enough, thank you."

Gwenella continued her conversation with the redheaded woman sitting next to her. Penelope somebody or other. Rachel was too tired to remember most of their names now. Hopefully the others would follow Gwenella's lead and end this farce. None of these so-called ladies were the kind of women Ben McGuire deserved, and she would have no part in matching him with such shrews.

If only she could go upstairs and sleep away the disaster the afternoon had become. Surely the next day's batches of cookies would go better, and the company would be less perturbing. But sleep seemed unlikely, for the feel of Ben's embrace would haunt Rachel long into the night. And to think, she'd given up a kiss from Ben for *this* bunch of harpies.

Be fair, Rachel scolded, offering cookies to the lady sitting next to the bay window. She really ought to stay out of the glare so she wouldn't blink so often. Just because "the blinker" wasn't her cup of tea, Rachel chuckled at her own joke, it didn't mean this woman or any of the others wasn't Ben's sort.

Once everyone had been served again, Rachel reseated herself beside a chubby brown-haired woman who had eaten at least a dozen cookies by herself. "Belle, is it?"

The woman nodded and spoke around a mouthful of sweets. "Aye. Actually 'tis Isabelle, but Gwenella says it sounds too provincial."

Rachel frowned. Another point against the leader of the group. Ben would not want his wife to be prejudiced. The owner of a general store served every sort of customer, and she knew by his letters that he played favorites to no one. Belle seemed unhindered in her willingness to talk. Perhaps this was the person to ask the question she'd wanted to all night, but was waiting for just the right moment to do so.

"Belle, you've lived here for several years, haven't you?"

Brown curls bobbed up and down in unison with her cheeks as she chewed the cookies. "Longer'n most an'one here. Excuse me . . . I almost choked."

"Take a sip of tea to wash it down." Rachel waited patiently while the woman gulped the tea, cleared her throat several times, then took yet another bite.

The woman's appetite was inexhaustible! "Can you tell me if Mr. McGuire has a favorite friend among any of these women?"

"They *wish.*" Belle licked her lips and wiped crumbs from her lap and onto Rachel's freshly swept floor. "Me too, for that matter. Ben has eyes only for ye, lass."

"Joanna . . . please."

"Well, *Joanna,* since you've brought up the subject we've

skirted around all afternoon''—Gwenella Duncan's voice commanded everyone's attention now—"what are your plans for handsome Ben? Have you come back to marry the poor besotted fool, or will you toss him back to us peasants when you're through with him?"

"Ben's no fool"—*if you were the last woman on this earth, I'd make certain you didn't get him,* Rachel vowed—"and he makes his own choices."

"Then why all these niceities? You invite us here and remind us all afternoon of everything he's done for Valiant in the past. You want to know which of us are married or spoken for and which aren't, then you ask Belle which one of us is his favorite friend." Suspicion narrowed Gwenella's eyes into gray slits. "You're working too hard to convince us of something about him. Now, I wonder what that could be?"

"I have no idea what you're talking about." Though she hated lies, Rachel wasn't about to give the banker's daughter the satisfaction of knowing about her matchmaking plan. In fact, no one would ever know, if she could help it.

"Oh, quit being so suspicious of everybody, Gwenella. Miss Th—Joanna's just wanting to know who her competition is if she stays in town. Isna that right, Joanna?"

Before Rachel could answer her, the heavy eater continued her admonishment. "Gwenella's just jealous because he won't give her the time of day, or night, ye can be certain."

"Do close your mouth, Belle."

Belle ignored Gwenella's warning. "Why should I? Ye just can't stand it because that ballyhoo ye're seeing—and I won't mention who since ye think 'tis such a secret—had the gumption to trust Ben alone with ye. Considering the way ye've thrown yerself at Mr. McGuire the past few years, I bet having yer *companion* feel unthreatened by yer being in the company of the handsomest man in the whole territory really churns yer butter, doesna' it, Gwenella?''

"Perhaps it's time to say good-bye. The storm has all our nerves on edge." Rachel noticed that all other conversations had halted and everyone leaned in a bit closer to listen to the argument that ensued between the two troupe members.

Belle rocked forward until she gained the momentum to launch herself from the davenport on which she and Rachel sat. "Ye're right, Joanna. 'Tis getting a wee late. Too late for me to change what I've done in the name of obeying her every whim and fancy. But no more, Gwenella. From what I saw here this afternoon, she's nothing like ye said. I can see why Ben loves her . . . and why ye never even had a chance with him."

"I have no idea what you're talking about, Isabelle O'Connor. Do you, Penelope? Alizabeth?"

Her cohorts chimed in simultaneously, "We don't."

Everyone in the room seemed to be waiting for Rachel's reaction, but she wasn't quite certain what she felt at the moment. Anger that the banker's daughter came there this afternoon to mock her? Pity that Gwenella's word was so questionable that she had to look to her companions to back it up? Confidence that Ben was wise enough to see through the vixen's charade of caring?

"I appreciate your vote of friendship, Belle"—Rachel smiled at the woman—"it means a lot to be accepted as I am now, and not whatever I'd once been or what people expect me to be."

Belle gathered her shawl around her. "Well, I for one intend to be back. That is, if ye care to have me call again."

"Anytime, Belle. Oh, and particularly the tea after next." If Belle and Ophelia Finck weren't friends already, she would do what she could to remedy the misfortune.

Others took the opportunity to make a quick escape from the animosity between the troupe and its deserter. Though polite invitations to future community functions were extended by nearly every visitor, not one felt genuinely offered. Perhaps the next day's tea party would prove more pleasant. But then, *anything* would be an improvement over this one.

When the troupe made no move to leave along with the rest, Rachel couldn't resist the impulse to test their character. "Oh, it's kind of you all to stay and help with the cleanup."

Gwenella was the first to gather her parasol and cloak, then head for the door—just the desired effect Rachel hoped for. Follow the goose, little goslings, she silently cooed, noting that Gwenella's neck did seem longer than most. Each one complied, affirming the lack of courtesy she suspected of them. Rachel took a curious pleasure in hearing them squeal as they hurried out the door and into the rain. She hoped the poor little darlings' shoes shrunk even tighter.

Belle rolled up a sleeve. "Where do I start?"

Friendship took seed. At least the afternoon wasn't a total failure. "That's kind of you, Belle. But I said that only to get rid of them."

Surprise filled Belle's face, then laughter made her double chin quiver. "And they took the bait." Her smile vanished. "And to think that I once thought they *had* to be my friends or I'd just die . . . just roll over and die. Saints and begorrah, I'm ashamed of meself."

"Don't be." Memories flooded Rachel, but she hurriedly pushed them away. "Sometimes we do things we're ashamed of, but if we try hard enough, we can open our eyes to the truth and not have to suffer the shame again."

" 'Tis true." Belle curtsied. "I never introduced myself properly to ye, and if ye don't mind, I'd like to start all over. Welcome to our fair city, Miss Tharp. I'm Isabelle O'Connor, and I'm very proud to meet ye. I hope we can be the best of friends . . . even long after ye're on yer way back to the big city."

"I'm pleased to be acquainted, Miss O'Connor." Rachel curtsied back, finally having the good time she'd hoped for all afternoon. What a shame the hour was so late and they couldn't spend more time getting to know each other better. "I'm Joanna Tharp, recently from Richmond, Virginia, and I'm pleased to meet you too. In fact, please come back tomorrow, Belle. I don't expect Miss Duncan and her group will stop by anytime soon. Tomorrow's tea party is certain to be better than this one."

Belle laughed and insisted she stay and help clean up, but Rachel refused. Both promised to talk at length the following day.

Not long after Rachel wished her a good evening and started gathering dishes, a knock on the front door interrupted her chore. She set the dishes down, then rushed to see what Belle had forgotten. "What's the matter, Belle? Did you—"

Ben stood on the porch, dripping from hat brim to boot. "I'm not Belle, but I thought I'd give you a hand with the cleanup."

"Come in before you catch your death." She stepped back to let him in. "You haven't been out there all this time, have you?" Rachel reached up and took his hat, setting free a stream of rainwater from its brim.

"Now I've gotten us both wet," he apologized, bending to shake the lower flounce of her dress. "Shake it a bit and it won't soak through your . . . uh . . . petticoats. And yes, I've been out here since three. I wanted to be around if that man you saw earlier decided to watch up close."

"I got *myself* wet." She wiped the wet hair away from his face and became enamored with the blotches flushing his cheeks. Were they a product of the cold, or her touch? Rachel fought an urge to kiss him and see if his entire body heated in response. But it seemed he had his own urge to resist, for

he started unbuttoning his shirt. "What are you doing?" she
demanded.

"Pulling off these wet things. If you don't mind, I'll borrow some of your father's clothes and let mine dry while I
help you clean up. Is the stove still hot?"

As he peeled off his shirt and bared a solid wall of corded
flesh to her, Rachel became speechless. At least outwardly.
Inwardly, approval volleyed through her thoughts. *Lord have
mercy, I'm in deep, deep trouble. And I'm trying to give that
away to some other woman! Ooohh, Joanna, you and I both
need our corsets adjusted!*

Rachel's heart slammed against her chest like a battering
ram. She licked her lips, feeling suddenly quite thirsty.

"Tell you what, I'll light the stove and get some water
heated for the dishes while you go upstairs and get me some
fresh clothes, if you don't mind. I'll just drape my shirt on
the back of a chair and set it in front of the oven to dry."

Rachel nodded and nearly ran up the stairs, afraid she'd
see more of him than she ought to, yet curious enough not
to want to miss a single moment.

Something wet hit the floor as she reached the landing,
and Rachel wondered if it was his trousers. Still another garment plopped, and she imagined longhandles gathered at his
ankles. No . . . his chest was bare. Ben wasn't wearing any
longhandles.

"Deep trouble," she muttered, trying to close off the images that invaded her senses. Images of the rest of his body,
bare, muscular, slick. "Deep, deep trouble!"

Now, where was the Tharps' master bedroom anyway?
She hadn't yet satisfied her compulsion to inspect each bedroom, using her time to familiarize herself with the lower
level of rooms since that was where she'd planned to have
the party. "I don't know which is Thadeus's room," she
worried aloud, looking first into one room, then another.

"Hey up there, it's getting kind of cold down here. Need any help?"

"Don't come up here!" *For heaven's sake, don't.* Having a nude Ben McGuire and numerous beds within kissing distance was simply tempting fate too much. She wanted to do what was right for him and match him up with a good woman, but heaven knew she never claimed to be that good herself. Temptation was difficult to ignore when its first name was Ben.

The next door opened to the room she'd discovered the previous night but refused to sleep in. Joanna's room. Red curtains, rose-budded wallcoverings, red everything. "I'll never find it."

Her search ended with the room across the hall from Joanna's. She swung open the door to the armoire and pilfered through Thadeus's frock coats and suits. The surge of triumph that filled her at finding the masculine garments whooshed out like the air from a punctured balloon. "These won't fit one leg, much less two."

Joanna's father was a short man, plump and barrel-chested. Nothing he wore would fit Ben's powerful physique. But Narcissia's clothing was another possibility. Joanna's mother was portly and favored evening wear that gave her room to breathe, as she often said. A smile curved Rachel's lips as she grabbed the heavy cotton nightgown and draped it over her arm. As an afterthought, she grabbed the blanket from the bed.

She raced downstairs, trying hard not to giggle for fear he'd hear her and anticipate her tactics. Caught up in her plans, Rachel remembered too late to announce her presence. She almost dropped the gown when she turned the corner to the kitchen and saw the near-nude Adonis washing dishes.

His hair waved in blond curls to his shoulders, uncorraled by hat and untethered by the strand of rawhide that she'd seen hold it in place. He might as well have stripped off his trousers, for the soaked cloth plastered his buttocks and thighs so tightly, it left nothing to the imagination. The other clothing she'd heard him discard was merely his boots and socks. The sight of his bare feet seemed so personal, intimate. His bare back glistened with such a sheen, she licked her lips to rid herself of the moisture that now beaded her upper lip. Ben turned and grinned at her.

Heat fused Rachel's cheeks as all playfulness escaped her. A near-nude Ben was no laughing matter; he looked far too dangerous and even more so soaked to the skin. She hid the gown behind her and thrust the blanket forward. "Here, cover yourself with this."

"My hands are soapy. Will you wrap it around my shoulders?"

And your waist. And your thighs. When he turned his back to her, she draped the gown over the back of the chair and wrapped the blanket around him. Rachel lifted his hair free of the makeshift collar, unconsciously letting her fingers glide through the thick, damp curls.

"Thank you," he whispered. "I feel much warmer now. No, don't, Joanna. Please don't move away."

His voice was so low, it could have been only a feather's rustle. Rachel felt his shoulders tighten slightly. Slowly he turned, then a fraction of an inch at a time, pulled her closer. Her fingers splayed over his chest, feeling the warmth of his body and his breath moving slowly across her neck.

His hands slid to her waist and drew her solidly against him. "Would you still deny me a kiss?"

Rachel marveled at the way he felt—like marble bound in velvet. She loved the steady pounding of his heart beneath her fingertips. She couldn't stop the sigh of longing that escaped her, neither could she give in to her yearnings. "I have to, Ben. It wouldn't be fair to you."

She would not play Joanna's game. Steal his kisses, rouse his passions, only to leave him brokenhearted and wanting. But how did she dare make him understand without revealing the deception?

"Let me decide what's fair," he whispered, pressing his lips against the path she'd accepted before—her forehead, her eyes, her cheeks. Each kiss became firmer, more demanding.

She sucked in her breath as his mouth halted only inches from her own. Would he stop? Could she stop him if he didn't? Did she even want to?

Ben's arms tightened around her, melding Rachel to him. God, how she wanted him to demand the kiss, to lose herself in the wonder of his embrace. But he believed in her. Trusted in her. Longed for more than she could give.

"Why won't you kiss me?"

His breath mingled with her own, sending hot tingles through her throat and to the nether regions of her desire.

"Don't tell me it's because you don't want me to." His hands traced the curve of her hips, her waist, lingering just below her breasts. "That would be a lie."

Her fingers now traced the strong slope of his shoulders as her body leaned into his of its own volition. Rachel looked closely at the man who held her, wishing he'd been in *her* life before Joanna Tharp's. Wishing more than ever she'd never read his letters. Praying that there was a way out of this agreement with Joanna.

His body shifted slightly, igniting every sensation within her. The need to touch and be touched was too strong, the pure joy of being held in his arms too powerful to deny herself this moment of heaven.

Yearning swept through Rachel like a fire out of control. The hunger in his eyes held more than passion. It offered promises kept. Lifetime commitment.

"Joanna love."

The endearment chilled the blood boiling in her veins. "I can't care about you!" she blurted out. "I won't care for you," she repeated, as if saying the words would make them true.

The rhythm of his heart slowed against her breasts, the warmth of his leg moved away from her thigh. It felt as if someone had tossed a bucket of winter water over them to cool their ardor.

"Did you just come back to Valiant to torment me, Joanna?" Ben moved away from her, shrugging off the blanket. "Or is this some kind of strange initiation I have to overcome in order to prove how much I care for you?"

Initiation? Would Joanna have put Ben through a test of some kind? Though the idea seemed distasteful, it would provide a way to keep him at a distance for most of the time she spent in Valiant. "I don't mean to torment you, Ben."

Nor myself. How am I going to get through this matchmaking if all I can think about is having you hold me?

"Torment me? Every moment you aren't in my arms you torment me." Frustration filled Ben's tone as he noticed the gown draped over the chair and lifted it. "Is this part of the initiation?"

A lovely blush spotted her cheeks. "It was meant as a joke. I knew Thad—*Father's* clothes wouldn't fit you very well, but Mother's could wrap around you and me together. The material is quite warm, you know."

This was a playful side of Joanna he didn't remember, and it pleased him. A grin began in his heart and spread to his lips, dousing the frustration that filled him too readily in Joanna's presence. "I think I'll wait for my things to dry, if you don't mind."

"But I do mind," she said huskily, her eyes rounding into

green saucers as one hand rose to cover her mouth. "Did I say that out loud?"

"You did, and frankly I didn't mind." He couldn't help but laugh at her panic. "I see things never change. Always talking to yourself."

The fact that she was still attracted to him renewed Ben's confidence. There could be a future for them together. The years in Richmond had not spoiled the possibility. "Ready to finish those dishes? I wash. You dry."

"You're still willing?" She grabbed a towel and followed him to the washtub.

"You look like you've never seen a man wash dishes before."

"I can't say as I have," she admitted. "But I thought you might be too angry with me to want to help anymore."

Dipping his hands into the soapy water, he scrubbed a teacup. "You've known me long enough to realize that I don't anger easily, and I intend to keep that promise I made to you on the day you left Valiant."

"And what promise was that?" Her fingers touched his as she took the soapy cup from him and dipped it into the rinse water.

Disappointment and hurt raced through him at the thought that it had meant so little to her that she hadn't remembered his heartfelt vow.

"That no matter where you went or what you did, if you ever came back to Valiant . . . to me . . . that the only way you'd ever go anywhere else again was as Mrs. Ben McGuire."

❖ 8 ❖

Mrs. Ben McGuire. It had a nice sound to it no matter how many times it repeated in her head. Though exhausted from the previous day, Rachel rose early. Cookies shaped like sharp-pointed shoes that waddled one after another had filled her dreams. She actually woke herself up laughing . . . twice.

But it was dreams of Ben that lingered most in her mind. Ben, at the station waiting for her. Ben, in church, leaving her breathless with anticipation of his kiss. Ben, in a state of undress that even a saint would find hard to resist.

He was everything his letters hinted at—a man who could turn a woman's heart inside out with just a wisp of a smile or a shared glance. A man whose thoughtfulness and concern for his adopted son had already earned her trust. A man who, no matter how much she tried to convince herself she shouldn't dwell on such matters, was definitely worth loving.

Rachel turned back the covers and got out of bed, hoping to find something to occupy her thoughts well enough to rid them of the way Ben made her feel every time he was near.

Get your hands busy and your mind will follow suit. The old family adage provided her with a possibility. Rachel plodded downstairs to the kitchen, deciding that cookie dough would keep her busy. She would get the baking done early enough to enjoy the rest of the morning, and have the house cooled down by the time guests arrived.

As the stove was heating, Rachel opened the cupboard to get the spices. A note lay across the jar of cinnamon, the parchment bent in half so that she couldn't readily decipher its contents.

"I wonder what he—" Rachel's reading halted as she read the words, realizing that Ben hadn't left the message, as she'd first suspected. Her hands shook as her mind raced to remember which of yesterday's guests had visited the kitchen. *Gwenella?* The obvious culprit hadn't left her seat all afternoon. Belle . . . yes. Penelope What's-her-name . . . no. The blinker . . . yes. And two others whose names she couldn't remember at the moment. But why would any of them leave such a threat?

Rachel scanned the warning again and repeated it aloud, hoping that the choice of words would trigger her memory and remind her of one of the women's speech patterns or turn of phrases.

> *"Joanna,*
> *I told you no games. I don't know what you're trying to prove with these so-called teas, but be careful what you say to whom. Gossip tends to die a quick death when spread to the wrong person."*

A quick death if spread to the wrong person? Though not stated outright, the implication was clear. Someone meant to kill her if she spoke out of turn. But to whom? And what could Joanna possibly know that might be worth dying for?

"The cookies can wait." She folded the note in half and headed upstairs to change out of her nightdress and into something more suitable for town. She might not be able to talk over this situation with anyone for fear they'd learn the truth about her real identity, but she didn't have to stay there and be a waiting target.

Though she had felt no sinister presence during the night and none that morning, the note instilled a certain wariness within her. Rachel hurriedly pushed the gown over her head, gasped when she realized she'd forgotten to unfasten the top button and that a strand of her hair was now tangled around it. While her hands worked at dislodging her hair, panic seized her with thoughts of someone creeping up behind her. Straining to hear the slightest creak across the wooden flooring, Rachel soon realized the Tharps' Aubusson carpets would muffle anyone's footsteps.

Unwilling to wait any longer for the wayward strand to extricate itself, she yanked hard and pulled the button off the gown. "Oooouch!"

The hair fell free and the gown flew over her head with one quick jerk. Like a blind woman whose sight had miraculously returned, Rachel scanned every nook and cranny for sight of an intruder. After a thorough search, she allowed herself a sigh of relief and a brief rub at the back of her neck where her hair had been yanked out from its roots.

She grabbed clothing that didn't have to go over her head to be worn. A red paisley blouse and matching skirt fit the requirements. Soft kid gloves and slippers completed her dressing and brought a welcome bit of relief to the tension that had filled her since finding the note. At least she wouldn't be accused of wearing tight shoes—the kid slippers fit perfectly.

Not wanting to spend any more time in the house by herself than was necessary, Rachel elected to simply brush her hair down about her shoulders and tie it back in a ribbon that matched the paisley. Staring at herself in the oval mirror, she asked aloud, "Now that you're dressed, what are you going to do with yourself, Rachel Sloan?"

Make sure you don't forget the stove, her reflection seemed to say as she stuffed the note in her handbag.

Minutes later she locked the door behind her, determined to visit Delaney's restaurant. Perhaps she could buy enough cookies not to have to make any today.

"Whatcha doing out so early this morning?"

Rachel nearly swallowed her tonsils. She spun around to see the boy and his dog rise from the porch. "J-Jimmy. Bowie. What are you two doing h-here so early?"

Jimmy frowned. "You told me to come by and you'd give me some cookies, didn't ya?"

Bowie snuffled, then licked at her ankles, leaving slobber on her hem.

The hand that had started to pat the dog stopped in midair, then finally scratched behind Bowie's ear. "Yes, I did. But I'm afraid I burned too many yesterday. Would you let me buy you some breakfast at Delaney's this morning?"

"Ham and eggs and biscuits with gravy?"

Bowie started panting, his face lighting up with the excitement that filled his master's tone.

"Whatever you'd like," she assured the boy, feeling guilty that she'd forgotten to save him any cookies. But the truth was, he'd come out the winner. She was doing him a favor sparing him from her first effort at hostessing. Even the unburned sweets hadn't been that good.

"I like just about anything." Jim's gait matched her stride toward town. "And what I don't eat, Bowie will."

She remembered hunger well. Never feeling as if she were full. Always taking anything anyone offered because she wasn't sure when or where she would get the next meal. "As long as I'm in town, Jim, you can eat whatever you like. Just charge it to the Tharp account."

Brown eyes stared at her. "Are you really that rich, lady?"

"Rich? Depends on what you call rich."

"Having money when you need it. Eating when you're hungry. Having a warm place to sleep."

"Then you must be more blessed than most," she answered, unable to lie to the searching gaze that would sense an untruth. Children always knew the truth when it was spoken and suspected when an adult lied to them. She would never do such a thing, because she knew how it felt to be betrayed. "I'm sure your father provides you with all those nice things."

"Mr. McGuire's a square man."

"You don't call him Father or Dad? Even Ben?"

"He's not my pa." There was no belligerence in the boy's tone, only a flat statement of fact. "There's a shortcut to Delaney's this way. You don't have to go by the store 'less you just want to."

"Let's take the shortcut." She followed Jimmy, glad that he seemed in such a talkative mood. "Did you agree to the adoption?"

"Yeah." Bowie barked in agreement as well.

If Jim talked as fast as he walked, she'd already know his life history by now. She reached out a finger to tap him into a slower gait. "If you wanted to be adopted, then why don't you like Ben?"

The boy stopped and faced her. "Did Mr. McGuire badger you into asking me this?"

The angry look on his face battled with another emotion she couldn't grasp at the moment. "Of course not. I think your father is the sort of man who would ask you outright, don't you?"

"He ain't done it yet."

As Jim resumed his walk, Rachel realized the emotion she hadn't been able to pin down a second before. The boy needed to tell, needed to confess whatever was bothering him, needed Ben to listen. Why hadn't Ben attempted to find out why Jimmy felt such animosity for him?

The fact that Ben hadn't already sensed his son's need worried Rachel. He wasn't the sort of man to leave a child stewing over problems. There was something deeper here, and she certainly didn't know how to advise the boy. But she could empathize with what it felt like to be thirteen and uncertain where one stood in the world.

"I don't know why you're angry with your father"—she matched his long-legged strides—"but I can tell you this, Jim. You can bet you'll always have a place to lay your head down with Mr. McGuire. And that may not seem like much, but sometimes having a safe place to come home to at night sure helps you survive the other trials you suffer during the day."

"Speaking of trials . . . here comes Mr. Whipple. Don't look him in the eye, or he'll talk till sundown."

Jim stopped and pretended to admire the store window they were about to pass. Rachel chuckled as she watched the boy eye a feathered bonnet as if it were the latest in military headgear. Despite his warning, she couldn't resist a glance at the notorious talker. At the moment their eyes met, she recognized him as the man who wouldn't move out of her way as she exited the train.

A jerk on her arm yanked her inside the millinery shop at the same time Whipple dashed into the nearest business.

As soon as the bell announcing their arrival ceased, Jimmy let go of her arm and whispered, "Don't have nothing to do with that man. He don't care nothing about nobody unless you're a voter."

"It didn't seem he wanted to see us any more than we did him," she whispered back.

"Why, Jimmy McGuire! How nice of you to pay a visit.

And Miss Tharp. I'm so glad you could take time to call."
A redheaded woman bounced into the room from a curtained-off area. "I'm planning to attend your tea this afternoon, if I can just get this hem finished in time. Work, work,
work. That's all I do."

"Clementine?"

"How nice of you to remember. Clementine Crawford.
Local dressmaker and seamstress." Pride stained her freckles
a deeper red.

Rachel surveyed the woman's merchandise, nodding her
approval. "These are lovely Venetian cross-stitches. And this
Antoinette pattern. The lace looks almost seamless. You
could set up shop anywhere in the East and do a healthy
business, miss."

"You really think so?"

Rachel could feel the woman's gaze watching her every
move, following her fingers across seams and embroidery.
"I know so. How did you manage to make this dart look
like a fold in the . . ." Rachel raved on and on about the
dressmaker's incredible talent. So much so that she began to
realize she was paying undue notice, and Clementine was
staring at her with a curious expression.

"I hear that you have a new wardrobe each season."

The shop owner said the word "each" as if it were the
pot of gold at the end of a leprechaun's rainbow. Envy filled
Clementine's eyes.

"One has to be quite knowledgeable if one is to know
quality." There, that sounded highfalutin and might ward off
the woman's further questioning.

The bell jangled again, followed by a loud "Hey there,
Clem! Needja to patch up my coonskin fer me." Alewine
Jones sauntered up to the counter as if she were bellying up
to a bar. "Run into some bushwhackers a ways down the
road to Saints Roost. None of 'em could hit a bull's butt

with a handful of banjos though. Missed me by a coon's tail.'' She jabbed a finger in and out of a hole shot clear through the tail that dangled from the cap, causing the fringe on her buckskin to rustle with her movements.

"Why, howdy there, Jimbo." She spied the boy and moved over to ruffle his hair. "Gotcha trailing that petticoat around, does he now?"

"I ain't doing no such thing." Jimmy dodged the hand that looked like it might be bearing grease of some sort. He bent down and whispered to the dog, "Stop that. It ain't your blanket."

A muffled snuff, grrrr, snufff, grrrr, snufff warned Rachel that the dog was doing all sorts of unmentionables upon something he shouldn't be. A silver-colored dress swayed on its stand, the taffeta rustling like windblown leaves.

"Ain't nobody said nothing about no blanket, Jim McGuire." Alewine grabbed the boy by the collar of his shirt and hauled him to an upright position.

"I know that, Aly." Jim's gaze slanted downward, then back at Aly, then downward again.

The salt-and-pepper-haired woman let go of Jim. "Shoulda told me I's barking at a knot, boy."

"Trouble?" Clementine craned her neck to see around the ruckus.

Rachel stepped in front of the dog and motioned to Jimmy with the back of her hand. "Is that your stomach I hear rumbling, Jimmy McGuire? You best go on along and eat something before you start work this morning."

Alewine's voice boomed so loud, it made the windows rattle. "And make sure you feed Bowie too, so he'll quit *chawing* on thangs, you hear?"

"Ohhh . . . okay. I gotcha." Jim bent over to pick up his dog, turn, and hold him in front of him so the shop owner couldn't see what Rachel and Alewine were trying to hide.

A loud ripping sound rent the air. Bowie went into his master's arms, trailing a jawful of taffeta.

Rachel stomped backward, pretending she'd stumbled. "Oh, look here what I've done. Ruined the whole thing. I guess I'll just have to buy it." She held up the dress and smiled apologetically.

A look of horror crossed Clementine's face. "Oh, you couldn't possibly wear that, Miss Tharp. The color's not right for you at all, and I'm sure I can repair the—" She finally noticed the mauled hemline and the slobber dribbling off its edge.

"I m-must have had something on my shoe." Rachel blinked twice. Realizing that batting her eyes was becoming a habit she mimicked, she abruptly stopped.

"Truth be, it might've been my boot that done it." Alewine fingered the material. "Shore is purty."

Clementine's eyes widened in response and held. "Will that be cash or on account?"

Rachel began to chuckle. The woman looked as though somebody had dropped an icicle down her corset. "On account of"—she paused and winked at Alewine—"if *you* buy it, she'd probably faint dead away."

But it was Rachel who thought she felt suddenly strange, for at that moment Sterling Whipple looked inside the millinery shop window, frowned at her, and hurried past.

❖ 9 ❖

"Lend me a hand, will ya?"

Flinging open the door to Tharp House, Rachel allowed in her unexpected visitor. The crimson staining the left side of her guest's buckskinned hip blossomed fresh despite the rain that attempted to wash it away. "You're bleeding."

"Not for long if I don't get it stopped. You gotta place I can lay for a spell? Feeling kinda dizzy at the mo—"

Rachel rushed forward to catch the woman before she hit the floor. She managed to break the fall but landed backward on her bottom, cradling the injured woman in a slick bear hug. "Miss Jones"—*what did she say her name was?*—"Alewine. Are you all right? Alewine, say something."

A muffled groan emanated from where the woman's face was buried in Rachel's collarbone. "S-somebody nicked me."

"Did you see who it was?" Rachel stared on in amazement as Alewine rose to her knees, wincing with pain yet not uttering a single sound. Was it someone nearby, lurking around her house? Fear settled deep into Rachel's bones.

"If I had, they'd be buzzard bait by now. The so-and-so hid behind a line of trees out at the Wild Horse."

Alewine stood and teetered slightly before lending a hand

to help Rachel up. Finally her golden eyes focused, looking slightly less dazed than before.

"Heard tell you got an honest-to-hellfire bathtub like they do in St. Louie. Seems as good a place as any to catch this hip juice I'm leaking."

"Can you make it up the stairs?" Rachel offered her shoulder under Alewine's right one. "Hang on. That will put all the pressure on your right side. Use me for a crutch."

Alewine did as she was told. The buckskin seemed glued to the frontierswoman's body and was difficult to hang on to, being so wet and slick from the rain. They made it half-way up the stairs before Alewine started to teeter backward and lose her balance. Rachel leaned forward, strengthening the hold she had around Alewine's torso. "Steady . . . steady! Lean forward. That's the way. Fooorwaard."

The arm that bent so desperately around her throat gripped so hard, Rachel feared she might suffocate. Seconds later her feet planted themselves firmly on the next step and held . . . along with Alewine's. The viselike grip eased.

"You know, this kind of reminds me of when me and old Rash drank ourself so drunk we had a helluva time getting up Ophelia's stairs. Kept falling down three for every four we made. Would've topped the rise if ol' Rash hadn't figured he'd just snuggle up in that fancy fluff carpet at the foot of the stairs and mount them jaspers when he was a might more sober. Made perfect sense to me at the time. Gotta say though, I'd druther not repeat the experience if you got it in ya to clear the peak."

"I've got it in me." Determination filled Rachel. Ben's friend might not expect Joanna to see her through this, but Rachel Sloan would.

"Gawldurn, ain't this a crackerjack of a house!"

Following Alewine's gaze as they cleared the landing and passed down the second-floor hallway, Rachel couldn't help but feel the same awe. "The Tharps always buy the best."

The moment the words were out of her mouth, she realized her mistake and tried to correct it. "Mother and Father, Grandmahmah and Grandpahpah, all the Tharp generations have insisted on quality purchases. Here we are." *Just in the nick of time.* Rachel breathed an inward sigh of relief as she lightly kicked the door open to the sitting room. "Do you feel well enough to undress yourself, or should I help?"

"Get me something to lean on, and I can shuck these things myself. Put a few towels down so's I don't get nothing bloody. I'll buy you some new ones from the mercantile tomorrow."

"We'll worry about that later. For now, I'll start heating water so we can bathe that wound and see how bad it is." She turned to leave and looked back at the pale-faced woman. "Are you sure you won't faint again?"

"I ain't never fainted in my whole however many years. You get them towels, little lady, and I'll be mighty obliged."

Rachel rushed to fetch all that was needed. She grabbed a gray chambray wrapper from Narcissia's wardrobe, certain Alewine would never approve of some of Joanna's more frilly nightwear. Barely opening the door to the sitting room, she stretched her arm around the oak panel and felt the towels and wrapper taken from her grasp. "I know the nightgown is too large for you, but it'll let you move freely once we get you bandaged. I'm going down to heat up more water, but I already had some ready for dishwashing."

The kitchen was still a mess from that afternoon's tea. Though better than the first, today's gathering had been just as frustrating. All the unmarried ladies such as Belle and Clementine might prove to be good matches, but none seemed the perfect bride for Ben. From all they said about him, she had learned that every man, woman, and child in town nearly worshiped Joanna's beau. Ben does this, Ben does that. Ben's so handsome. You can trust Ben.

As Rachel primed the pump and watched water fill two more huge cooking vats, she wondered if being worshiped was enough to make a man like Ben happy. Didn't he say in his letters he wanted a woman to live and learn with him? That he wanted them to be equal partners in his store, his home, and in raising their children?

Testing the water already heated on the stove, she decided she'd have to mix a bit of cool water with it or it would scald Alewine. *The same way with Ben,* she realized, adding cooler water to the pots. He didn't need someone to fawn all over him as Gwenella Duncan might, or to worship him as Clementine Crawford would. What he needed was a woman who ran hot and cold, a woman who would make him live every moment but keep him challenged.

No one seemed to fit that billing in Valiant other than Ophelia Finck, and though she didn't believe in intuition for the most part, Rachel's told her to tread lightly if attempting to match Ophelia with Ben. If only there were someone else Ben truly respected and could learn to love.

"Hey there! Didja forget me?" Alewine called.

"No, I didn't—" Rachel hollered back, then realized she had done just that. She'd forgotten Alewine Jones and the respect Ben held for the frontierswoman. A woman who would certainly make life interesting every moment and would definitely keep him challenged. The only problem—she wasn't much of a female.

A slight dilemma Rachel had plenty of experience in handling. Couldn't she sew the prettiest fashions east of the Mississippi? Didn't more than one of her former employers, even Joanna herself, admit that Rachel knew just how to enhance a woman's attributes so even the dowdiest-figured patron felt feminine and alluring? Wasn't it her obligation to try *every* available female in Valiant before making her decision?

Why, then, with such a prime candidate as Alewine, did she feel suddenly so . . . so . . . *what? I should be happy for the two of them.* Ben and Alewine were great friends. That was a wonderful start for any marriage. Ben would treat Miss Jones like a woman dreams of being treated. And in return, Alewine would work beside him, love him, and make an exciting mother for Jimmy and the rest of the children two such life-loving people would birth.

Children. *Ben's* children. For just a moment Rachel allowed herself to switch places with Alewine in the images she conjured, but they wouldn't form. In the deepest part of Rachel's heart she knew why. Even if she did allow the dream to become reality and accept Ben's courting, she would be caught in a net of lies and he would never trust her.

Taking a deep breath to foster strength she didn't feel, Rachel whispered, "You did this to yourself, Rachel Sloan. The consequences aren't so bad, are they? You got everything you wished for. A nice home to live in for a while. Money and fine clothes."

Why, then, did she still feel so unsatisfied?

She grabbed potholders to carry one of the pans upstairs. The best thing to do now was to satisfy Ben's seven-year dream and give him someone special to love. It was time to put her plan into action and see if it had any merit.

Rachel closed her eyes to remember the face she'd found so mesmerizing upon meeting the frontierswoman. She almost missed a step, splashing water from the pan and soaking her face and collar, just enough to make her blink away the image that had risen in her mind's eye. Cleaned up, Alewine Jones just might make a beautiful bride.

She hurried upstairs, stopping just short of the sitting room door. "May I come in?"

"Unless you're bashful."

Good, she was afraid Alewine might be. Having sewn all manner of garments for wealthy ladies the past four years, Rachel was accustomed to seeing them in all levels of undress.

She almost dropped the pot of water again. Standing before her was a woman of unparalleled beauty. A white towel draped around full breasts was tucked in the center, exposing a bronze cleavage that had been well hidden beneath the buckskin shirt. Any woman would envy the slim waist that flared to such finely curved hips. A second towel rode low over one, then slanted toward another, leaving the wound visible for doctoring. Alewine's legs seemed longer than when they'd been encased in buckskin and were shaped by years of ''doing'' rather than being ''done for.''

''Whatchoo gawking at?'' Alewine's gaze started toward the knife lying next to the heap of buckskin on the floor. Something lacy peaked out from under the shirt.

''Nothing.'' Rachel dumped the water into the tub and deliberately kept her eyes from focusing anywhere on her visitor. ''You just look more female without your buckskins. I'm surprised, that's all. You clean up pretty good. I'll be back in a minute. I've got to go get more water.''

''It's only a graze. No need to bring much more.'' Alewine swayed and grabbed the rim of the tub, steadying herself. The water splashed back and forth as she jostled the tub.

''You need a bath.'' *If my plan is going to work.* Rachel formulated which dress of Joanna's she could alter to fit Alewine's more statuesque form.

''The rest of me ain't hurt.''

''That's true.'' Rachel met the woman's challenge. ''But we both know you need a place to rest up a little before you try to go home. If you can honestly tell me when the last time you took a bath was, I won't feel so stubborn about making you take one.''

'' 'Fraid I'll soil your sheets?''

"Afraid someone will see how you *can* be if you choose to?''

Alewine looked startled. Rachel knew immediately she'd locked on to some secret fear the frontierswoman held. She supposed it took one impostor to recognize another.

"I'll sleep on the floor.''

Fists shot to Rachel's hips. "Not in this house, you won't.''

"Then I'll sleep on the front porch.''

"You *are* afraid. So afraid that you want everyone to think you're rough and tough and not one ounce female. Well, if that's so, then why do you wear this?'' Rachel picked up the lacy chemise she'd spotted beneath the soiled buckskin. Though it had been cut to fit only hip level, its length hadn't been the surprise. The fact that the wilderness woman had chosen to wear one at all proved the biggest curiosity.

"Give me that,'' Alewine complained, and attempted to grab it from her. "Ooohh!'' She clutched her hip, pain etching her face. "Damn you, Joanna Tharp, if you tell a soul about that, I'll skin you like a rabbit.''

Rachel dropped the chemise and grabbed Alewine by the shoulders. "Get in the tub and just lie back before you hurt yourself any more.''

Alewine reluctantly obliged. When she was settled, Rachel took a cloth, dipped it into the water, and lightly pressed the wound. The hip jerked away in response. Rachel refused to be intimidated by the unfeminine growl that exited Alewine's throat. She squeezed warm water over the injury, until Alewine relaxed and let her continue the necessary cleansing.

Upon careful inspection, Rachel was relieved to know that her visitor was not in as serious trouble as she'd feared. The bullet had passed clean through the fleshy part of the hip. "Are you in much pain?"

Golden eyes stared at her. "Could be worse."

"Why don't you press that against you for a while?" She held the cloth over the wound and waited until Alewine's hand tentatively moved to grip the cloth. "I'll get more water and then some salve. Fortune smiled on you after all, Miss Jones. You'll be sore for a while, but nothing's cracked or shattered."

"For a society gal, you sure are putting yourself out. Ain't nobody gonna give ya any backslapping for helping the likes of me."

"Backslapping is overrated, Miss Jones. All it ever gave me was a stiff neck."

A loud guffaw rent the air. "D-don't make me laugh, it hurts too much."

Rachel emptied the remainder of the water into the tub and searched the cabinets until she found a medicinal supply that was surprisingly fresh, thanks to Ben. When she returned, Alewine was in a more pleasant state of mind. She even allowed Rachel to wash her hair—a badly needed scrubbing.

"I do believe your hair is white, Miss Jones. I thought it was more salt and pepper colored." Rachel grimaced as she wondered exactly what it was she was sudsing out of the woman's locks to make the difference.

"Keeps anyone from guessing my age."

"Is that important to you?"

"Most of the time . . . no."

Who or what are you hiding from? Rachel wondered, but didn't voice her question aloud. A person's privacy should be respected. Perhaps someday Alewine would trust her with the truth, just as she might trust the frontierswoman with her real identity.

"Why did you come to me for help?" She'd been so busy cleaning her guest, Rachel hadn't remembered to ask the one question that had nipped at her all evening. She poured water over Alewine's hair, rinsing out the suds.

"Ahhh. That's better'n it's felt in nigh on two years."

Rachel jerked back her hands. Two years! No wonder it looked partially black. Alewine started chuckling, her nose wrinkling and her mouth appearing even more comical in its upside-down position. She sat up and turned to face Rachel, rivulets of water streaming from her undried hair.

"I was just funnin' ya, Jo. I clean it onc't every couple'a weeks, whether it needs it or not . . . 'cept in the winter." She laughed again, her shoulders shaking with mirth. "Doc's delivering a baby over in Tascosa. Ben's gone to Clarendon to visit with Old Man Colston and his wife, Hannah, so's I couldn't bother him neither. Said he'd be back 'round noon tomorrow. Jim's minding the store, but couldn't ask him to shuck his chores on my account. Figured you's the only one in town I wouldn't be putting out too much if I bled up your doorstep. Besides, I took a hankering to ya this morning in the millinery. Anyone who'll go up against Clementine for a mutt like Bowie can't be as bad as you used to be."

"And how bad was I?" Rachel dried Alewine's hair with a towel and wrapped it around her head. She handed the nightwear to the frontierswoman, then turned around as Alewine dressed.

"Well, most knew ya to be a fine, upstanding little twist of petticoat that had too much too soon. A few thought you were mean and deceitful and full of spitefulness, eager to hurt anyone who stood in your way."

Rachel heard the wet towels fall against the floor and the wrapper slip over Alewine's head. She turned to confront her ward. "Were you one of those few?"

Golden eyes stared at her, appraising her. "Not till that last day."

"Then, who?"

"Ophelia, but I guess you know that plain enough. And Joshua Duncan. And Whipple, of course."

"Why does that man's name continue to come up all the time?"

"Just who the hell are you, lady?"

Taken aback, Rachel busied herself gathering the towels and soiled clothing from the floor, wishing now she'd never opened up this powder keg. "Joanna Tharp, of course."

Alewine gripped Rachel's hand. "Yeah, and I'm a horse trader and mule skinner from Valiant, Texas. So now that we've got our secret lives out in the open, how 'bout telling each other who we really are?"

❖ *10* ❖

IGNORING ALEWINE'S QUESTION, Rachel hurried into the bedroom and started turning down the covers. "Why don't you make yourself comfortable, and I'll get the salve and bandages?"

When she finished fluffing the pillows, Rachel turned to find her guest peeking into the jewel box on the top of the armoire, then quietly sliding out the top drawer of the dresser to do the same. Rachel spun around and pounded the pillow, elaborately fluffing it more.

All too familiar with Alewine's curiosity about Tharp House, Rachel chose not to embarrass her. "There, that ought to do it. Are you ready to be done with this?"

She could almost feel the frontierswoman's body brush by. When she turned, Rachel found the woman standing at the window, peering out. Lightning blinked, illuminating the room in an eerie glow that momentarily brightened the waning daylight. Seconds later thunder rattled the panes.

Alewine let the curtain fall back into place and sauntered forward, her steps slightly more unsteady than before. "Like to check the streets before I turn in."

"Better lie down here." Rachel moved out of the way and allowed Alewine to sit on the edge of the mattress. She grabbed the rocking chair near the window, scooted it next to the bed, then took a seat.

The wilderness woman looked out of place amid the delicate cream-colored linen sheets. Her bronze skin seemed even more sun-weathered peeking out from the gray wrapper's high collar and sleeves. Seconds ticked by as each woman stared at the other, and Rachel wondered if her guest would ultimately let her minister to the wound.

A growl of thunder rumbled its discontent. The room blinked once, twice, then began to take on the early shadows of twilight.

"You gonna just sit there and gawk at me, or patch me up?"

"Patch you up," Rachel replied. "How would you prefer we do this? Standing or lying down?"

"I'd *prefer* we didn't do it at all." Alewine snorted, rising from the bed. "But since I hafta, why don't I just hike this here hem up and you slap a gob of that salve on me?"

Rachel examined the wound carefully. Now that it was clean, she could see that more than simple bandaging was needed. "I'll light some lamps so we can see what we're doing. You need a few stitches."

"You fetch whatever you need, *Jo*." Alewine tucked the gown's hem up into her collar to free her hands, exposing a statuesque figure that would enhance any seamstress's designs. She placed one hand against the front of her hip, the other behind it. "I'll keep pressure on it till ya get back."

After lighting the lamps, Rachel searched the medicine supply. A subsequent search in her trunk provided a needle and thread, while the kitchen yielded candles and the necessary wax. She'd read somewhere that using a touch of slightly warmed wax on a fresh stitch would seal the skin tightly together. Rachel just hoped she hadn't read it in one of those dime novels she loved, and that it was truth rather than fiction.

A check of the water heating on the stove assured her it was hot enough to sanitize the needle and thread. She lit the candle and let the wax melt. Finally, when all was ready, she went upstairs to finish her task.

" 'Bout time,'' Alewine grumbled through clenched teeth that now held the hem that must have worked loose from its anchor in the gown's collar. "Figgeth you's fetchin' Clem to sew me up"—she paused, working the chambray around in her teeth to be understood better—"sinth Doc ain't in town."

Rachel tugged the hem from Alewine's mouth and tucked it once more into the gown's collar. She would need both of her own hands as well. "No need. Miss Crawford's good, but you won't know you've been sewn when I get through with you."

"Spoken like a true Joanna Tharp, though we both know you ain't."

Rachel nudged Alewine backward. "Lie down and don't start talking with your hands the way you do. You need to be very still."

Waiting until Alewine complied, she took a cloth and gently wiped the wound clean again. "Why must you insist that I'm not who I say I am?"

"Well, little Miss Sewer-upper"—puzzlement etched Alewine's brow—"because Joanna couldn't tell the eye of a needle from a hole in her daddy's outhouse."

Rachel laughed despite her need to waylay Alewine's suspicions.

"And the real Joanna would never agree to let the likes of me step foot in her house, much less waller in her sheets."

"If you'd lie still, you wouldn't have to wallow," Rachel insisted, frowning at the woman's elaborate hand gestures.

Alewine's brows veed together. "I ain't known to be the patient sort. This gonna take much longer?"

Rachel glared right back. "It'll take as long as it takes, Miss Jones. Once I'm done stitching, I have to add the salve. After that I'll smooth some wax over both sides and then I'll be finished. You'll be good as new in about a week."

Alewine sat up and complained loudly as she gripped her hip. "A week! Woman, I got a freight line to run and horses to stable."

"Lean back. You're just making your wound seep." Rachel gently nudged her guest back against the pillows. "Quit worrying about everything. I'll put a notice on the freight office door that says it'll be closed for a week. If nothing else, I'll just have to see to those horses myself."

"I know'd you ain't Joanna Tharp fer sure now."

"Will you please control those hands?"

Alewine lay back and threaded them together behind her head as if she didn't have a care in the world. Still, her eyes betrayed her, for they watched Rachel's every move.

"Like I asked before," the woman demanded, "who the hell—"

"Did your mother ever wash your mouth out for cursing, Miss Jones?" Rachel admonished as she began the stitching.

"Hell, yes . . . I mean . . . she shore dang did." Golden eyes focused on Rachel's dexterity. "Durn if that ain't the fastest sewin' I seen this side of the Cimarron!"

"Turn and let me get the other side."

"I'm mighty obliging to you, whoever the hell—heck— you are." Alewine turned, smoothing the sheets appreciatively. "Didn't have to take me in, but ya did. 'Bout the neighborliest thing anybody's ever done fer me. And jist fer that, I take back 'at bunch of yowling I hollered at ya the other night at Delaney's."

"Apology accepted."

"Figure I owe you now. If you ever need me, you kin call on Alewine Jones, you kin bet. Trouble is, I don't know who I owe this heap a' gratitude to. Shore ain't Joanna Uppity Tharp."

"You aren't going to leave it alone, are you?" Rachel whispered, then realized she'd spoken the question aloud. She smoothed the salve to moisten the thread. Ben was right. She was taking on Joanna's habit of talking to herself.

"Leave it alone? Nope. I'm 'bout as stubborn as a tick on a tendon," Alewine challenged. "Might as well 'fess up. I ain't agin pesterin' the truth out of ya."

Did she dare tell? Could she trust Alewine to keep her secret? If not, how could she possibly keep this woman from discussing her suspicions with Ben when he returned?

Perhaps a partial truth was in order. One that would satisfy Alewine and her own curiosity over whether or not the frontierswoman was the right choice for Ben.

"I can tell you that no matter who you think I am"— Rachel tested the wax, then smoothed a thin layer over the stitches—"I'm someone with Ben's best interests at heart."

Alewine jerked slightly.

"Too hot?"

"Just wasn't 'specting it."

The woman's body tensed as she steeled herself against the second drop of wax Rachel applied to the other side.

"Just what do you think are Ben's best interests?" Alewine asked between clenched teeth.

"A wife. Children." Images of blond-haired, blue-eyed babies being bounced on Ben's knee brought a smile to Rachel's lips. The peaks of her breasts budded against her bodice, aching with the desire to have his children nourished there.

"From the way you been treating him, like a polecat with his juices hiked, I'd say you ain't alookin' to fill them wife shoes anytime soon. And you best get to noticin' there's aplenty herebouts who'd gladly step in and help him birth up a slewful of young'uns. Hell—heck—what female in her right notions wouldn't? What I ain't got figured yet is why you keep alookin' over all them gals at those there pinkie parties ever' afternoon. Ain't no way he's gonna want nobody but you."

"Is it that glaring?" Rachel reviewed the past few days and couldn't determine the moment her matchmaking scheme had become noticeable. Was Alewine's shrewdness spurred on by something more?

"Please stand." Rachel concentrated on wrapping both sides of the hip now, finally asking the one question she'd hoped to broach since her patient's arrival. "Have you ever wanted to set *your* hat for him?"

"A coonskin? Ain't exactly the sort that'll stretch a man's galluses, now, is it? 'Specially a man like Ben McGuire."

Rachel tucked the end of the bandage in and gently lowered Alewine's gown. "Finished! Now look at you. Good as new." She waited until Alewine moved over to the oval mirror and stared at herself. Just as Rachel had hoped. Both surprise and appreciation was reflected in the golden eyes that stared back at her. "I think Ben would have to buy a whole new stock of galluses if the men of Valiant ever saw how truly beautiful you are," she complimented sincerely.

Alewine's hand rose to toy with the gown's high collar as the other pressed one cheek. "There was a time . . . but that was only a young gal's wishes."

"Tell me about those wishes, Alewine." Rachel stood beside her guest, watching Alewine's reflection take on a faraway expression. For just a moment the frontierswoman seemed as if she might confide in Rachel, but the expression hardened, the look in her eyes becoming a golden glint. Still Rachel felt Alewine had long since left Narcissia's room behind and was traveling some distant memory.

Alewine smacked one fist into the open palm of another. "Wishes are for innocents. The rest of us . . . well, we should count ourselves lucky protecting somebody who really deserves 'em."

A chill ran over Rachel at the anger in the woman's tone. As if it were high noon, Alewine seemed to be having a faceoff with herself. What could she possibly be guilty of if she didn't consider herself one of those innocents? And whom was she protecting?

"I didn't mean to distress you." Rachel touched Alewine on the shoulder hopefully to bring her thoughts back to the here and now. When she swung around, looking fierce and foreboding, Rachel added, "We can talk more about this in the morning, when you're feeling better."

Alewine blinked. Her fists unballed, and she offered Rachel an embarrassed laugh. "Guess I wronged ya a couple a' times lately. I been apestering you to 'fess up your secrets, thinking you's trying to flamboozle me and Ben and the rest of Valiant. But can't say as I'm ready to spill my own what-led-me-heres."

Her features softened. "I'm plenty 'shamed of the way I've nagged ya, and I'd be for begging your pardon. If there's anything I can do to make it right, you just name it. Alewine Jones will see it's done." She spat in her hand and offered it to Rachel. "Let's shake on it."

Staring aghast at the palm, Rachel didn't know what to do next. She didn't want to seal the pact in the rough manner Alewine proposed, neither did she want to dismiss the offer completely. It might work too well into her plans for matchmaking the next day. How could she accept graciously without offending the frontierswoman?

"No need to shake," Rachel assured her, "your word is good enough for me."

Satisfied, Alewine nodded, drying her hand on Narcissia's gown. "Done."

"There is a way you can make it right with me, as you say," Rachel informed Alewine as she moved over to Narcissia's armoire. She took out the silver taffeta gown she'd bought at Clementine's dress shop. With a tuck here and there she could hide the ruined hem and add a bit of lace to make it seem as if the dress naturally gathered on one side. Only Clementine's eyes would discern the difference, and Rachel doubted the dressmaker had the courage to question Alewine about the alterations.

"Since you need to rest up anyway, and as long as you're in this house, I want you to come to my tea parties." Though she had meant to persuade Alewine to let Ben woo her, there might be yet a better way for Rachel to encourage the courting. If he returned from Clarendon early enough the following day, she could send a message for him to stop by. Once he got a glimpse of Alewine in her feminine regalia, perhaps nature would take its course.

"Ophelia Finck will be there and Clementine," she informed Alewine. "Of course, I would want you dressed appropriately for the occasion. I could alter this gown so it would fit you perfectly. And you said it was the prettiest one you'd ever seen."

"You want me to go in that?" Alewine started backing up. "I ain't been in no gut clutcher since . . . well . . . since I got me some sense. Ain't no way in hell—heck—I'm gonna go to no pinkie party wearing a dress."

"You gave me your word."

One golden eye narrowed as Alewine pointed a finger at Rachel. "Not about no dress I didn't. You hornswoggled me into this, Joanna-whoever-you-ain't. Roped me in like I was a greenhorn what didn't know better. I ain't goin'."

"Your *word*, Miss Jones."

"Hellfire, snake piss, and cow turds, woman!" Alewine stomped her foot, unfortunately the one connected to her injured hip. Her face contorted in pain.

Rachel laced her arms together under her breasts. "Stomp a little harder. That will only add days to your stay."

Alewine didn't stomp her foot again, but her toes tapped an obstinate rhythm on the floor. "Just what do I have to do at this here pinkie party?"

"Tea party."

"*Tea* party, then. My mam always called this here fanger a pinkie 'cause it's the only one I managed to keep clean." Alewine pretended to sip out of a make-believe cup, extending her smallest finger out so far, it looked as if it might take wing. "I figured them wimmen must've been told the same thang the way they's aholding them out so's not to dirty 'em up."

"How do you know that?" Rachel didn't recall Alewine at the other parties, and she was definitely a guest who wouldn't go unnoticed.

The bronze skin deepened at Alewine's high cheekbones. "I had me a look-see in yer winder."

A fondness for Alewine rose instantly within Rachel. How many times had she stared in windows, eager to see how someone else lived, wishing she could be a part of whatever was taking place but knowing she would never be asked. "Join us tomorrow." She knew the turn the freightliner's thoughts would take. "Just be yourself. It ought to make for an interesting party."

"That'll sure give a few of 'em the vapors."

Rachel chuckled, certain the next day would be unlike any she'd spent in Valiant so far. "We'll make a pact. I'll be on my best behavior if you'll do the same."

"This is about as good as it gets." A gleam of mischief filled Alewine's eyes. "You got my word on that."

❖ 11 ❖

As soon as you get back, come to Tharp House. Alewine injured. She's staying with me. Must talk to you. Am hosting a tea, so there will be company when you arrive.

Joanna

Ben studied the words once more to make sure he'd read them correctly. Concerned about the extent of Alewine's injury, he thrust the note at the gambler. "Better remount," he advised, unhitching the reins from the post in front of the general store. "There's trouble at Joanna's."

"There's trouble here too." Nicodemus Turner nodded at the stone-faced boy standing on the sidewalk, leaning his chin against the top of the broom handle and deliberately focusing his gaze anywhere but at Ben.

There probably would be an argument between them when he returned from Joanna's, Ben realized, but his son needed to learn there were times and issues that took precedence over spending hours with friends. He'd make a point of giving Jim a couple of extra days off.

"I won't be long," Ben promised his son. "I appreciate you watching the store yesterday and this morning, but I have to see about Aly. Mind things for me a while longer, and I'll be back as soon as I can. Nick, you coming?''

The gambler was already in the saddle and reining half-quarter before Ben finished the question. "Miss a chance at introducing myself to a roomful of Valiant's prettiest?" Nick straightened his cravat. "Not likely."

Spurring their horses down Main Street, the two men passed the church and rounded the corner to Tharp House. Surreys and buggies lined the carriageway that ran alongside the house on the east and in front.

"Looks like the only trouble here may be the lack of a man who appreciates such festivities." Nick reined to a halt and dismounted. "Care to be the first to bask in their sweet attention, or shall I go ahead of you?"

Ben finished hitching his reins to one of the fence pickets. "You keep them company. If Alewine's here, she'll be upstairs."

"From what I've seen of that strip of buckskin, she's definitely not the tea-party temperament. You go see about her. I'll keep the ladies entertained."

A blood-curdling scream rent the air, issuing from inside Joanna's home.

The two men exchanged glances, then hurdled over the fence. Ben raced ahead of Nicodemus, shouldering his weight against the door. The gambler's added momentum caught Ben off-balance. Arms and legs tangled. Fingers reached out to grasp for something to stop the fall, finding only air. Ben crashed to the floor and, a second later, felt the air rush out of his lungs as Nick sprawled on top of him.

Women shrieked. Bodies darted for protection. One rustle of petticoats moved close and halted inches away from the two rescuers. The nose belonging to the woman standing above Ben snorted loudly before she burst into hilarious laughter. The other women in the room seemed to breathe in a collective gasp.

"Well, would you look at that? If it ain't two of Valiant's *up*standing citizens!" Alewine pointed at them as Nick rolled away. She bent down to wink at Ben, offering him a hand. "You fellers shoulda dropped in a mite sooner. Ya done missed the excitement."

"Anybody hurt?" Ben asked, rising to rest on his elbows.

"Just a few feathers ruffled, you might say." Alewine laughed, looking as if she were the coyote that swallowed the rooster.

Ben sat up, prepared to yank her across his lap and paddle her for scaring ten years of growth out of him. Alewine wasn't hurt. What kind of game was Joanna playing now? Just as he reached out to accept Aly's help, his hand stopped in midair.

Gone were the boots and buckskin, replaced by slender pumps and silver taffeta. The rustle of petticoats as she took a step closer forced his gaze upward. Standing before him was a slim-waisted beauty with dark stains of gooey-looking food covering her well-defined cleavage and freshly scrubbed face. Gone was that god-awful shine of grease used to protect her skin from the elements.

The question that filled Ben lost its voice at the sight of Joanna moving alongside Alewine. Dressed in a Nile-green challis tea gown that deepened the hue of her eyes, her beauty struck him like a hard blow to the stomach. He could rarely remember a time she'd worn anything but red, and the effect was stunning. Joanna looked different . . . delicate, yet strong.

Surely the simple changing of color could not create such a difference, could it? Perhaps it was her very presence at his friend's side that seemed the most puzzling of all. Joanna's drawing room was the last place he ever expected to see

Alewine. The fact that Joanna had not only befriended the freightliner but gotten her into women's finery told Ben that there was a lot to learn about *this* newly returned Joanna Tharp. Seven years had made considerable differences within her—changes that made her more desirable, if that were possible, changes that let everyone else glimpse the kindness he'd noticed in her youth, and changes his heart whispered might heal the wound she had inflicted upon him before she left.

Needing time to let his senses regain balance, Ben forced his attention from Joanna to focus on the changling at her side. A million questions raced to mind, but all he could do was simply say, "Why are you dressed like that?"

Alewine thumbed toward Joanna. "It was all her doin'. Better get a quick look, 'cause fast as I kin get out of this here priss parlor and trot up them stairs, I'll be for shucking this gut clutcher. You won't see the likes of me in it agin." She glared back at the woman sitting on the davenport with her head bowed. "Don't need no *education* to figure out the right time to skedaddle."

"Oh, Aly, how could you?" Rachel tried to wipe some of the mess off her guest's gown, but only ended up smearing it more. "Now everything is ruined!"

"Now, Joanna, it's nothing that can't be taken out with a little scrubbing and lye." Ophelia Finck's voice held a note of authority. "No need to make any more of this than there already is."

Joanna allowed the saloonkeeper to join the circle of confusion, giving Ben a glimpse of some of the other faces in the room.

Ophelia pointed the tip of her cane at the dark-haired banker's daughter whose head remained bowed. "Gwenella started it. And I believe she's ready to apologize now, aren't you, Miss Duncan?"

Every eye in the room trained itself on the leader of the Tight Shoe Troupe, who had openly bragged that she would attend the tea party that afternoon and make it miserable for Ophelia. What none of them had planned on was Alewine Jones's presence!

Gwenella raised her bowed head. Chocolate pudding dripped from her bangs, dangled from her eyelashes, and smeared one cheek. From the imprint on Alewine's bodice and both women's faces, Ben was certain whatever had transpired between the two had ended in a cat fight—but more of a mountain-cat variety than a homestead pet.

A low hissing sound exited Gwenella's mouth. "I'm sorry I called you stupid. I was mistaken."

"This ought to be interesting." Nicodemus lay back with his hands behind his head. Slanting toward Alewine's gown, where the hemline rose dramatically to one side, his gaze lit with approval. "And a most spectacular view, I might add."

"Get up from there, you low-lying cayoose." Alewine grabbed his hand, jerked him to a standing position, then let go as if she'd touched a cactus. Spitting in her palm, she rubbed it furiously against her dress. "What in tarnation d'you do to me, gambler?" Alewine eyed him and shook her hand free of his touch. "How come it burned me like 'at?"

Nicodemus rubbed his own palm, puzzlement creasing his brow. "It was as much a surprise to me as it was you, Miss Freightliner." A smile curled his lips. "A heated moment."

Ophelia tapped his shoulder with the cane. "Douse it, Romeo. You probably just scooted across the carpet and caused some friction between you. Both of you, get up."

"Durned right." Alewine's glare was hot enough to wither a fence post. "And if I catch you agawking at my unmentionables agin, Nicodemus Turner, you best hightail your butt to Boston, 'cause the bullets'll start blazing." The glare eased when it focused on Ophelia. "Sorry, 'Phelia. I know'd he's Nash's baby brother and all, but Miz Turner must've parceled out all her polish to Nash and forgot to save a lick of it for Nick."

Alewine hiked her skirt to one side and draped it over her forearm. Despite her recent injury, she took the stairs two at a time, calling back over her shoulder, "Sorry to you too, Jo. This here prissing and cooing jist ain't fer me. Ain't the marrying kind anyway. Match him up with somebody else."

"Who are you trying to match with Alewine?" Ben searched Joanna's face for answers.

"I'd like to know the answer to that question myself," Ophelia echoed, her hands crossing over the cane's handle.

Joanna's lips formed a perfect O as her gaze darted back and forth from Ben to Nick, then finally settled on Nick. Ben got the distinct impression that the gambler might have been second choice. Which meant . . . she was trying to match Aly up with *him*? Suddenly the teas she'd been hosting took on a whole new perspective.

"Ohhh, no one in particular," she announced. "I just thought if any man in Valiant saw how pretty she can be when she wants to, she could have her choice of husbands."

"A noble cause, but"—Ben waved in the direction Alewine had taken—"apparently wasted effort."

Nicodemus straightened the ruffles at the end of his sleeves, his gaze aimed at the second landing. "I beg to differ, Ben. A good challenge always raises the ante."

Nick and Alewine? The probability seemed as absurd as Joanna trying to match him and Aly together. Then again, did a romance between Nick and Aly seem any less unlikely than he and Joanna reestablishing their own courtship after such a long time? "Yes, anything worth having has its challenges, doesn't it?"

"And there's no time like now to grab the buffalo by the horns."

"That's bull," Ophelia corrected him.

"I do that well too." Nick grinned. "Want me to fetch Miss Bullheaded upstairs and take her home? There's nothing like living dangerously, is there?"

"Got things to set straight here before I can go," Ben admitted, glancing at the door to see how it had fared his and Nick's rush. Fortunately, it had been partially open, so the force of their bodies had done little damage. "Stop by the store and tell Jim I'll be there as soon as I can."

Joanna looked unusually nervous. "What do you mean, *set straight*?"

Ben's gaze swept down the front of the black lace panels that formed the bodice of her tea gown. He'd meant the door, but she shouldn't have given him the opportunity. He'd mulled over a certain question all the way back on the ride from Clarendon. "I want to know the reason you're deliberately avoiding me."

She raised a finger to her lips as if to hush him. "The guests will hear."

"Then get rid of them, because I mean to have an answer."

Ophelia turned and tapped her cane three times. "Tea party's over, ladies. Any of you women enough to continue this 'tea tasting' is welcome to join me for a sip at the Lazy Lady. Beer and sarsaparilla's on the house."

Gwenella jolted from the davenport. "Well! I never!" Her troupe rose beside her, like buzzards lining a fence.

"You're right, you'll never." Ophelia sashayed to the door. "Or at least won't ever admit you did." She pressed a hand on Ben's cheek. "Bye, Benjamin. Don't be too hard on the filly. After all, she's the first Tight Shoe with the gumption to invite me to a party. Coming, Nicky?"

Nicodemus half bowed to Ophelia. "Wouldn't miss this for the world, but let me fetch Alewine. She won't pass up free"—he winked at the ladies—"sarsaparilla."

"Out of my way, gambler." Alewine barreled down the stairs dressed in her buckskins. She swept past the saloon-keeper and her escort. "Stuff that sarsaparilla where the—"

"Aly, wait! Your hip!" Joanna protested, racing to the door to stop her. Nick and Ophelia moved out of the way.

"I'm jist fine!" the frontierswoman called back over her shoulder. "Quit mother-henning me, Jo."

Alewine's departure started an exodus. Everyone grabbed their parasols and shawls, bid their farewells, and left. Ben leaned against the door frame and stared at the departing buggies, thankful the previous day's rain had settled the dust and didn't stir up the roadway. His hand ran along the door's top hinge and discovered that it wouldn't need replacing at all, merely tightening.

He hoped the trouble between him and Joanna could be as easily repaired. The thought disturbed him. Was there trouble between them, or had he simply imagined it? Yet since she'd returned to Valiant, Joanna had done her best to make sure there was always a crowd around her.

Unable to endure the sound of another cup rattling against its saucer as she collected the dishes from the party, he demanded, "Are you afraid to be alone with me?" He hadn't meant his words to sound harsh, but they did.

The rattling stopped. "Whatever do you mean?"

Ben could hear the false innocence in her voice, much like the tone she'd used years before to convince him she loved only him. "Please don't lie, Joanna. It doesn't become you. *I deserve the truth.*"

"I'm not lying."

He turned to find her staring at the dishes in her hands.

"I just wanted to get reacquainted with everyone," she

insisted, finally raising her gaze to his. "And give Ophelia and Alewine a chance to be accepted among the townswomen."

The sincerity in her last statement almost convinced him. But he knew there was more. Sensed it. The sooner he found out why she didn't want to be with him, the better. "Then spend this evening with me."

"I'm tired."

"Tomorrow, then?"

"I've promised at least two more parties." She turned from him and stared out the window. "I'm just not ready for us to resume our courting. I've told you before, I must have time to settle in. To get used to . . . *things* again. Please quit hounding me."

"I'm not hounding you." Ben studied Joanna, wondering if there would ever be a time he didn't love her on sight. Wishing she might one day feel as strongly about him. "You win," he whispered, rubbing his chin between his thumb and forefinger, "for now. But don't expect me to remain so patient, *querida*." The Spanish endearment rose unexpectedly, and he smiled, knowing one day he would not only tell her what it meant, but show her all the love compelling him to whisper it. "It's hard to keep my distance, when all I want to do is take you in my arms."

He couldn't remember a time he'd ever wanted to touch her so much. Not in the past, not even in the dreams that sustained him throughout her absence. For a moment Ben allowed himself to imagine what it would be like to indulge the fantasy that rose in his mind. To watch each silken curve bare itself to his sensual exploration until at last she lay naked beneath him. But that would never happen if he forced the issue. She must come to him willingly, in her own time, and because she wanted to do so.

He waited for her to speak, but finally grew impatient with

her silence. What did he have to do to prove to her she could trust him? "I'll just tighten up this hinge," he announced, reminding himself that anger did no good. Love wasn't something someone dictated. It came from a knowing. And Joanna just didn't know her own heart yet. The simple fact that she'd returned to him said she *wanted* to love him, and that would have to be enough for now. But he had to see her again soon . . . and alone. "I'd love to take you on a picnic Sunday after church."

"Ben." His name was like a vow upon her lips. "Be patient with me. I care deeply for you. Perhaps more than I have a right to. But I truly need time to make sure I won't hurt you."

For an instant he thought he saw great sadness fill her eyes. Perhaps he shouldn't take advantage of her at that moment, but his heart refused to overlook the opportunity presented to him. The need to touch her became too great. Ben reached out and curled a knuckle gently under her chin, raising it so she had to meet his gaze. "Go with me to the picnic?"

She nodded and sighed. "Yes, Ben. I'll go."

A blink seemed to rid her of the vulnerability he'd glimpsed.

"But don't count on convincing me how much we should be together. I haven't belonged anywhere in a long, long time."

But you have, he argued silently. *There's a special place in my heart that belongs to you and always will, if you'll just accept it.*

❖ *12* ❖

Rᴀᴄʜᴇʟ ᴛᴏᴏᴋ ᴀ bite of roasted chicken and savored the rich taste. She never wanted to have tea and cookies again. The aroma of baked cinnamon apples and fresh yeast rolls wafted through the batwing doors that separated the kitchen from the dining room at Delaney's. Memories of her mother's Christmas baking filled Rachel's thoughts, bringing with them a lump of homesickness that welled in her throat and brought tears to her eyes. Ten years' worth.

Glancing around the dining hall and eating counters, she noticed families sharing meals together, a couple holding hands across the table from each other, three women chatting and laughing, obviously sharing supper with chosen friends. A feeling of family blended among the crowd—an invisible bond that forms between people who live in the same town, work to make it a thriving community. People who had the right to call Valiant, Texas, their home.

She returned the fork to her plate and quickly grabbed a goblet of water, trying to swallow back the lack of belonging that engulfed her. Having supper with Ben and Ophelia, and the absent-at-present Jim, should have eased some of her loneliness. Yet Rachel knew she could never truly belong here. She had lied to them all and to herself.

As if her thoughts had been read, one of the three women she'd spotted having such fun frowned at Rachel.

"Something wrong with the food?" Ben asked, gently touching her arm.

His compassion almost proved her undoing. She shook her head and took an even larger gulp of water.

"She's probably swallowed something the wrong way," Ophelia announced on the other side, pounding Rachel's back three times.

Rachel's nostrils contracted, her shoulders hunched, and her throat tightened. She held up a finger to signal for the saloonkeeper to wait while she regained control. Blinking back the sting in her eyes, her nose finally opened and her throat eased, allowing the water to continue toward its original destination. "I—I'm fine," she stammered. "Just a bit queasy."

"It's all those cookies. Too many sweets," Ophelia diagnosed, slicing off a hefty bite of chicken. "Baking all day, cleaning up after everybody all night. Don't you think you've had enough of those tea parties? Nearly every woman from here to Clarendon has paid a visit." The slice disappeared into her mouth, followed by a forkful of potatoes and green beans.

"Not everyone," Rachel gently argued. "Who are those ladies over there?" Nodding toward the three women, she added, "Particularly the one dressed in the silk polonaise."

"The what?" Puzzlement filled Ben's tone.

"Matilda Whipple." Ophelia gave him a store-owner-such-as-yourself-should-be-more-informed look. "That costly little creation she's wearing is made from silk polonaise."

"You don't remember Matilda, Sterling's wife?" Ben asked. His puzzlement deepened, creasing his forehead.

Should I? Rachel instantly squelched the question, sensing from Ben's expression and the narrowing of Ophelia's eyes that she had just made another blunder. *Think fast, Rachel, how are you going to get out of this one?* Whoever Matilda was in Joanna's past, it was clear the woman didn't particularly care for her. "Oh, is that Matilda? Why, she's changed considerably since I left. I almost didn't recognize her!"

Ophelia's upper lip curled. "She's changed about forty pounds' worth. Looks more than that without her corset on. You'd think she wouldn't be caught out in public without it, but guess she's up to riding without reins tonight. Been living high off her daddy's horses, you might say. He's built an empire supplying the army with horseflesh. She's the darling of her daddy's eye and that skirt-chasing jackanapes of a husband don't mind being part of the shine."

" 'Jackanapes?' " Rachel had never heard the word before.

The saloonkeeper's gaze darted about the room. "I was trying to be polite. Want me to tell you what I really think of Valiant's pompous politician? Picture this—try crossing an ape with the stubbornnest jack—"

" 'Phele, there are children here." Ben's tone was hushed but brooked no argument. "Speaking of which, I hope Jimmy's not much later, or I'm going to have to send his food back to Cookie to keep warm."

Not to be put off completely, Ophelia leaned closer to Rachel to finish with a conspiratorial whisper, "Calling Whipple a donkey butt just doesn't do that sidewinder justice."

"Mama, that lady said donkey butt," a little girl's voice echoed from the table behind them.

Ben tried to look gruff but failed. He and Rachel shared a glance that lit with laughter, though neither dared let their mouths grin.

"Here." Ophelia reached into her handbag, pulled out a coin, and handed it to the child. "Put that in tomorrow's offering and pray for my sinning ways, will you, sweetie?''

The child grabbed the coin, oohing and ahhing as she showed it to her brothers and sisters.

Rachel waited until Ophelia turned back around. "You really don't like her husband, do you?''

"No, I don't. And if I were you, I'd stay as far away from him as possible,'' the saloonkeeper advised. "The man has two never-ending goals: getting more voters and getting more money. You're a new voter and you certainly have the money. That makes you a prime target.''

"She'll stay away.'' Ben craned his neck to one side, as if he were trying to see past the diners and stare at something beyond the front glass of Delaney's restaurant.

Before Rachel could ask Ben why he'd made such a decision for her, he scooted out his chair and stood.

"There's some kind of trouble. Michael's heading this way, and he looks none too happy.''

"Who's Michael?'' Asking may have been her second blunder this evening. Perhaps Ophelia would accept it as simple forgetfulness. "I can't seem to recall him.''

She watched Ben meet the tall, dark, bearded man at the door. Dressed in a duster that had clearly seen recent days on the trail, the wiry stranger had the look of a predator in the blue-gray eyes that quickly surveyed the room, then settled on Ben. Their exchange of words was brief. The somber expression on Ben's face as the two men parted, and the fact that he grabbed his Stetson from the hat hook next to the door, didn't bode well.

"You shouldn't recall him at all. That's Michael Austin Edwards. He's been sheriff for three years.'' Ophelia forked another slice of chicken. "One tough hombre, if you're toting meanness. A good friend and gun hand when you stand on the right side of the law. Unmarried and definitely worth the chase.''

Ben returned, pulled out two bills, and dropped them on the table. "I apologize, ladies, but it seems my son needs my attention. I'll do my best to get back before dessert is served. But in case I can't, I'd appreciate it if you'd settle up with Delaney for me. If that's not enough, tell him I'll be by before church tomorrow."

He looked upset. Perhaps there needed to be a buffer between parent and son. Rachel rose. "Shall I go with you? I'm really not all that hungry."

Ophelia placed a hand on her arm. "We'll wait for you here, Ben. Take your time. Joanna and I haven't had a chance to really talk, and could use some time alone."

Refusing to sink back into her seat like a chastised child, Rachel waited for Ben's reply.

"I appreciate the offer, Joanna, but I'd better handle this on my own."

She seated herself and watched him leave, her thoughts racing with concern. Was Jimmy hurt? Why was the sheriff involved? Had the boy gotten into trouble of some kind?

"Better learn now it's best to let those two come to terms with each other all by themselves. You can try to help, but it won't do any good until they find a way to communicate on their own."

Eyeing her companion, Rachel wondered how closely Ophelia followed Ben's life. It was true the woman knew everything that went on in Valiant and had been awarded the unspoken title of "gossip queen." But how much of her interest in Ben's and Jim's life was curiosity rather than actual concern for Ben and his son?

"Tell me about the adoption." Ben had never volunteered the information, and she'd respected his privacy.

Ophelia brushed bread crumbs off the folds of her tightly stretched overskirt. "Nothing much to tell. A year ago Ben caught Jimmy stealing from his store. When the circuit judge came around, he gave the boy two options: go to a home back East for wayward boys or wrangle employment. No one wanted to hire him because of the crime. In these parts a thief is usually hanged without any questions. But Jim was barely twelve, and nobody had the heart to hang him. Ben stepped in and not only offered a place to work, but gave him something better—a home.''

She sighed. ''The boy was smart enough to take Ben up on the offer. And thanks to Ben's good heart, Jim's learned to rein in some of those street-urchin antics of his. But he's still got a ways to go before he becomes the man his father is.''

''Are you in love with Ben?'' Rachel asked, knowing the answer to her matchmaking dilemma had been at her disposal all along.

The ping of Ophelia's fork dropping against the china plate in front of her should have warned Rachel she'd over-stepped one of the woman's boundaries. But it wasn't until she saw the crimson stain flushing the saloonkeeper's cheeks that Rachel realized how angry she'd made Ophelia by merely asking.

The woman rose like a gathering thunderhead, towering over Rachel at the table. ''*That* is none of your business, Miss Tharp, but I'm making this mine. I've stood and watched you gauge every woman in Valiant. Watched you try to make Alewine into something she isn't. Now you're asking *me* if I'm in love with Ben. Just what are your inten-tions for Ben McGuire? Are you or are you not going to stay and marry that good man, or have you set out to break his heart again?''

''Please sit down, Ophelia, everyone's staring.''

Ophelia grabbed another coin and pitched it over to one of the boys behind them. ''Add that to your sister's tomor-row.'' She stared at the children's parents. ''I feel a slewful of sins coming on." She sat down and waited until those staring at them resumed their own conversations.

"I didn't want to confess this to anyone." Rachel avoided a direct answer. "But it's true, I have tried to meet as many women as possible. But not to hurt Ben. It was to see if there was someone who might make a better bride than me. If I've learned one thing, it's that Ben deserves to be loved. He deserves someone who will remain in Valiant and make it her home. I asked if you're in love with him, because, if you are, then you should try to win him over, that's all."

"Win him over?" Ophelia's teeth bared themselves sharply as the saloonkeeper grabbed her knife and sliced another piece of chicken. She sawed on the poultry so hard, the slice flew off the plate and landed in Jimmy's long-forgotten meal. "Are you mocking me?"

Rachel scooted back her seat, feeling the hidden threat in the woman's handling of the knife. "Why would I mock you?"

"I know you invited me to your tea party only so you could pretend old rifts were forgotten. And *you* may have forgotten how you dared me to take Ben away from you years ago, but, Miss Tight Shoe, *I* haven't. I'm not accepting the challenge this time. The man loves you, and we both know it." Her eyes narrowed into ebony slits. "I refuse to be anybody's second choice once, much less twice."

"I'm not issuing any challenge." Rachel sensed the friendship she'd believed had blossomed between them wilting even as she denied the accusation. "I'm trying to step out of the way."

"Play the innocent changeling with everyone else, *Joanna dear*. I'm not fooled." Ophelia finally gave up trying to slice the poultry further and wiped her hands with a linen napkin. "I admit, you had me curious. Even to the point that I thought you weren't Joanna at all, but some conspirator who had come to Valiant to scam Ben and the town. But I was wrong. Only one person could be so cruel to play with people's hearts like you have since you've been here.''

Her voice got louder. ''You sure as hell are every inch the mean-spirited, scheming, conniving, selfish witch you've always been, Joanna Tharp! If it weren't for Ben expecting us both to be here when he gets back, I'd leave your black heart right there. Don't utter another word to me the rest of the evening, or I swear, I'll cane you baldheaded! Then we'll see who looks best to Ben.''

Despite the threat, Rachel could not remain silent. ''You're wrong about me, Miss Finck. If you'd only give me a chance to . . .''

''I'd like an explanation, son.'' Ben sat on the edge of the bed that filled the jail cell's west wall.

''Don't got no reason.'' The thirteen-year-old scooted over as far away from Ben as he could, then shrugged. The wolf-dog lay his head on Jim's lap and darted his gaze back and forth between masters.

Ben looked askance at Sheriff Edwards, but Michael shook his head. The lawman thumbed backward, signaling he would be inside his office if needed. Ben returned his attention to the boy, wondering what it would take to convince Jim to talk rather than offer those frustrating shrugs that resolved nothing. ''You had to have some reason for tying Mrs. Whipple's corset to the courthouse door.''

Another shrug. ''Thought it would make everybody laugh.''

''Some will. Others are going to look at it as stealing. Again.''

''They gonna hang me?'' Jim's chin shot upward, his brown eyes rounding with worry. Bowie whined.

Ben started to brush the hair from the boy's forehead, but

Jim shirked away, slinging the hair back himself. "I'll talk to Sheriff Edwards and Mrs. Whipple. You don't have to worry about hanging, but you will have to apologize to Matilda and do whatever chore Sheriff Edwards decides is fair punishment for the crime."

"All right." Jim stood and stuffed his hands into his pockets, preparing to face his jailer. Bowie jumped off the cot and stood alongside Jim, tucking his tail as if he'd been a coconspirator.

Uncertain what else he expected, Ben was surprised by Jim's acceptance of the terms. It was almost as if he'd purposely gotten into trouble and wanted the punishment. "What's going on, Jim? Why did you decide to act up now, when you haven't in months?"

"At least you care where I am. You ain't got your nose stuck up Miss Tharp's petticoat."

"Don't talk about her like that." Ben didn't mean to sound as gruff as he did. His anger was directed not at his son, but at himself. It was painfully clear. Jim's misdeed was nothing but a dogie's cry for its mother's attention. Ben had been so wrapped up in trying to be with Joanna that he'd neglected to spend time with Jimmy. The boy had been given his undivided attention the past year, and he was feeling threatened by Joanna's arrival.

He had to convince his son that Joanna's presence in their life would make them a better family. He could grow up not only with a father, but a mother to teach him and love him.

"I've been unfair to you lately, Jim. Asking you to watch the store longer than I usually do. Spending my time courting Miss Tharp instead of helping you build that hideout of yours. I've already promised to take her on a picnic tomorrow after church, so I can't break my word. You're welcome to go with us if you like. Afterward, I'll spend the rest of the day with you alone."

"So you say." Jim wiped his palms on his pant legs. "I
don't want to go to no picnic, but if you got any time left
over, you can help me finish up the north wall. I'm supposed
to meet Aly out there after church. That is, if I ain't too
punished."

"That's up to Michael. Best be asking him."

Jimmy moved over to the iron bars separating him from
freedom. "Sheriff Edwards, can you come here a minute?"

The lawman sauntered in from the next room. "Ready to
'fess up?"

"Yeah, I done it." Jim looked at Ben, then back at the
sheriff. "Figure I gotta apologize to Mrs. Whipple, but what
else you want me to do? Ain't got no bail money. Spent my
savings on a knife."

"Want to post your knife as bail?"

"Couldn't I have another punishment instead?"

Michael's blue-gray eyes lit with laughter as he bit away
the smile that lifted his mustache. "The church needs its
pews polished and the baseboards repainted. That sounds like
fitting punishment to me, and would do the town a service
too."

"Sounds fair to me," Ben agreed. The look on Jimmy's
face nearly made Ben laugh. He could almost see the boy
mentally counting off the hours to be spent indoors.

"Hey, tomorrow's Sunday." The boy's relief spurred his
words into an all-out gallop. Bowie's tail wagged like a frenzied pendulum. "I can't do no polishing and painting tomorrow 'cause there's church services." He faced his jailer,
his expression earnest. "I ain't trying to get out of doing
'em, Sheriff, but it just don't make sense to do it till Monday,
after I've finished up for Ben. Folks can't sit down on fresh-
polished pews, and everyone knows the smell of paint makes
Wilhemina Harrison pass plumb out. And Wilhemina's gotta
go to church or Mrs. Harrison'll have a conniption. And if

Mrs. Harrison has a conniption, Mr. Harrison will—''

"Point taken, boy," Sheriff Edwards announced, jangling the keys as he unlocked the cell. "I'm letting you out on your pa's promise that you'll apologize to Mrs. Whipple in the morning, and that you'll show up at the church Monday about three. You can work from three to seven every day until the painting and polishing are done. Then we'll consider this crime duly punished. Got your word on it?"

"Yessir."

He grinned broadly. "Then go and repaint. Sin no more."

Ben groaned. "You ought to be locked up for that one, Edwards."

"And, Jim—" The sheriff ruffled the boy's hair.

"Yessir?"

"Your pa once rode a buggy over Sterling Whipple's top hat . . . trouble was, he never apologized."

"Thanks a lot." Ben urged the boy and his dog out of the cell ahead of him. He shot Michael a half-angry, half–I-can't-believe-you-chose-this-moment-to-tell-my-son-that look as he passed the lawman.

"Don't mention it, friend." Mike guffawed. "Just trying to do what I'm paid for . . . keeping the peace. Sometimes that means between father and son too."

❖ *13* ❖

CONVERSATION WAS SPOILED. The peaceful family atmosphere she'd felt earlier had fled along with her appetite. Try as she might, Rachel couldn't endure another moment among present company.

Jimmy sulked about who knew what, building a green-bean fortress alongside the chicken he wasn't eating. Ophelia continued to fume, her anger radiating like heat waves. Ben attempted to enliven the conversation, but got only brittle one-word replies from Ophelia and little more from Rachel. He looked so puzzled, she felt sorry for him.

Her stomach churned from the sheer tension of hoping Ophelia would not discuss what had transpired between them while he was gone. "If you'll excuse me, I'm a bit tired. Perhaps I'll be better company tomorrow."

Ben's hand rested over Jim's. "Son, are you going to eat your supper or play with it?"

"I'm not hungry."

"Then why don't you walk Miss Finck back to the Lazy Lady? I'll see Joanna home."

"Can I stop in and say hello to Banjo?" The boy looked expectantly at his father.

"Banj has been asking about him," Ophelia informed Ben.

"I told him Jim was having to handle the store for you a few days. I'll make sure he doesn't stay too long."

"Come *straight* home." He let go of his son's hand. "You've got church in the morning, and you need a bath before you go to bed."

Ophelia rose and crooked her elbow. "Well, latch on here, Jimbo. We best get this escorting over with so you and Banj can have time to swap a few chords. He'll be pleased to see you."

Jim linked his arm with hers and headed for the saloon.

Though the tension diminished as soon as Ophelia was out of sight, Rachel yearned to leave the restaurant behind and walk off the rest of the discomfort she felt. Gathering her handbag and wrap, she decided to wait outside while Ben settled with Delaney.

The night had cooled considerably, making her glad she'd thought to bring a shawl. The gauze Bertha that formed the bodice of her muslin dress left her shoulders bare and did little to ward off the chill being stirred up by the breeze. She draped the shawl over her hair and wrapped it around her shoulders.

"Cold?"

The warmth of Ben's concern sent a shiver down Rachel's spine.

"A little," she admitted, knowing the chattering of her teeth was not a product of the night wind, but a reaction to the man wrapping his arm around her and pulling her close against his side.

"That better?"

Much, much, much better, her body answered, her right arm worming a path beneath his frock coat to encompass his waist. A strange flush swept over her skin as Rachel felt herself melting against him, like butter on hot bread. Unconsciously, she held him tighter and tried to control the sudden weakness in her knees.

"B-better," she managed to whisper, her cheeks tightening with a rush of heat.

Falling into step with his leisurely stride, Rachel discovered she fit too perfectly against him and dangerously relished the clean, fresh scent that seemed uniquely Ben.

Twilight cast violet hues over the buildings and roadway, offering a dreamlike quality to the distance. Even the crickets and locusts ceased their usual banter, leaving only the soft whisper of wind to sigh as it raced along the prairie grass.

Rachel glanced up at the stars, wondering why they shone even brighter than the previous nights she'd spent in Valiant. Perhaps they just *seemed* brighter. It was as if each suspected something special would happen but were far too impatient to wait. One by one each star attempted to outshine the others before having to settle back into the cluster. Their impish twinkles made Rachel laugh. "What a beautiful night," she whispered, then finally spotted the moon. "Isn't that strange? There's a ring around the moon."

"Not so strange as it seems." Ben stopped. "If you look closely, it has only one ring. That means either bad weather will hit in twenty-four hours or less, or a maiden is in need of kissing. The more rings it has, the sooner the storm hits. Or the sooner she gets kissed."

"Is that a local legend?" Rachel peered closer, wishing there were a dozen or more rings and the second half of the tale were true.

Ben laughed and kissed the top of her head. "It's a McGuire tradition handed down for generations, I'm afraid."

Surprised by the kiss, Rachel turned and tilted her face up to his. His nearness flooded her mind, intoxicating her senses. He had wonderful eyes, but then, that was in keeping with the rest of him. Their color was hidden to her now, but they were no less mesmerizing in the twilight.

He slid his arms around Rachel and pulled her so close against him, their hearts began to pound in the same rhythm. He said nothing. Words weren't necessary. Ben looked down into her face with the most tender expression Rachel had ever received. Her heart sped up, and a deep yearning flared within her.

She tried desperately to look away, told herself it was the right thing to do, but Ben was far too distracting. His eyes, his mouth, his jawline, were much too compelling. She concentrated on his chest, trying to ignore the muscular span that pressed so warmly against her breasts, but that proved her undoing.

As naturally as day gave way to night, their lips met. His kiss was soft at first, then became bolder, scorching the outer edges of her soul. Rachel's senses reeled with the impact of desire coursing through her.

The wind seemed to cease. The lights of town became distant beacons. Night no longer existed. There was only the pleasure of being in Ben's arms. She loved the feel of his strength beneath her fingertips, the unreadable expression in his eyes, the taste of passion upon his lips.

Knowing she had no right to be there yet unable to deny her heart's request to know this moment in Ben's arms, Rachel gave herself over to the sweet sadness that engulfed her. Entwining her arms around his neck, she returned his kiss, conveying all she felt in the sweet melding of their mouths.

It was a kiss of regret. A kiss of apology. A kiss of goodbye.

The sigh brushed against her mouth as his lips left hers wanting more, needing all.

"Joanna, I've loved you for so long. Doesn't this feel right to you too?"

Rachel wanted to scream and cry, *Yes, Ben. It feels right.*

Not only right but all I've ever dreamed of. Love me, Ben. Me. Not Joanna. Don't whisper her name on my lips. Feelings she'd never experienced before riddled Rachel with conflicting emotions—anger, disappointment . . . passion. Her body was hot, sensitive to Ben's every movement. It was as if she were waiting, expectant, eager for—for what? For him to sweep her into his arms and make passionate, heart-rending love meant for Joanna?

Rachel had no idea what to do with herself. What to say to him. Her own heart was beating too wildly, her breath coming too rapidly, her misery too deep to answer him. ''I'll walk myself home, Ben.'' She wouldn't lie to him anymore. Couldn't. ''I'm not sure what I feel is right.''

She deliberately moved away and hastened her steps. Perhaps if she walked fast, the strength would return to her knees and the distance would ease the pain of wanting Ben but denying herself the pleasure.

His hand reached out and caught her wrist, halting her abruptly. Rachel felt the strength of his fingers and remembered how easily his slightest touch had turned her body into a sea of shifting sand.

''I'll not let you walk home in the dark.''

''You don't need to,'' she found herself saying. ''I know . . . *remember* the way well now.'' Yet something in her wanted him to insist, to let reason flee her thoughts and allow her dreams of remaining in his arms to flourish just a while longer.

''If I promise not to kiss you again . . . at least tonight, may I walk you all the way home?''

Yes! her heart cried. ''If you like.'' She tried to sound reasonable.

''We have to talk, Joanna.''

We do, she reminded herself, praying that the night would never end and tomorrow would never come. She couldn't confess all in the same twilight that had gifted her with his embrace. She deserved the cold light of day to confess her sham, not the security of shadows.

"Joanna, you've got to realize that you can't continue to run away from me and expect me to—"

"To what, Ben?" There was hope for him yet. "To wait for me? No, I can't, and you shouldn't."

She winced when she heard him curse and his fist hit the side of the building they passed. "That was a foolish thing to do!" Rachel grabbed his hand and felt something warm and moist soak through her glove. "You're bleeding!"

He tried to jerk away, but she refused to let go. "It doesn't matter."

"It does matter. I won't have you hurting yourself for someone like Jo—someone like me."

"I quit hurting a long time ago. Now it's a matter of persistence. When I fell in love with you and promised you no other woman would ever take your place, that wasn't just a schoolboy's infatuation, Jo. I can't give you less than I am, no matter how much it hurts. I don't know why you're trying so hard not to love me, but my heart says if I believe hard enough, you'll feel it too. I'm not about to give up now. It's like surviving the forest and reaching the timberline, only to give up just as you spot the peak. I waited seven years. Guess I can wait longer."

It was then that Rachel wished she *was* Joanna. She'd never believed in devotion before, had no concept of the kind of people who honored it. All she knew of love was that it was an emotion easily shed when times got tough and she became just another mouth to feed and a back to clothe. But this was a man who truly believed in forever. A forever she had only dreamed of. An eternity of belonging.

For a moment she simply looked at him. Rachel felt the

heat of Ben's gaze on her, and it was almost as if she did belong to him.

If he touched her again, she would be lost.

"You belong to me," he whispered, reaching out to touch her. Somewhere, distantly, in the back of his mind, Ben knew this might only frighten her away, but he would be damned if he stopped. She was not the same high-handed, green-eyed, perfect-figured Tight Shoe he'd fallen in love with all those years before. She'd changed. Joanna was gentler, compassionate, more eager to be a part of the community. But all that didn't matter now. Touching her did.

Slowly he removed the shawl and feasted his gaze on the silken slope of her shoulders, delving his fingers into the curls that cascaded softly down the nape of her neck. He pulled Rachel close and kissed her.

For a few seconds his world careened. Long-dormant sensations burned through him, searing reason from his thoughts, leaving a driving need that ached to be appeased.

She didn't pull away and that fact crumbled the bastion of control he'd kept in check for so long. His tongue begged to taste her, savor her to satisfy the craving aroused in his youth yet hungered for even as a man. A whimper escaped her lips. Fingers delved into his hair, her lips moving hungrily against his own.

All that he'd dreamed of holding forever pressed against him, tempting him. But Joanna-the-dream had been a sham. Nothing could be compared to the unbridled, obsessed, consuming passion Joanna-in-the-flesh aroused within him.

The years of waiting faded. Damn every night he'd lain awake wondering if and praying that she would return. She was in his arms *now* and that was all that mattered.

He wasn't even aware of what he was doing, but suddenly Ben cradled her in his arms, carrying her like a beloved bride over the threshold of her porch. Nothing short of himself could stop what their hearts had set into motion this night, and he trembled at the power and repercussions of that responsibility.

Sounds caught in her throat, mingled in his mouth. Breathless moans of desire, hot, moist, demanding, stirred him to the depths of his need. But reason—whether it was self-control, honor, or fear that he might suffer an unhealable wound to his heart, filled him with caution.

He shouldn't . . . no, he *wouldn't* make love to this woman now. Not like this. Not until he knew for certain she would never leave him again. He'd dreamed of her too long, wanted her too much to accept a limit on how long they would share their lives, needed to know she meant forever.

Ben set her gently on her feet. "I think we've appeased the legend for now. We better stop, or I won't be able to say good night."

Or good-bye, Rachel thought as she watched him back away silently into the darkness. She already missed the heat of his body, the strength of his arms . . . missed the taste of him.

"Good night, darling. I hope your dreams are filled with hundreds of hazy moons."

His voice was like the wind, brushing over her in a soft sigh. Rachel trembled, locking her arms around her to hold in the memory of his touch. Thank heaven for Ben's staunch code of honor, or she would have given herself to him completely. She waited until he turned the corner to Main Street before going in and closing the door behind her.

A long, hot bath did little to ease the tension that coiled inside her. Even the material sliding over Rachel's skin as she pulled on her nightdress reminded her how easily Ben had awakened her to the yearning pulsing inside her.

Night sped by as she tossed and turned, unable to find peace, achingly aware that the other half of the bed was as empty as she felt, and would remain so when she told him the truth come morning.

No matter how impractical it seemed, no matter how much she tried to reason it out, Rachel knew something wonderful and promising had occurred between her and Ben, something that a life could be built on, but something Ben thought he was sharing with Joanna Tharp.

Rachel moved to the window, looking out into the night, feeling more alone than at any other time in her life. Ben would never truly belong to her. *So, what am I supposed to do,* she wondered miserably, *pretend this never happened? Pretend I don't love him?*

Hot tears trickled slowly down her cheeks as she felt the hopelessness of her situation. Tears of shame. Of longing. Of love that had to be denied.

Worst of all was the reality that no other embrace would ever satisfy the love beating in her heart for Ben, nor offer the sense of belonging she felt in his arms. No other home would ever be enough unless Ben lived there with her.

Her future loomed like a nightmare from which she might never wake.

❖ *14* ❖

SUNDAY MORNING DAWNED cold and thunder rumbled, promising rain. Rachel chose her clothes carefully, a dark brown merino skirt and muslin chemisette. She decided to dress warmly in the event the storm crossed over the vast prairie and sent the good citizens of Valiant scrambling for shawls and topcoats.

Sudden pounding on the front door startled her and made Rachel drop the cameo she'd been tying around her high-necked collar with a brown silk ribbon. "Just a minute!" she shouted, bending to see if the wayward treasure had rolled under the bed.

She felt around and came up empty-handed. Rachel's cheek pressed against the mattress while her fingers stretched farther, anticipating the feel of the ivory-carved oval silhouette. Nothing.

At first she thought the thunder had increased in intensity, then she realized it was the pounding that had increased. "All right, I'm coming! I'll be right there."

One last stretch rewarded her persistence. "There you are!" she scolded the cameo as if it were a living being. Threading the ribbon through the back of the pin, she quickly dashed downstairs, tying it as she went. When she finished,

Rachel swung open the door with a flourish, prepared to berate the early caller for being so demanding. "Ben, what are you doing here so early? Church isn't until eigh—"

Her words halted as glacial blue eyes stared at her with icy regard. The planes of his face looked sharper somehow, his jaw etched in stone. The grim line of Ben's mouth warned he was angry, but at *whom*?

"I've brought your guests. They arrived on this morning's train . . . from Richmond."

"Who?" Dread knotted in Rachel's stomach even as she asked the obvious and strained to peer around him. There was a handful of people who would leave Richmond for Valiant, and none of them would be coming to visit *her*.

To Rachel's dismay, her worst nightmare had come true. Thadeus Tharp was helping his wife from the carriage. Exiting behind the plump Narcissia was Joanna's six-year-old son, whose company Rachel had enjoyed on several occasions when he holidayed from boarding school. Now the Tharp family had come home to Valiant!

I am in the worst trouble of my entire life. Rachel pressed a palm over her mouth to keep it from gaping. *What am I going to say to them? Did Joanna tell them about the plan?* But all the concern over the Tharps' reactions was nothing compared to the worry over what Ben might say . . . and what he must be feeling.

"Good to see you, Mr. and Mrs. Tharp . . . Samuel." Rachel opened the door wider to allow them in. Ben and Thadeus returned to the carriage to carry in trunks.

"Miss Sloan, how good to see you. Isn't that one of Joanna's old things you're wearing?" Narcissia patted perspiration from her brow, then did the same to her neck. The woman's gray hair looked almost silver against her pale skin.

A lie got you into this mess, Rachel reminded herself, *don't let another dig you in deeper.* "Joanna gave me last year's wardrobe. You may remember that I sewed this for her last fall.''

"Yes, yes, I do remember." Narcissia's eyes teared up. "For the charity cotillion in October." Fanning herself, the plump matron strolled across the room to the fireplace Rachel had lit earlier to ward off the growing chill. "My Joanna was the most beautiful belle there."

"Shall I draw you a bath?" Rachel easily resumed her role as paid employee, but felt no resentment. She well remembered how unpleasant those gaseous fumes were riding the train from Wichita. Between smoke and ash, it was no wonder the poor woman's eyes were misting. "You must be tired from your trip."

"More exhausted than you can ever imagine, Miss Sloan." She gave the blond-headed boy who had taken a seat on the bottom step of the stairway a disparaging look. "He's been quite a handful, our Samuel."

"Our Samuel" held none of the endearing tone the woman had given "my Joanna." But then, the Tharps had never been overly fond of their role as grandparents, easily agreeing to their daughter's demand that Sam be sent away to Elizabeth Peabody's school in Boston.

The sound of trunks being set down behind her urged Rachel to redirect her concerns to the two men handling the baggage. "Will you be staying long?"

Thadeus removed his top hat, his ruddy cheeks puffing like a well-used bellows. "Just long enough to settle things, Miss Sloan."

Rachel suspected she was one of those "things" to be settled.

"Would you and the missus and your grandson like to attend church this morning with me and *Miss Sloan*?" Ben's eyes softened as he included the six-year-old in his request, then turned to marble as he emphasized her name.

The knot in Rachel's stomach tightened, burning her throat with rising nausea. *Serves you right*—she swallowed back her discomfort—*you have no one else to blame but yourself.* Unable to meet Ben's gaze directly, she moved over next to the boy. Maybe Ben would wait to aim those silent daggers of accusation since Sam would be watching too.

"We'll forgo this service, Benjamin," Thadeus announced. "Please give our apologies to everyone. I know they're expecting to welcome us officially, but we're all in need of bathing and rest first. The journey and what led to it have been quite an ordeal, I don't have to tell you."

"Perhaps I should miss it too?" Rachel knew she was only putting off the inevitable. Church or no church, Ben would have his say. As well as the Tharps. She suspected she was the "what led to it" part of the Tharps' ordeal. "I can heat up the Tharps' bathwater and prepare something to eat."

"That won't be necessary, Miss Sloan." Thadeus draped a hand around his wife's shoulders. "We're all much too tired from our journey. We'll eat later."

"I'm hungry," a tiny voice announced.

Every eye focused on the small figure balancing his elbows on his knees and staring up at the four grown-ups.

"You'll have a bath and take a nap first, young man." Thadeus Tharp's stern expression bowed the boy's head. "We'll not be selfish and keep these fine folks from worshiping the Lord. You can eat later."

"A drink of water always makes me feel better when I just get off a train." Rachel gently urged the child to let her guide him toward the kitchen. Her Maker would grieve if she let attending services force a child to go hungry. "Why don't we get a drink and warm up some water for your grandparents?"

"All right." Sam's dark eyes filled with gratitude.

"We *will* be going to service after I help get this trunk upstairs."

Rachel tried to ignore the demand in Ben's tone as she led Samuel into the kitchen. She knew there would be a reckoning, and nothing she could do would put it off. But right now the child was more important than her worry over what might transpire later.

She gave Sam a glass of milk instead. While he drank it, Rachel readied the stove, put water on to heat, then folded several cookies and a slice of cheese into a napkin. She grabbed the apple from the fruit-filled bowl in the center of the dining table. "Here, I wish I could take time to make you something more substantial," she offered, bending down to hand him the goodies. "Stick these in your pocket. No one but us has to know about it, all right?"

Obsidian-colored eyes stared up at her. "You won't tell on me?"

She crooked her smallest finger in front of her face, suddenly aware that Sam's eyes differed from Ben's. "If you won't tell on me for giving them to you. Shake on it?"

"Stubby swear." The boy's tiny finger curled around her own and sealed the deal.

"Stubby swear?" Rachel had heard the finger shake called by lots of names, but never that.

"Miz Narcissia calls this my stubby finger." Sam held up the smallest finger on his other hand. "So this is a stubby swear."

Miz Narcissia? It galled Rachel for the Tharps not to allow their own grandchild to call them Grandmother and Grandfather. "Then stubby swear it is. A pact between you and me. Now, you and I should get back in there before they start wondering what's keeping us."

Rachel tried not to watch the boy's pockets as he returned to the drawing room, but the apple bulged too blatantly. Fortunately, Joanna's mother had already hastened upstairs and the two men were intent upon following behind her, carrying the woman's heavy Saratoga trunk.

"You're in luck. They're not looking." She waited until the trio disappeared beyond the landing before taking the boy's hand and tiptoeing up the stairs. "If we can just get to your mother's room without anyone seeing us, we're safe."

Sam's small shoulders bobbed up and down as he tiptoed elaborately with her and kept a finger pressed against his lips to hush Rachel.

When they crept past the doorway leading into the sitting room, Rachel heard: "Why has she been sleeping in *my* room? There are plenty of others."

Knowing there would be a thousand questions to answer if Joanna had not let her parents in on the reason Rachel had come to Valiant, Rachel wanted only to disappear from sight.

"Is this it, Miss Sloan?" The boy tugged on her hand and led her into Joanna's room.

"Yes, now quickly, take everything out of your pockets and put it under your pillow."

Samuel rushed to obey. Soon he looked extremely pleased with himself. Rachel felt a twinge of guilt about teaching him to hoard things. A habit of hers that rose from many a night wondering where the next meal was coming from. No, she reasoned, she was showing him how to survive and grab life as it was offered. Some might look on it as hoarding, maybe even stealing, but Rachel believed everyone had a right to learn self-preservation.

"You ready for church?"

Startled by the deep voice that stood only a breath behind her, Rachel nearly jumped out of her skin. She squealed.

"He didn't see, did he, Miss Sloan?" The boy backed up against one side of the bed pillows, threading his arms behind him.

"See what?" Ben asked, staring at her accusingly. "What else are you conspiring, *Miss Sloan*?"

Telling him would be too easy. The look of disgust riddling Ben's face was unwarranted. She'd merely fed a hungry child. But Rachel refused to break the boy's confidence in her. Her first lie was so insurmountable, how could another one possibly hurt? And it wouldn't be a total untruth. "Sam's got a special way to make bargains. It's called a stubby swear, and he doesn't let just anybody see it, do you, Samuel?"

Sam shook his head.

Ben eyed the pair of conspirators, then finally focused on Rachel, making her all too aware that neither of them had fooled him.

"I think we'd best be on our way to church, *Miss Sloan*"—he continued to stress her name sarcastically— "I've got a feeling you have a lot to repent this morning, and me . . . well, I'd best bend my knees a little harder. I need a reminder about judging lest I not be judged."

Rachel's fingers stiffened as Ben pressed his own over hers, helping her hold the hymnal instead of sharing songbooks with Jimmy, who stood opposite him. It seemed such a natural sharing—one that any man in love with his Godfearing wife would do. Yet, singing with Ben and standing next to him in church made her feel all the more miserable.

Her lie magnified tenfold beneath the sanctuary's rafters. Ben's anger faded, like mud that could be wiped away, as the church service continued. She'd thought his statement about judging had been a taunt, but Ben meant what he said earlier. He sank to his knees and prayed earnestly.

When he rose, she noticed his face was strained, his eyes brimming with unshed tears. Her heart clenched as if someone had roped it and tightened it. As the minister ended the service and people began to file out of the church, Rachel followed. She took advantage of the slightly pushing crowd and leaned into him. "I never meant to hurt you," she whispered. "Please believe that."

"I don't know what I believe in anymore." He knuckled away a tear as he half turned and refused to look at her. "Somebody needs to dust in here."

The tone of his voice pierced her with its defeat. The impact of her lie became too glaringly clear. She'd taken away his hope and his belief in the dream he'd lived for seven years. Rachel wished she could shrink from sight, but her feet felt as if they'd been staked to the ground.

Someone nudged her and complained, "Step aside, Joanna. Some of us want to get home before the storm blows in."

"I'm not Joanna," she whispered, not caring who heard. The enormity of what she'd done settled into her like a bad seed that couldn't be weeded out. When Ben learned the truth, he would probably always believe she did it only for the sake of the house. She allowed those behind her to pass. *Go home,* she bid them silently. *Go home and be glad you have one.*

She was the last to leave the church, unable to watch the friendly exchange of good-byes and offered invitations among the townspeople. Rachel had started to feel a part of Valiant, liked its people, even looked forward to the challenges the Tight Shoe Troupe and Ophelia presented. Now she would have to leave, once she told Ben everything.

Wind blasted her face, brushing a strand of hair into her eyes and whipping up the hem of her skirt. Rachel smoothed back the hair, wishing she'd thought of wearing a snood to hold it in place. She turned so that she met the wind face-on and her hair would blow behind her.

Where had Ben gone? Why had Jimmy not walked to

church with them earlier? Was there still trouble between them?

She shielded her eyes with her arm as she fought the strong breeze to search the varied groups who had not yet left for home.

She spotted Ophelia talking to Alewine and a cluster of young boys. Jimmy stood alongside Alewine, looking as if he had no intention of being with his father. From the way Aly elaborately gestured, Rachel could tell the buckskinned woman was enthusiastic about the conversation, and the boys were enthralled with her tale.

". . . then me and Ben, we just pounced on 'em like they was standing in sweet grass insteada' that ol' hog waller." Alewine snorted. "By the time we got through with them cayoots, all of us smelt worse than skunk piss."

Jimmy laughed the loudest.

Ophelia tapped her cane against Alewine's arm. "We're at church. Watch your mouth."

"Thanks for reminding me. Good a place as any to 'fess up to my no-good ways." Alewine slapped Ophelia's back so hard, Ophelia's top curls shifted position beneath her hat.

Though Aly's pat had been offered in a good-natured manner, Ophelia looked as if she might bring the walls of Jericho down on top of Alewine's head. Rachel stepped in before the crowd of boys had to choose up sides and determine which of the pair was more saint than sinner.

"Have any of you seen Ben?" she asked.

"Saddling up horses over at the livery." Alewine nodded in the direction he'd taken. "Said something about a picnic. Though it looks like it might get a little soggy."

"If you see him, would you tell him I'm not going? We shouldn't go with these clouds flowing in so brisk."

"Tell him yourself. Here he comes." Ophelia pointed the cane tip behind Rachel.

Jimmy dug his boot tip into the dirt. ''He won't be no help now,'' the boy complained to Alewine. ''He'll have his mind on *her*.''

Before Rachel could question the resentment in the boy's voice, Ben reined to a halt a few feet away.

''Mount up.'' He extended her the other horse's reins.

''We shouldn't go,'' Rachel insisted, noticing the pulse throbbing in his jaw.

''You can tell me the truth in front of God and all of Valiant, or you can let me ride off my temper between here and the canyon. I'd rather have this discussion in private.''

Alewine whistled long and low, her gaze darting from Ben to Rachel, then to Jim. ''I'd say the storm's already hit, Jo. You best hang on to your saddle horn.''

''I'll go,'' Rachel conceded. She cared too much to let the whole town see that he'd been made a fool of.

❖ 15 ❖

THE SILENCE OF the horseback ride was deafening. Ben rode ahead of her, forcing Rachel to follow or be lost. She couldn't catch him to tell him she knew very little about horses, so all she could do was pray the beast wouldn't throw her.

The rush of wind taunted Rachel as if it were her conscience taking voice. *Schemer,* it blasted against her face. *Selfish, selfish, selfish,* it berated in rhythm to the horse's ground-eating gallop. *Liar!* the wild current of air battered her clenched teeth and siphoned the warmth from her throat.

Despite every reason to turn and run the other way, Rachel raced toward the reckoning. A dozen strategies for explaining the deception catapulted into her mind, only to sink into the quagmire of her guilt. All had flaws. Each gave only half-measures of truth. None would ever be enough to ease the hurt and humiliation she'd caused Ben.

Suddenly, her mount slowed to a trot. His ears twitched and his front legs volleyed from left to right in a strange prance. "What's wrong?" she asked, watching as Ben reined to a halt ahead of her.

"This is as far as we go." He gave a command to Rachel's horse that urged the pony forward, though cautiously.

Her curiosity became an exclamation of wonder as the horse moved up alongside Ben's and she saw the land that stretched before them. A wide chasm split the Texas prairie, extending deep into the earth. The wind-carved stone fanned like multicolored flounces of a flamenco dancer's skirt, then snaked its way south.

"Where are we?" Her awe-filled tone was hushed with reverence.

"The Palo Duro Canyon. Coronado's true find in his foolish search for the golden city of Quivera." A sigh as deep as the canyon beneath them escaped Ben as he added, "A man whose obsession destroyed his life."

The pain in Ben's eyes made her aware that he compared himself to the explorer in some misguided way. Rachel looked closer and noticed the glimmer of tears at their base. When she reached for him, Ben jerked away and dismounted.

She dismounted too, watching him use the moment to wipe away the emotion he refused to shed in her presence.

"I wanted to tell you before." Though she fought to keep from crying herself, all she managed to do was bite her lip until she tasted blood. "But every time I tried, you did something so thoughtful, so wonderful, I didn't have the heart to hurt you, Ben."

Disbelief and anger blended on his handsome face. Rachel's hands shook so badly, she could barely hobble the horse. The deceit she'd dealt him was unforgivable. How she wished she'd listened to her first impulse before talking to Daniel, before allowing Joanna to tempt her.

"Didn't have the heart to hurt me?" Ben repeated in a quiet tone that shouted with contempt. He grabbed her by the shoulders.

She started to flinch, but wouldn't. He had a right to shake her until her teeth rattled, but he didn't. The deliberate restraint of that righteous anger struck a more powerful blow than any that could have been dealt physically.

"Is this some cruel joke?" His eyes narrowed into sapphire slits. "Did you ever once consider *my* heart, Miss Sloan?"

The full force of his words registered on Rachel's conscience. Blood drained from her face. Choking on her remorse, she gulped back hiccups that almost prevented her from answering his question. Her chin lifted as she steeled herself to face her accuser. "I did consider you, Ben. Whether or not you'll ever believe me again, it's true."

The facts came rushing out. She placed no blame even though she'd been forced to read the letters to spare Samuel a wrong. She even admitted that Joanna's threat to make employment impossible for her in the East was not the deciding motivation for the deception. "The truth is I had come to admire the man I met on paper. I envied Joanna for having someone who loved her so much that his single-minded goal in life was to make her dreams come true."

Confessing that she'd meant well seemed shallow even as Rachel told him that she'd hoped to soften the blow of ending the courtship. Their gazes met, held. "I knew I'd made a mistake the moment I stepped off the train. Even though you were too blinded by love to see me for what I really was, others suspected. Ophelia. Possibly Gwenella Duncan. Alewine, for certain. That's why I hosted all those frenzied tea parties. I thought I could match you up with someone better than Joanna. Someone who would love you as much as you deserve to be loved. I'm so sorry I hurt you, Ben. I truly meant to help and messed everything up completely."

What a mess he'd made of his life! Ben stared out into the vast canyon that seemed small compared to the cavern that had become his heart. He sat on the buffalo grass, sinking deep into the prairie loam. Acceptance came slow and with painful reality. Joanna had not cared enough to return. She'd concocted this elaborate lie to evade him. All his dreams, his hopes for a future with Joanna, his efforts to mold himself into a man she would be proud to call husband, had been an obsession that played itself out. Like Coronado's.

Still, why did he feel so glad she wasn't Joanna?

"I hope you'll forgive me one day, Ben."

"Forgive you?" Ben came to grips with his own folly. Joanna's look-alike was guilty only of wanting more than she had. From what she'd told him, the woman had honorable intentions. Anger fled, replaced by a fury directed at himself. "Forgive you for what? Trying to spare a small boy humiliation and a man the heartache of being old enough to know better? Your reasons sound pretty noble to me, miss. In fact, downright compassionate."

"Not so noble," she whispered.

"There's something you haven't told me." He sensed it when her voice cracked, in the slump of her shoulders, the way she would not meet his gaze. When had he started noticing her every move? he wondered. Why had he found her so much more beautiful than before? Shouldn't he be feeling a pang of disloyalty to Joanna?

"There's nothing more."

The halfheartedness of her reply assured Ben he was right. Could she be deceiving herself as well? "You came here for another reason than wanting to be kind to a man you read about in letters. For all you knew, I might have been lying to Joanna. Saying all those things to woo her home."

"But you didn't," she replied. "Everything you said was true."

"Even so, you didn't know that. Why did you come, Miss Sloan? Hell, I don't even know your first name."

"Rachel."

"Rachel," he repeated, thinking that it suited her far better than Joanna. All their differences suddenly became clearer. Instinctively, he'd sensed it from the moment she'd stepped off the train and into his arms. The darker green of her eyes, the more delicate shape of her face, the waist that had not been affected by Samuel's birth. Then later, her thoughtfulness and gentle ways, her willingness to befriend Alewine. Her forgetfulness about the past. All those things had stared him in the face, but he'd been blinded by his love for Joanna.

Thunder rumbled directly over them as lightning streaked the sky. Clouds sagged lower, heavy with their unshed moisture. He stood, suspecting they should be leaving, yet unwilling to go without discovering what had led Rachel Sloan to this desperate deception. He wanted to know, needed to understand, refused to wait any longer. "I deserve to hear *every* reason you came to Valiant."

Faced with the final explanation, Rachel floundered. How could a man who seemed at home everywhere in Valiant understand the need that drove her to search for a place where she could belong?

She walked to the edge of the cliff and stared out into the prehistoric panorama. For the first time in her life, she wondered if she dared trust someone with the truth that broke her heart and drove her to a life of endless searching.

"My mother and father had too many mouths to feed when I was fourteen," she began slowly, threading her fingers in and out of each other as she talked. "Said I was big enough to take care of myself. And I was, more or less. I was paid to carry groceries for the local merchant. Made extra money sweeping the floor at Lou's barbershop. Seemed like I worked from dawn to past dark most days. It kept me fed and bought me good hand-me-down clothes, but allowed precious little time for anything else. Still, no amount of work kept away the fear of being alone when I tried to close my eyes at night.''

She rubbed her arms to ward off the chill of anguished memories. ''I spent years finding employment few others would take. Finally I learned not only to sew, but to sew well, which eventually led to my position with the Tharps. Joanna realized we looked so much alike that I could model for her fittings when she tired of them. I found a security unlike any I'd known in a very long time.''

Rachel sighed. ''Working for her had its difficulties, of course. Other than being snobbish and demanding at times, she was exciting to be around and made me see a side of life I didn't realize existed.'' Shrugging, she admitted, ''And Joanna paid well.''

She knew she was prattling, stalling, hoping the storm would force them to leave this discussion until a better time. But the man looked like he'd taken root in the soil. His wide stance and hands shoved into his pockets warned he wasn't about to move, come rain or hail . . . or hell itself.

Just say it, she told herself. *What does it matter if he doesn't understand?*

It matters, her heart insisted. *But say it anyway.*

''I've always had this horrible feeling''—the words rushed out. She found herself grappling with the emotion that rose to slow those that followed—''that I might never be more than part of a litter. Somebody easily given away.''

Her eyes began to burn, but she blinked back the tears, afraid that if they started, she'd never be able to stop them. ''I'm afraid I'll never know what it means to have a home of my own or someone there waiting for me to return.''

She glanced up at him and the compassion staring back at her burst the dam of her restraint. The tears began to fall, scalding her cheeks with the pain of unloved years. ''A home, Ben, even a make-believe one, was too tempting for me to resist." Rachel wiped her eyes, trying to keep her vision from blurring. "I'm sorry for deceiving you, for wanting a home, even a temporary one, so much that it caused you such hurt."

When Ben moved closer she turned, unwilling to see pity in his eyes. Two warm hands encompassed her shoulders, softly kneading the nape of her neck. Her muscles tensed beneath his touch as she fought the urge to lean back into the warmth she felt from the powerful body standing behind her.

"Rachel Sloan, whoever you are, I think you're someone I'd like to know very much," he whispered against her neck. "I'm sorry Joanna used you. Sorry that she'll never know how much I loved her."

When his hands returned to his sides, Rachel faced Ben again. "But she can. You've just proven to me that you can forgive anything, Ben. I don't know her reason for not letting you come to Richmond or what she's hiding from her friends there. But whatever it is, you're the man, the only man, who can see her through it. The only one who loves her enough to forgive her anything. There's still a chance, don't you see?"

"She's dead."

Joanna? Dead? "When? *Why?*"

"She was killed by her lover's jealous wife during a rendezvous. It seems Joanna had been seeing a certain politician in the neighboring county and his wife got wind of it."

The tears Ben refused to shed earlier sprang from a deeper hurt than Rachel imagined. Not just from the deception and Joanna's death, but from the death of his dream he'd held fast for so many years.

"*That's* the ordeal the Tharps spoke of," she realized aloud. She felt ashamed she'd been so insensitive to their grief and worried only about whether her deception would be revealed. "Poor little Samuel. What will happen to him?"

With emotion breaking his voice, Ben continued painfully. "That's the real tragedy here. Joanna lived long enough to request that I, not his grandparents, raise her son. A request the Tharps are only too eager to grant, I assure you. They told me when I met them at the train, mind you, even knowing the child could hear what they were saying, that their lives would have to be pared down during the social seasons and that simply was unacceptable to them. They brought Sam to live with me. Can you believe their callousness?"

Anger tightened Rachel's cheeks. Anger that grown people, blood kin, could throw a child away as though he were no longer of any use. To damage an innocent heart that would never know when to trust again. Thank God, Joanna loved her son enough to give him the best home she could offer the boy. Ben McGuire would never let Samuel go unloved and homeless.

Though Rachel was uncertain Ben was Sam's father, never did the possibility seem more likely. "You must have known from the very beginning I was a fake," she announced, then realized her thoughts had slipped out.

His forefinger traced her lips. "Frankly, I was too charmed to notice."

A flash flood of desire washed through her. Lightning brightened the sky, illuminating Ben's face and the sincerity darkening the blue of his eyes. They took a step closer to each other as if some intangible force pulled them.

Her pulse went berserk. She whispered his name. With a low growl he framed her face in his hands, then kissed her deeply, passionately, putting all his need into it. She returned the kiss in kind, melting against him, finding the one place she wanted to be more than anywhere else in the world.

He moved his hands boldly over her back, tracing the curve of her waist, the slope of her hips, pressing the hard evidence of his desire near that part of her that ached for his more intimate touch. She gasped with need, inflamed by a burning urgency that knew no reason, compelled by an emotion so powerful that Rachel was caught up in an enchantment stronger than any lie.

He kissed her again and again, as if he thirsted and could not be quenched. She sensed the change, felt the desperation in his kiss. No, she screamed silently, wanting more than passion. She needed love.

Suddenly she felt tainted. Less valued. Anger filled her. Rachel backed away from his embrace, trying to curtain off the window into her heart that she'd exposed to him. "I'm not Joanna, Ben. I'll never take her place. No matter how much I look like her. No matter how much you want me to *be* her. Take me ho— Take me back to Valiant. I can't live here anymore."

The words Ophelia had spoken at the restaurant the previous evening filled Rachel's thoughts. Her heart shattered in two as she repeated them to the man who had lain claim to her love. "I refuse to be anyone's second choice."

◆ 16 ◆

Tiny PELTS OF rain cooled Ben's passion as Rachel backed away from him and prepared to unhobble her horse. The roan shied from her touch, making it difficult for her to complete the task.

"We'd best get back to town or we'll be soaked," she insisted, shielding her eyes against the rain as she glanced up at the angry clouds above.

Even a well-seasoned wrangler couldn't control a frightened horse that easily, and from Rachel's hesitance as she approached the roan again, Ben realized she was an inexperienced horsewoman. He unhobbled his Appaloosa and secured the reins so they wouldn't drag in the brush. With a swat to the horse's spotted flanks, he yelled, "Hyah!"

"Why are you scaring him off?" Rachel nearly stumbled backward as her foot slipped in the wet grass. "Won't this one run away now?"

"If we aren't careful, yes. But Crockett knows his way back. He'll turn up at the general store. If Aly catches sight of him and we don't arrive soon after, she'll send someone to search for us. We'd best get back as soon as possible so we won't worry everyone." That is, Aly would send someone if she and Jim weren't caught out in this too, Ben worried silently.

How could he have let his grief and anger that morning at finding out about Joanna's death and Rachel Sloan's deception put them in such danger? She may have owed him one hell of an explanation, but her life was not part of that debt. As if to punctuate the threat, lightning struck a cottonwood so close, it sizzled like a thousand stinging bees. The pungent odor of charred wood filled the air.

The roan pounded its fear against the ground, screaming defiance against keeping his front legs in captivity.

"We're riding double. If lightning spooks the roan, then I'll control the reins."

Rachel shook her head. "I don't want to ri—"

"Don't risk your life because you're angry at me." Ben's voice was low, almost undetectable in the fury of the increasing wind. He took slow steps forward, encouraging the horse to calm. The roan danced sideways, its nostrils flaring and head bobbing.

"Easy, fella. I know you're frightened. But I just want to undo these so we can take you back to the livery. Yes, that's right. Easy. Easy now. It'll be dry there, and you can have a bucket of oats. We'll brush you down and get you out of this weather. Easy. Eeeasy."

Ben directed a warning toward Rachel, keeping the same low monotone. "He might spook the second he's free. Step back, but do so slowly."

Once she was out of harm's way, Ben gently took the reins and wrapped them around one hand, the other hand stroking the animal's neck. Making certain he stood where the roan could see his every movement, he unhobbled the animal's legs and mounted with the speed and skill of experience. The horse reared and screamed its insult.

"Ben!" Rachel yelled, rushing forward.

"Stay back! He'll kill us both!"

Two wills fused into a singular purpose, each intent upon

mastering the other. The roan crow-hopped, curling its head and shoulders into itself. Its flanks twisted, and he shot skyward. Ben rode the maelstrom of horseflesh. His teeth clamped together. Knees braced. His right hand clutched the lifeline of reins. Unbridled power churned beneath him as catapulting bucks and bone-jarring impacts of hooves attempted to rearrange his bones.

Ben expected another crow-hop, but the roan took Ben by surprise and reared backward.

"The cliff!" Rachel screamed.

With all his might Ben dove across the roan's mane, thrusting his entire weight upon the horse's neck and shoulders. The momentum spurred the animal forward, away from the canyon's edge. Ben hung on tightly, certain he would be killed if the beast had the presence of mind to crow-hop before he could reseat himself. But the roan bolted into the prairie instead.

"Wait for me!"

Ben heard Rachel's scream, yet could do nothing but hold on tightly. He knew if he let go, he would be trampled beneath the animal's hooves. "Easy, fella, easy," he crooned into the wind, hoping the roan would hear him, praying he could keep his own fear from consuming him.

He repeated the words, took his courage in hand, and inched backward toward the saddle.

"I can't run that fast! Wait up!" Rachel yelled behind him. A loud "oooff!" echoed over the prairie.

He heard her fall. Imagined her hem tangling in a root or a low-lying mesquite branch. He heard another shout and another, but soon her words became distant. Ben tried to get his bearings, to remember where she was, but he could only concentrate on his hold . . . or die.

If he could slide back . . . just a little. The roan lunged, hurdling some obstacle in its path. Ben's hands jerked loose.

His body took flight. Arched backward. Images of Joanna, Alewine, and Jimmy sank through his consciousness.

The impact of earth against his buttocks and back jolted one face to the forefront. The face of a green-eyed stranger. The face of the woman who'd taught him too late that he should have been living the passion and not worshiping the dream.

Rachel ran as fast as she could, praying that he was still alive. The rain distorted the distance that separated them. Her hem caught on brambles. Thorny mesquite tentacles seemed to reach out and grab at her. Still, she ran.

Though she'd seen the horse throw Ben off, she could have sworn it hadn't been but a half-mile away at most. The Texas prairie mocked her, testing her courage and challenging her stamina.

At last she found him lying on his back, eyes closed. His breathing was shallow. She knelt beside him, wanting to lift his head into her lap but afraid to move him. "Ben"—she leaned over his pale face, pressing her lips against his forehead—"Ben, can you hear me?"

When he didn't move, didn't utter a sound, she began to cry.

Ben lay still, wondering if that mournful sound was his soul crying for the life he'd wasted. He'd allowed himself to be alone. Told himself that it would prove to Joanna how much he loved her. That no other woman could ever fill her place in his heart. If that were so, why hadn't he discovered the deception before the Tharps told him of Joanna's death? Why hadn't he questioned all those differences in the woman who'd professed to be Joanna that he knew were too good to be true?

Yet if he had, he wouldn't have held her in his arms,

kissed her. Wanted her. She would have still been a stranger to him.

Slowly, Ben realized he was not mourning the wasting of his previous life, but the possibility of one in which Rachel might become something more than a counterfeit love. He tried for years to achieve all that he and Joanna had discussed about their future. To do everything according to her preference and expectation. To become a man worthy of her social status.

Now a woman had stormed into his life that made him realize he wanted more. Ben strained to open his eyes . . . to see clearly for the first time in seven years.

Emerald eyes stared back, tears shimmering in their depths and mixing with the rain that pelted them. But he wasn't ready to face her just yet.

She'd deceived him. Attempted to scam not only him, but the whole town. He couldn't just ignore every code he lived by because she stirred a passion in him as no other woman had before. He had to get his thoughts in order. Nothing made sense anymore.

"You're alive," she whispered.

Relief flooded her face with a beauty he could not resist. His hand acted upon its own and reached out to wipe away the tears trickling down her cheeks.

"You can move!" Excitement punctuated each word. "Is anything broken?"

He hadn't given his state of well-being a thought, but once he did, Ben felt as if he'd been stampeded over. He bent one knee, then the other, then finally sat up. "All in working order, it seems."

"Can you stand?" Rachel rose and held out a hand.

Ben accepted the help, discovering that though bones weren't broken, they hadn't quit shaking. He stood, waiting a moment for the world to stop whirling. "Next time we'll take my horse"—his attempt at humor failed—"and let yours loose."

She offered her shoulder to him to use as a crutch. "Next time we'll take a buggy," she argued. "Can you walk?"

"If there ever is a next time." He tested one leg, then the other. Though slightly wobbly, strength returned to them in a few minutes. "My legs aren't the problem."

Rachel touched Ben on the shoulder, neck, forearms, and chest, everywhere but where he actually hurt. The pleasant way she smelled was thick in the air around him, causing a sweet ache to form in the pit of his stomach. Ben groaned.

"Have I hurt you?"

"No," he lied.

"Then, where *do* you hurt?"

Everywhere aches when you touch me, he acknowledged silently. "I landed on my . . . uh . . . well, you know."

"Your buttocks?"

"Are you always so frank?" Ben ignored the soreness and headed toward town. If they didn't get out of this rain, he would be stove up for days.

"Are you always so bashful?" She kept in step with him, continuing to offer him her shoulder to lean on.

"The last thing I am is bashful. You ought to remem—"

"I'm not Joanna." Anger erupted inside her again. "And the one thing she didn't share with me is anything about your intimacy."

Ben apologized. "Look, it's going to take all we've got to get back to town in once piece, Miss Sloan. It'll be easier if we're not angry with each other. I didn't break anything, but I'm hurting enough to know I won't last long out here in this weather. Let's start walking so we'll be closer to Valiant if you should have to leave me behind."

Her arm tightened around his waist. "I wouldn't leave you."

"Pardon me if I don't rely on those words." Ben took painful steps forward. "It isn't the first time I was expected to trust them."

The sight of two riders wearing yellow slickers and riding with Crockett in tow renewed her strength to continue. Her body trembled with exhaustion from having to walk mile after mile over the mushy prairie loam. Hope that Ben had been right in predicting that a search party would look for them had washed away miles and prayers earlier.

"Over here!" She waved, hoping she didn't fall when shifting Ben's heavy weight upon her shoulder. "We're over here!"

Ben waved and whistled. Rachel jerked away, the sound too abrupt and shrill on the desolate plain.

An answering whistle signaled the riders had heard. Horses thundered across the prairie, heading straight for them. Ben sank to his knees. "It's Aly and Jim. I'd know that whistle anywhere."

Rachel moved closer and bent beside him. "They found us. We'll be home soon. Hang on just a little while longer."

"Thank you"—he reached out, threading his fingers through hers—"for staying with me when I needed you."

"It's nothing more than you would have done for me." She returned the appreciation with an equally gentle squeeze.

"That's true." He turned morning-glory blue eyes to meet her gaze. "But it's something Joanna would never have done."

A thrill raced through Rachel, giving her a sense of accomplishment and an appreciation for his honesty.

His lips softly brushed hers. It was a kiss of gratitude. A kiss of amends. A kiss of hello.

"They don't look hurt to me," complained the wearer of the smallest yellow slicker as the riders reined to a halt in front of them. "Just wet."

Alewine dismounted, heading directly to Ben. "Then you'd better look a little closer, James Donald. I don't know about you, but I ain't never seen your pa on his knees 'cept in church. Get off your backside and help me get him up." She glanced at Rachel. "You hurt?"

"I'm f-fine." Rachel stood, touching her lips unconsciously to hold in Ben's kiss. The gritty taste of mud mingled with the rain sprinkling on her mouth. She wiped the offending taste away with the back of her hand, then cleaned her fingers with a fistful of her merino skirt. The hem was already ruined anyway, so good manners be damned. "Ben took a nasty fall. Nothing's broken, but he's sore."

"A fall? From Crockett?" Jim sounded incredulous.

"I taught you better than that, boy," Alewine scolded. "Think how he came in. Were his reins trailing him?"

"No." Jim helped Alewine walk Ben to the Appaloosa and mount. "Crock was reined in so he wouldn't get hurt."

Ben grimaced as he settled low into the saddle, revealing all too well where he hurt most. "I fell from the roan. Got bucked off." Offering Rachel a hand to mount up behind him, he added, "It's a long story. One I'll tell you once we're home and out of these wet clothes."

Jim heaved himself into his own saddle. "This ought to be a good one. I ain't never seen Ben bucked off. *Ever.*"

Alewine remounted as well, looking from Rachel to Ben, then at the thirteen-year-old. "Well, if you ask me, I got a feeling this ain't going to be the last time your pa's gonna have some sense knocked into him . . . long as Jo's in town."

The boy rode point to spot trouble. Alewine rode behind to make sure the couple suffered no more misfortune without receiving quick assistance.

Rachel's awareness of Ben became even more heightened with her arms threaded around his chest for support. She could hear the steady beat of his heart in her ear as she pressed her cheek against his back. His rain-drenched clothes molded to him like a second skin, yet she could feel the heat their closeness kindled between them. An ache grew within her to hold him even closer, a throe of sensations stimulated by the rhythm of their hips rocking back and forth in concurrence with Crockett's gait.

"I need to say something, whether you listen or not." Though husky in tone, determination motivated Ben's words. "Since I first saw you at the depot, I've felt this unexplainable attraction to you."

A chill raced over Rachel's skin, and she wished she could back away without fear of falling.

He pressed a hand over hers, preventing her from unthreading them from around his waist. "I mean something different than what I felt for Joanna. Your eyes were . . . *are* a deeper green. The way you move. That little smile you give when you're pleased."

Rachel tried not to smile, but his compliment eased the resentment that had instantly flared at the comparison.

"But the real difference is your strong spirit. I've watched you face some of the most forceful citizens in town and still keep your patience. You've been kind to those that others have no time or use for because they don't do quite what's expected of them. Alewine, Ophelia. Even Jim. But most of all, I've watched you face the danger we shared today without complaining once." He was silent for a moment, then added, "You're quite a fascinating woman, Rachel Sloan. I hope you'll stay in Valiant long enough for some of us to get to know you better."

His compliment blanketed her in its warmth, warding off the chill of the decision that must be made once they reached town. Where could she go now? Certainly not back to Tharp House.

"I guess what I'm trying to say"—Ben softly stroked her hands—"is that I've loved only one woman, and I've learned that it was a misguided love. I don't imagine it will be easy for me to trust again. And I'm not sure I can ever love again. But I do hope that one day we can put this deception behind us and become friends."

Suddenly her hands felt bereft of warmth.

"Hold on, we're jumping a deadfall."

"Friends?" *Hardly.* Rachel was grateful the lightning-struck tree lying in their pathway forced her to strengthen her grip around Ben as Crockett easily cleared the jump. She wanted to hold on tightly, suspecting there might never be another opportunity to do so again. "Perhaps we will be."

How was she supposed to push away the feeling of being in his arms? To forget the intoxicating taste of his lips. To cool the passion that smoldered within her every time he looked at her?

She would never settle for less than his love . . . for less than he'd offered Joanna.

❖ 17 ❖

THE STREETS OF Valiant were vacant. The rain had driven everyone indoors, evidenced by the amber glow of lantern light shining in the hotel and saloon windows. Ben signaled for Alewine to catch up. When she did, he thanked her again for coming to his rescue. "If you'll check with Nash and find out if the roan made it back, I'll make sure Rachel gets home. If it didn't, tell him I'll agree to whatever price he thinks fair."

"Rachel?" Alewine's brow arched inquisitively at her. "Didn't think you looked like no Jo."

"It's a long story, Aly. I'll tell you tomorrow." Ben reined Crockett away from the livery.

"No, *I'll* tell you," Rachel insisted, twisting around in the saddle to make certain the freightliner understood that she would tell her the truth herself. "Thank you for rescuing us."

"Weren't nothing. You'd do it fer me."

Rachel turned back around. Yes, she would help Alewine any way she could. Valiant had given her a handful of friends in the short time she'd been there. She counted Aly among them. As Ben commanded the Appaloosa to move down

Main Street toward the church, she asked, "Where are you taking us?"

"To Tharp House, of course."

"I can't live there anymore. Stop here and let me off." The reality all that entailed nearly overwhelmed Rachel. No more fancy roof over her head. No fine clothes to wear. The funds would no longer be hers to use as promised. Joanna was gone, and the stable employment that had supported Rachel so well disappeared with her death. Rachel had nothing but the soggy chemisette and skirt.

He swung the horse around but refused to rein to a halt.

"I asked that you let me down, please," she reminded him, trying to hide the despair that engulfed her. With the Tharps in Valiant, all her belongings were locked away in their Richmond home. After all she'd done, would they ever return them to her?

"You can stay at my place tonight. There's plenty of room with me and Jim."

Rachel's heart took on a faster rhythm. Sleep under Ben's roof? That's one torment she would spare herself. She may be soaked to the brain, but she wasn't addled. "I can't."

"You're right." Ben changed his mind and his direction once again. "You shouldn't. I wasn't thinking of the scandal that might cause. Everyone's going to know soon enough about Samuel. And with them thinking you're Joanna and unmarried, her reputation will suffer. If you stay with Jim and me, that would only add to the slander unless you had a definite purpose for being there. I don't care what they'll say about me, but it might be hard on Jim and Samuel . . . and yourself, of course."

"Of course," Rachel repeated, caring only that he agreed with her over the foolishness. "Why don't you take me to Ophelia's? She'll put me up for the night." Particularly after

Rachel gave the woman what would probably prove the gossip to end all gossip—her real identity.

"You can't stay at 'Phele's. It's not the sort of place for a woman like you."

His concern made her hesitate. How did he know what kind of woman she was, or what would he say if he knew half the places she'd spent nights in her youth? Rachel had accepted warmth and company wherever she could find it to ward off the cold of night and the chill of being a throwaway child.

"You don't have any money of your own, do you?" He steered the horse toward the boardinghouse.

"Most everything belonged to Joanna." *Even you,* she added silently against his back. The only garment she called her own was the linen wrapper she slept in. She had refused to spend her nights as Joanna. But the letters that filled the same box as those Ben had written to Joanna were the real treasures she refused to leave behind. Letters she'd hidden beneath Narcissia's bed for safekeeping and to shield them from whoever was leaving the notes.

No one, not even Joanna, knew of their existence or what they contained. She'd never told a living soul about them and refused to let anyone learn of them now. Tomorrow she would ask the Tharps to allow her an opportunity to gather her things. Surely they would give her a few moments alone upstairs. She could wrap the nightdress around the box and no one would see what she hid. Rachel would willingly give up everything she owned here and in Richmond, but those letters were irreplaceable. *All* of them.

"Why don't you let me help you get a room at the boardinghouse?" Ben suggested.

"What, and give Ophelia even more gossip than she'll already have?"

"Consider it a loan. You can pay me back when you—well, *later*. You know."

No, she didn't know. She had no idea where even her next meal would come from. Rachel needed to leave Valiant. Head as fast and as far away from Ben McGuire as possible. But that was as unlikely as the Tharps deciding to raise Samuel after all. "All right. A loan, then, but just for one night." Pride refused to allow more. If she had to wait tables at Delaney's, she would, providing the good citizens of Valiant didn't run her out of town.

Ben reined to a halt in front of the boardinghouse. Rachel dismounted, then offered him a helping hand. He managed to get down by himself without too much trouble, then dug into his pocket and handed her several coins.

"That's too much." She returned the extra to him, but he refused to accept it.

"Eat something. You've had a long day."

"I'm not hungry."

"Then save it for breakfast. I'll send Clem over with something for you to wear. Mrs. Abernathy won't take kindly to you soaking her mattress in that."

"Send Ophelia instead." Rachel lifted her hem and petticoats until they were inches off the sidewalk. "I should talk to her tonight. It's best to go to the source when you want gossip spread right. No doubt the good people of Valiant will know the truth if the Tharps had any visitors at all this evening. I wouldn't want Ophelia to be shortchanged."

Whispers rippled across the restaurant as Rachel stepped inside. Furtive glances shot her way, following her progress to the empty table she wished were anywhere but in the middle of the dining hall. Still, she refused to cower beneath their curiosity and met every eye directly, offering a smile of hello that was not totally sincere. She recognized a few

patrons. Matilda Whipple and her friends. Nash Turner
looked sympathetic, and she smiled back, grateful for a
friendly face in the crowd.

"Yeah, what do you want?" asked the aproned woman
who apparently had no qualms about showing her dislike.
She set an empty goblet in front of Rachel and deliberately
poured it too full so Rachel would have to scoot back out of
the way.

Rachel gave her order, then added, "And a dry tablecloth
would be nice too."

"We don't serve the likes of you in here, missy," the
woman said. "Nobody treats Ben McGuire the way you
did."

She'd expected this. The dislike on every patrons' face
was deserved. "I don't expect you to like me. Any of
you"—her eyes encompassed them all—"but I do expect to
be served food I order and pay good money for."

A buzz of insults rippled across the room.

"Good morning, Rachel," a welcome voice announced as
the door to Delaney's opened and admitted Ben, Jimmy, and
Samuel. "May my sons and I join you?"

Silence layered the restaurant as mouths gaped open.

"Please do." Rachel waved them into the chairs adjacent
to her own. *Thank you, thank you, thank you, Ben.* He would
never know what he'd just done for her. She smiled at the
unkind waitress. "I believe we need a new tablecloth, miss.
This one seems to have something spilled on it."

"What's that all about?" Ben asked, watching as the
woman turned and grumbled her way beyond the batwing
doors that separated the dining room from the kitchen.

"Just expressing her discontent with the morning crowd."
Rachel placed a hand over Ben's arm. "Thank you for
having breakfast with me. I hope you're feeling all right this
morning."

"Most of me is"—Ben leaned closer—"but, and I do mean butt, there's still that part that isn't."

A giggle erupted from her throat. Ben chuckled too.

"Why're ya laughing?" Sam's voice squeaked.

" 'Cause they got eyes for each other," Jimmy explained in a you're-so-dumb-and-I'm-older look. "Old people always laugh at things for no reason, turkey puke."

"Snake snot." Samuel retaliated the namecalling, then stuck his tongue out at Jimmy.

Jimmy thumped Samuel on the side of the head.

Samuel lit into him with flailing fists, wailing at the top of his lungs. "He hit me! He hit me!"

Rachel hid her mouth so her grin wouldn't show. How many times had her own brothers and sisters fought like this? A glance at Ben showed he was trying hard not to laugh either. She realized the crowd stared at them, but she didn't care.

It felt good to be herself. Not to have to hide who she was anymore. To react the way she would instead of what was expected of Joanna Tharp.

"As you see, Rachel"—Ben pulled the squirming six-year-old off his now older brother—"I've got my hands full. Sam, be still. We'll settle this after you've eaten."

"Yeah, shortcake, we'll settle it laaaater," Jimmy sneered.

"James Donald, you best be remembering that you and *Shortcake* are brothers now and have to live under the same roof."

" 'Long as he don't sleep in my room." Jim sunk his chin into his palms, propping his elbows on the table. "Can we eat now? I can't think when I'm hungry."

"That's 'cause your brain thinks it's a pea. Pea brain. Pea brain. Pea brain," Sam chanted.

"Boys!" Ben's tone silenced the argument. He sighed and shrugged his shoulders. "You can see what I'm up against."

The waitress came and replaced the tablecloth. Ben waited until she took their orders and left before continuing his conversation. "I need someone to care for Sam while Jim and I run the store the rest of the summer. When school starts, both boys will be in class for a good part of each day. Jim will, of course, help me after school until closing time. So you'd only have to cook and clean and take care of Sam after school till we get home on most days. What do you say?"

"Will you please, Miss Rachel?" Samuel asked, staring up at her with dark, doleful eyes. "You're the only one I'll know here when Miz Narcissia and Mr. Thadeus go back. My mother went to heaven."

"What are you proposing?" Rachel asked Ben, her heart clenching at the thought of Samuel being left alone among strangers. Though Ben would provide for Sam, he was still a stranger to the child.

She noticed Matilda Whipple leaning over in her chair when she said the word *proposing*.

"I'm asking you to be my housekeeper."

"Will I be required to stay in your home?"

The politician's wife leaned over farther.

"Yes, I think it's best under the circumstances."

Matilda fell out of her chair.

Nash Turner, who sat a table away, helped the woman off the floor. Rachel heard him whisper to the busybody that if Ophelia caught her spreading any vicious rumors that couldn't be verified, she'd suffer worse than having her corset tied to the courthouse door.

"Is there bad blood between Ophelia and Matilda?" Rachel kept her voice low so no one else could hear.

"A long time ago. It's just that Nash tends to put the fear of God in anyone stealing Ophelia's scoop on town gossip. He's desperately in love with 'Phele, has been for as long as

I can remember. If she'd only show him an ankle, he'd demand to marry her before sundown, saying that it was the right and proper thing to do since he'd seen her in a state of undress. But she says she's too set in her ways. Says she won't marry him till he gets up the gumption to actually *ask* her the question. Then who knows what she'll do? She says she'll probably keel over from rot for having to wait so long. Speaking of which, how long do you need to give me an answer?''

"An hour or two after we leave here," she whispered. By then she would know if anyone else in town would give her employment. But more important, she would either have the letters back in her possession or leave town so she wouldn't have to face Ben after he read them.

• 18 •

Rᴀᴄʜᴇʟ's ʜᴇᴀʀᴛ ꜰᴇʟᴛ as if it had shimmied up her throat and drummed like tom-toms. She studied the drawing-room ceiling, the window, the sideboy and its rows of de-canters, everything in Tharp House but the people who owned it. When she'd asked the Tharps if their daughter had mentioned the arrangement between herself and Joanna, Rachel hadn't expected the long silence that followed.

Narcissia fanned herself elaborately, not taxing the rest of her plump arm by moving only her wrist. "Although Joanna told me of your arrangement, Miss Sloan," she finally said, "she did not mention anything about you using *my* room while you were here. And I must say, you spent the money she gave you extravagantly."

Relief swept through Rachel, erasing the volumes of explanation she'd been rehearsing all the way there. "I'm sorry, Mrs. Tharp. It's just that I thought Joanna would want her old friends to know she'd returned. You know how she loves to give parties. In fact, she suggested that I give one or two." The five she gave may have been extravagant.

"Joanna also said the whole house was at my disposal, and your room was the prettiest. You have such wonderful taste, and I must confess I couldn't resist. I beg your pardon.''

The flattery worked. Narcissia nodded understanding momentarily, then her brows knit as she frowned. "But this foolishness must be stopped. Have you already taken steps to let the town know you're not Joanna?''

"*You* haven't?" Surprise filled Rachel.

"We'll be leaving as soon as I can gather a few of Joanna's things. I want to take some of her childhood t-treasures back with me to Richmond," she stammered, dabbing at her eyes with the handkerchief she clasped in one hand.

Thadeus stood and moved to the window, looking out. "Which leads us to the necessary arrangements for your belongings, Miss Sloan. Are you here to gather your things?''

A sigh of relief escaped Rachel. "Yes. It will take me only a moment. I know right where everything is." She stood and started upstairs to retrieve the letters.

"There's no need to go upstairs." Narcissia's tone halted Rachel. "We've gathered it all and stored everything in the kitchen. Did you come afoot or have you a way to transport it to wherever you're going?''

"Did you get it all?" They wouldn't know to look under the bed. They couldn't possibly have found the letters.

Narcissia's brows arched, her eyelids lowered in a haughty stare. "Would you care to look through your trunk to make sure?''

She didn't dare insult them. It was just her word against a dead woman's that this deception had not been her own idea. The Tharps could file charges if they decided to be hateful about the circumstances. "That's not necessary.''

There seemed only one way to know for sure if she worried needlessly—ask. "Did you find the carpetbag I stored under your bed, Mrs. Tharp?''

"The small green paisley one?" Thadeus questioned.

Swallowing hard, Rachel stammered, "Y-yes."

Thadeus motioned for her to precede him into the kitchen. "I thought it might be yours because of the color. Narcissia tends to buy blue, and Joanna"—his voice cracked—"she loved reds so. I've put the bag on top of your trunk."

Rachel almost ran into the kitchen and had to resist the urge to open the carpetbag immediately to make sure all the letters were there. Instead, she turned to Thadeus and held out her hand. "Thank you, Mr. Tharp. My prayers will be with you and the missus. Next time I'm in Richmond"—if I ever get there again, she added silently—"I'll come by and pick up the rest of my things."

Thadeus opened his frock coat and took out a rather large sum of money from a hidden pocket. "Buy what you need to replace them. And take all those gowns Joanna gave you. She gave them of her own free will. They should be yours. I'm afraid I can't allow you to visit us in Richmond anymore, Miss Sloan. You look too much like Joanna, and it's difficult for us—Mrs. Tharp—to be in your presence."

She pushed the money away and shook her head. "You keep it, Mr. Tharp. I'll make my own way. And I don't want Joanna's things. Mrs. Tharp may want to go through them at a later time. God grant you peace."

She would have liked to give them all a piece of her mind. It was so unfair. Rachel had tried everywhere in town short of the saloon, and that was one place she wouldn't work. No one wanted to hire her. Even Belle's family wouldn't, and Belle had tried hard to persuade them.

All because she'd lied to Ben. Deep down Rachel envied the kinds of friendships Ben enjoyed, but wished there were at least one friend of his that might be willing to forgive her.

Aly. The frontierswoman's image sprang clearly into her mind. Aly might know of *someone*, anyone, who would need a hand. She did not want to depend on living under Ben's roof to earn the money to return to Richmond. Surely there had to be another way.

At least Ophelia had been willing to let her store the trunk at the saloon. Afraid to tempt fate again, Rachel carried the carpetbag with her. The Tharps were honorable and the letters remained undisturbed. Hopefully, Aly would be at the freight office and she could get this settled soon. The way her luck was running, though, Alewine was probably on the road, hauling cargo.

A glimmer of good fortune welcomed her inside the office. Alewine tore a pair of spectacles off her face and stuffed them under the counter she stood behind.

"Well, what're you doing here?" Aly blinked several times. "I didn't figure you had a petticoat to your name, much less something to transport."

"I'm not here to send anything. I need a place to work."

"Here? You?" Alewine started chuckling. "I could just see you and old Rash bickering over who's gonna muck the stalls. No . . . no . . . wait a minute . . . better yet. See which one of ya's gonna hitch Ol' Jaw Stomper ever' morning." She h'yucked-h'yucked.

"Jaw Stomper?"

"Yeah. You don't do it right, that ornery old mule will high-kick ya and stomp your jaw 'fore you can even clear the box. No, Rachel. This ain't no place for the likes of you."

Tears bubbled into her eyes. Rachel sank into the chair where customers waited their turn to send their parcels.

"Ohh, now, girlie. Don't do none of that. I can't abide no squalling. Awww, Rachel, come on, now." She looked around the office. "Shoot, I can find something you can do here. Maybe."

Rachel willed the tears away, partly so as not to distress

Alewine anymore, but mainly because they only made matters worse. She'd learned that crying got her nothing but puffy eyes and a drippy nose. "You don't have to, Aly. That's kind of you, but I've been offered a place to work. I just thought I might find something better."

"Well, why didn't you say so?" Alewine looked relieved. "Who's the lucky boss?"

"Ben."

"Ben? You gonna work in his store?"

"No, he needs a housekeeper. I'll be staying out at his place."

"That so?" Alewine's head cocked from one side to the other as if she were inspecting Rachel's face for every detail. "You sure you're up to it?"

She started to say she had no choice, but she did. She could either take his offer or put Alewine in a position the frontierswoman was too kind to squirm out of. Rachel valued her friendship too much to cause trouble. "No, I'm not sure, but it's best for all concerned. Just cross your fingers for me that it works out. He's my only hope."

✦ *19* ✦

It was almost twilight before they turned onto the lane where cottonwoods formed a leafy canopy overhead. The team of horses leaned into their traces, their heads bobbing faster. Crockett, who had not been tied to the wagon but left to follow, galloped around them.

"He's eager to be home," Ben said.

Rachel sat up straighter on the driver's box, full of curiosity about Ben's place. "How much longer until we're on your land?"

"We're already on it."

Samuel tapped on Rachel's back and she half turned. "Can I sit with you and see?"

She helped him crawl over the driver's box and nestled him onto her lap.

"It's just an old farm," Jimmy grumbled, propping his elbows up on his knees and leaning against the back of the wagon. "Nothing special."

"In Texas, this is called a ranch, Jim. There's a difference." Pride, not criticism, filled Ben's voice.

Nothing special? Every blade of grass, every stem of wheat, every lowing cow, filled her with awe and appreciation. This was Ben's home. Built by the sweat of his brow.

Everywhere she looked she saw a golden sea of ripening wheat, winnowing in the wind. Waving him home.

The lane broadened and before them spread a wide clearing. The house lay off to the left, a huge log cabin with a stone chimney running up its two stories. On the other side, a vegetable garden had been planted and looked well used.

Smaller buildings horseshoed the mainhouse. Ben caught the direction of her interest. "That one just left of the cabin is the smokehouse. There's a woodpile stacked behind it." His finger pointed to where Crockett stood. "That's the corral and barn."

"Where did you get all the wood? I haven't seen that many trees in the entire Panhandle."

"Had wood hauled in from Colorado. Took some doing, but it was worth the cost." The pride of ownership filled his tone as he allowed the team to hurry the last forty yards to the corral. "There's a building you can't see from here. It's our springhouse. It's behind the cabin. If you'll look real close, you can see the southeast wall."

As he jerked the brake, Rachel remembered the springhouse from his letters. It was his greatest accomplishment at the ranch. Though the same offshoot tributary of the Canadian River that fed the Wild Horse also gifted Ben's land with much-appreciated water, he had discovered an artesian spring three years before and built his house near it.

"I'd love to see it," she said, though she knew every detail by heart. He'd built the springhouse in the fashion of a Seneca's longhouse. Encased in an elongated wood cabin without flooring, the spring had been dammed with stone on one side to form a bathing pool, safeguarding the other side for drinking water. A huge tub with four clawed feet had been brought in from St. Louis and stationed in the soft sand near the bathing section's bank. A gift to Joanna should she prefer to have the spring water heated in the winter.

Ben tied the reins to the brake and jumped off the driver's box, then wiped his palms on his thighs before helping Rachel down. "We're home, Rachel . . . boys."

Swallowing hard, she felt overwhelmed by the dueling emotions inside her—fear that she was making a mistake and excitement that she had finally arrived at the place she'd always dreamed of being . . . under the roof of the man she loved. A roof she'd told herself was the wrong place to be.

Never did Ben leave home without returning to it filled with the pride of accomplishment. He'd spent years, like most of the townsfolk, in a soddy, fighting off wind and rain and the cold of winter. Watching Rachel's expression of appreciation, he was grateful for the obsession that had driven him to an excess of achieving. If he chose to remain in Valiant, his ripening fields would provide a harvest of plenty for his sons, the house would weather the winter, and the store would provide a steady income to secure the boys' futures.

But living there would be difficult now. Everything was such a reminder of his failed hopes and dreams, Ben wondered if it might not be best to start all over somewhere else.

When he swung Rachel down from the wagon, his hands lingered at her waist. The thought of touching her there without the barrier of gingham made him conscious of how much he wanted to experience that pleasure. Ben dropped his hands.

"Come, let me show you the house, then I'll tend to Crockett and the team." He deliberately avoided her eyes so she would not see the attraction coursing through him. He suspected she had agreed to be his housekeeper only as a last resort. It mattered to him that she stayed, and Ben wanted time to learn if his interest in her stemmed from more than her likeness to Joanna.

"Let me get my carpetbag first," she insisted, asking Jim to hand her the bag.

"Leave them. We'll get them in a minute," Ben said. "I want you to see the house first. Welcome to my home, Rachel Sloan." His invitation was sincere, yet Ben felt he was offering more. "I hope you'll make it your own for as long as you choose to stay with us."

Samuel ran ahead of them, but Jimmy claimed the lead.

The interior was shadowed with afternoon light and smelled of soap, sage, and wildflowers. Rachel wondered how he managed to run a store, grow wheat, and keep such a clean house as well. Small wonder he needed help.

A scrape echoed across the room from where Jimmy stood lighting a lamp, then another. Light flared, bringing the room's elegance into focus . . . and the color. The drapes hanging from each window, the floral cushions on the rosewood davenport and matching chair, even the braided rugs that spread over the high-polished oak floors were all hues of red.

Ben looked expectantly at her, and she smiled wanly, trying to muster the approval he awaited. She'd promised herself no more lies. "It's . . . uh . . . unlike anything I've ever seen before." *It's so Joanna,* she wanted to add but didn't.

Longing to take back the remark as soon as she'd said it, Rachel could tell she'd disappointed him. He turned and excused himself.

"I'll go brush down the team. Jimmy can show you to your room. Explore on your own, if you like. You'll be the one cleaning it, so you might as well make yourself familiar with the house. We lock no doors here. Inside or out."

He patted Sam's head as he passed. "You and Jim will share rooms for the time being. I have only one room other than mine and Jim's finished. The other two aren't quite ready for taking up residence.''

''I ain't going to share with no crybaby.'' Jimmy crossed his arms over his chest. ''I'll sleep on the davenport.''

''No one's sleeping on the davenport in this house when there are plenty of beds for everybody. This is not something we'll barter over, understood?''

''Yeah.'' Jim grabbed the six-year-old's hand. ''Well, come on, crybaby. But you better not wet my sheets, or I'll rub your nose in it.''

''I don't wet the bed. Only babies do that.'' Samuel looked up at Rachel askant. ''Do I hafta sleep with him?''

''You heard your father.'' She gently shooed him to follow his new sibling. Ben was his father now; as his paid housekeeper she had no right to defy his word. Still, as the days progressed, perhaps she would find a way to help the two boys learn to like each other. ''Go on and put your things away. I'll be there in a minute.''

When the boys disappeared into one of the rooms behind the L-shaped stairs, Rachel refused to let Ben go without answering the question that bothered her. ''Why is Jimmy calling Sam a crybaby? I've never seen the boy cry.''

Ben sighed. ''When the Tharps brought him to me this morning, he did.''

''Because they left him?''

''No, he seemed almost relieved to be out of their company. He didn't start crying until he asked me a question and I gave him my answer.'' Ben's eyes darkened. ''He asked if I was going to leave him somewhere when I got tired of him. Because if I was, he said I might as well take him there now and save us both the trouble.'' Anger carved Ben's expression. ''Can you imagine the level of hurt inside that would force a six-year-old to make that kind of statement? I wanted to take a bullwhip to the Tharps.''

She didn't have to imagine. Rachel knew the hurt first-hand. "What did you tell him that made him cry?"

His eyes focused on Rachel and held. "That I'm a fairly patient man, so I didn't think he had much to worry about. I said he would probably be grown-up and have a place of his own before I got tired of him." Ben added softly, "That's when the boy started crying."

A strong desire to throw herself into his arms engulfed Rachel, and it was all she could do to withstand the impulse. He had no idea what his reassurance to young Sam meant to her. Had no idea that he'd also reassured her that there were still special people in the world too kind to throw away innocent hearts. "Thank you, Ben."

"For what?"

For everything. For asking nothing more of Sam than to be a little boy. "For giving Sam and Jimmy a home," she said instead. "For offering me work when you should hate me for what I did. It must have been difficult considering the lie I told you."

"Not so difficult when I considered that I had been lying to myself. You just made me see the truth. There's no blame in that." He half bowed, like a cavalier welcoming his lady. "Now, go acquaint yourself with the rest of the house. I'll settle the team and bring in wood for the stove. Let me know if your room is to your liking. I can exchange it for mine upstairs if you prefer. But I thought you might want to be near Sam for a while. The Tharps say he sleepwalks since his mother's death."

His eyes swept over her with a look that held a hunger of its own. "You might want to start supper soon. You have three healthy men to feed now."

* * *

A survey of the house confirmed Rachel's suspicions. Ben had decorated each room to Joanna's taste—ornate, impractical, and in every shade of red possible.

The lower story not only contained the kitchen, drawing room, and one of the fireplaces, but the boys' bedroom and the one she'd been assigned. A stairway led up to the second story, where Rachel discovered a long hall ending at the stone fireplace that rose from downstairs and provided heat for the upper story as well. Ben's bedroom, a sitting room, and two unfinished bedrooms filled the remainder of the space. It was a huge house that must have taken a lot of time for Ben to build, and her respect for his efforts continued to grow.

When she'd finished touring and returned downstairs to start supper, Ben was already preparing the cookstove. She marveled at the span of his shoulders as he reached for a pot hanging on a peg over the stove, and appreciated the solidness of his thighs as they bunched against his trousers when he bent to lift a trapdoor in the floor. An earthy aroma of potatoes and other stored vegetables wafted through the room as he slipped first one leg, then the other, over the edge and disappeared into the dark cellar.

His deep, rich voice echoed from beneath the floor. "I'll have to build you a ladder tomorrow before I go to work, so it'll be easier for you to do this. Jim and I have just been jumping down and heaving ourselves out of here. It'll be nice not to have to pounce."

Two hands rose in the open space and offered a handful of potatoes. "Just a minute, we'll need a few more."

Rachel waited until he gave her another batch, then added carrots and a jar of green beans as well. She placed them on the counter and waited for him to exit.

"That's all right. I can get up myself. Scoot back."

Rachel observed the play of muscles as he planted his

palms on the floor and pulled himself out. When he glanced up, a grin stretched across his lips, rewarding her with a flash of white teeth. Embarrassment flushed her skin. He knew exactly what she'd been remembering—the way he looked without the barrier of his shirt while washing dishes.

Ben twisted and sat beside her, allowing his legs to dangle below. "Is it too hot in here?" he teased. "The stove heats up fast."

"A little." Rachel resisted an urge to push him back into the cellar. He didn't have to look so pleased with himself. It was going to be a looooong, loooong summer and school term. "I think I'll wash while the potatoes are boiling."

"Your trunk is in your bedroom, if you'd like to change." He stood and wiped his hand on a towel hanging on a peg near the stove.

"And my carpetbag?" She tried not to sound concerned, yet wanted to know where the letters were at all times.

Puzzlement creased his brow. "In the same bedroom. The only things I stored elsewhere were Joanna's wardrobe. Mrs. Tharp said you refused to take almost everything when you left this morning. But she insisted that Joanna gave them to you. Said it wasn't right to keep them under the circumstances. When she asked if I would see that you got them, I told her I'd store them upstairs in one of the extra rooms till you make up your mind whether or not you want them."

"I've made up my mind. You shouldn't have wasted your time."

Anger clouded his face, his palms rising as if someone held a gun to his back. "I'm sorry, Miss Sloan. I figured you didn't have much with you. She'll just donate them to some other nee—"

"Needy person?" Rachel lifted her chin, feeling petulant and arguesome when she should have thanked him for his thoughtfulness. "I have been taking care of myself for as long as I can remember. Neither you nor I need any more reminders of Joanna Tharp. I want nothing of hers.''

But you, her heart argued.

''Good!'' He marched out of the kitchen and headed upstairs. ''Then I'll pack it all away in the barn.''

''You do that.'' She followed him, balling her fists on her hips. Let him be upset that she dared to deny his precious Joanna influence over her life anymore, just because he refused to do the same. The proper thing to do *was* to put away her things. If he was too obstinate or obsessed to do it, then he'd just have to stay angry with her. ''They'll be out of the way now!''

''That's just dandy with me!''

''Fine, then we agree.''

He leaned over the handrail to the second-floor landing. ''We don't have to agree on anything but the fact that you are a good housekeeper and cook for my sons. Do I make myself understood, Miss Sloan?''

''Perfectly, Mr. McGuire.'' She spun around on her heel and stormed into the kitchen.

into a . . . um computer. Maybe you top I need my mute
reminder of human frailty, I want no one to feel—"

"You're not as afraid—"

"God." He made his way off the kitchen to finance up—
stairs. "I'll just wait until I'm done."

"Wait," he . . . She rolled and arms tolling her arms on her
hips. Let him forget that he need to keep up you look
through billions over her the suggests, just because he re—
fused to do the same. They knew there he no way it still
away her thing. If he was not obstinate as obsessed in the
he may hold you have to play story with an . . . They fill it
called the day over.

"Then a just away without—"

"You, then she was."

He turned over the himself to the second floor timber
tolks like I knew company engulfing for the tori shadows
are a give houseclean and grief tones scene. His Lundle
record understand, Miss Mabel.

Finally, Mr. McCourt . . . she just ached from the heat,
and turned find the interior.

✦ 20 ✦

THOUGH THE SUN would not sink below the western horizon for hours yet, Ben couldn't endure another moment inside the general store. Few had come in to purchase goods, but far too many visited to see if he'd survived the scandal of Rachel's deception. He had heard it in their whispers, saw it in the stolen glances when they thought he wasn't looking. At one point Matilda Whipple even approached him and asked why he was being so kind to someone who had lied to him. He'd told her the truth. Rachel was not so much to blame as Joanna. If he could forgive the dead woman, then shouldn't he also forgive Rachel?

Ben untied his apron and hung it on the peg by the counter. "Jim, what say we close up early today and work the south acre? I'm feeling a bit cooped up, and it would be a good time to get it ready for winter seed."

"I can't. Remember, I ain't finished painting. Got the polishing done though."

"Then I'll see if Rachel and Sam want to join me. If you get done in time, ride on out and give me a hand. We'll work till it's too dark to see."

"I'll paint as fast as I can. Don't plow it all up, all right? Save me some to do."

"Will do. But paint the woodwork right, or Michael will make you do it again!" Ben hollered after the boy, glad that at least there was one element of their existence the two of them never argued over—a love of tilling the ground with the sweat of their backs. He would miss it if he moved.

He hung the CLOSED sign in the window, locked up, and headed for the ranch.

The ride was filled with curiosity over how he would be received in his own home once he got there. He'd been pleasantly surprised by the fine supper Rachel had cooked the previous night and the hot breakfast waiting for him and Jim that morning before leaving for work. Accustomed to waiting till lunch to grab something to eat at Delaney's, he'd forgotten how good home-cooked biscuits, gravy, eggs, and fryback tasted. She was one helluva cook. He'd give her that.

But she had been one silent cook as well. When he'd told her he and Jim wouldn't be home for lunch, she merely nodded. When he asked if she would prepare buffalo rump for supper, she'd said only, "All right." When he thanked her for breakfast and made sure Jim and Samuel did the same, she'd sparingly given all three of them one short "You're welcome."

Guess he didn't pay her to talk.

The three miles that separated his spread from town went by in a blink. As he approached, he wondered how the place had looked to Rachel yesterday when she'd seen it for the first time. A twinge of sadness filled Ben as he realized Joanna would never see all he'd done to please her. Never enjoy the house they'd planned together down to the last room. Never sleep in the feather mattress he'd had Aly freight in.

Joanna would never see any of it . . . but Sam and Jim would reap the benefit whether he sold the place or remained in Valiant. If he stayed, the boys would share equally. His sons would become his life now wherever he lived.

As the lane widened into the clearing that fronted his home, Ben saw the six-year-old look up from where he played and race toward the front door.

"Raaaachel!" Sam shouted, disappearing inside.

She came to the door, wiping her hands on her apron. The boy peeked around her hip, as if afraid Ben might mean them harm.

"You're home early." She stared up at him and brushed back a strand of hair that had pulled loose from the chignon at the nape of her neck.

"I wanted to work the fields today." She looked beautiful, sunlight detailing the structure of her face, every slender curve of her body. "Would you and Sam like to go with me? Get some fresh air?"

She half turned. "I was just starting to bake cinnamon rolls for the boys."

"I'll help you when we get back. In fact, we'll have something easy for supper so you don't have to do much cooking. We'll save the buffalo rump for another day."

Samuel stepped from around her. "Can I drive the team?"

"If you'll pay careful attention to my instructions. They're not a toy. You can hurt them and us if you don't heed what you're doing."

"I promise."

"Let me hang this up and put away the dough. I'll be right there." Rachel started untying the apron even as she disappeared into the house.

"Grab gloves out of the drawer closest to the stove!" Ben shouted. "There should be a couple of pairs. Mine are out in the barn."

Hurrying to change teams and harness Buchanan to the plow, Ben went about the chore whistling a tune of expectation. After letting the others free, his hands stroked the

Belgian's withers, shoulders, and flanks as he spoke softly to the mountainous horse and told Buchanan his plans for the afternoon. Ben believed in sharing not only the work with the great beast, but the dream as well. It took both of them to till the land properly. Both of them to trust the other would pull his share.

"He seems to be agreeing with whatever you're saying," Rachel announced from behind Ben as Buchanan's head bobbed up and down.

Ben turned, his gaze traveling over her briefly as he realized she had brushed her hair and repinned it. Even flour no longer smudged her cheek. He smiled, touched by her effort to be well groomed for him. "He's eager to be free again."

The huge Belgian leaned into his harness, carving deep grooves into the ground. The redolent scent of upturned earth and summer layered the air, promising new life, a rich harvest . . . a new beginning. But the sight of Ben's powerful forearms bunching over Samuel's smaller ones to instruct him, the broad span of his back as he commandeered the horse that outweighed boy and man twenty to one, was the most powerful image of all to Rachel.

A trembling began in her belly. The man, the boy, the horse, carving their future deep into the earth, created such a sight of total beauty that she finally understood why men had fought and died in war to save their land.

Within an hour Jimmy and Bowie joined them. Rachel followed behind the three, breaking up clods and watching Ben teach his sons to till the earth. Once, when she glanced up, she nearly stumbled over her hoe. Ben had taken off his shirt, gifting her with the vision she'd yearned for for the last hour—to see him in his natural form. Try as she might, Rachel could not keep her mind on her task. Her gaze kept straying to the rigid cords of his shoulders, the flexing of his arms, the tapering slope of his torso.

Occasionally he turned and caught her watching, but she'd quickly lower her gaze and concentrate on the clod she should have been pulverizing.

She sensed rather than saw his approach. Felt the heat emanating from his body. Working the hoe madly, she prayed she had the willpower not to look up.

"Are you all right, Rachel?" Concern filled his voice. "You look a bit piqued."

"I'm f-fine," she managed to say, but a pain in her back demanded that she straighten. "Oh, God," she whispered, catching sight of the golden trail of hair that erupted from somewhere near his taut abdomen and veed over his chest. Her eyes met morning-glory blue that no longer held mere concern. "It's my b-back," she stammered.

"You rest a while. The boys and I will finish up."

Rachel merely nodded, unable to speak.

When at last Ben called a halt, his pants were dark with sweat. The boys looked like they had been dunked into the river and needed wringing out. Even Bowie drooped.

"First one home gets to brush Buchanan down!" Ben challenged. The boys raced ahead, Jim's long-legged stride outdistancing Sam's in bounds. Bowie had them both beat.

"That's not fair," Rachel announced, willing Sam speed. "Jimmy can take three steps to his one."

"Don't worry," Ben laughed, easily matching her pace. One hand held tight to the Belgian's reins as they made their way home. "I'll let the loser feed him. I just wanted to teach Sam that life won't be fair. But even so, there's always a reward for trying."

"Second best doesn't sit well with some folks." She knew how that felt.

"Maybe it isn't second best at all," Ben said. "Maybe

it's just discovering that if you can't be first one way, you can win in a different way.''

Ben McGuire wasn't a man who gave up easily. She admired him for his persistence. Rachel changed the subject, too tired to consider the possibilities of Ben's statement. ''I've never seen Sam so happy or sunburned.''

''No?'' Ben reached over and tapped her nose. ''Guess that'll be two of you.''

Her hands covered her nose before she realized what she'd done. The gloves she wore smelled of dirt and perspiration. When her hands jerked away, Ben laughed and took off one glove.

''Here, let me get that for you.''

He wiped something from her cheek. Desire streamed through her like the sunset sinking over the horizon. She had to get her mind on something else, anything but the way his touch filled her with yearning. ''Sam's lucky to be here. You'll be the father he's never known.''

''I'm the lucky one,'' Ben said, gently anchoring a strand of hair behind her ear. His face wore a look of satisfaction. ''I now have two sons and a new friend to share all this with. That makes me a fortunate man.''

By the time they reached home, Rachel was stumbling with exhaustion.

''Go into the house and get some clean clothes. There's a red bandanna hanging on a peg just inside the springhouse. Tie it around the doorknob and we'll know you're bathing. We won't accidentally catch you unawares that way.''

''No,'' she gently argued. ''I'll prepare supper so it'll be ready when you're through with Buchanan.''

''I'm the boss, right?''

Rachel nodded, suspecting he would use his station to

have his way, yet grateful he would overrule her stubbornness.

"Then get your bath and forget supper for the moment."

She eyed the water warily. A toe in the bubbling surface confirmed her suspicions. It was freezing! But she couldn't go to sleep feeling so grimy and smelling so obnoxious. The scent of summer she'd admired earlier also brought with it the unpleasant odor of sunshine-induced perspiration. Gritting her teeth, Rachel took the plunge.

"Ye gods!" she shrieked, coming up for air. If it was this cold in the summer, no wonder he'd bought Joanna a bathtub. Just the thought of reacting the same as her former employer spurred Rachel to dunk herself again and again. She would learn to enjoy the water's chill if it was the last thing she did.

Later Rachel was surprised to find that exhaustion had fled and she felt revived. A fragrant aroma greeted her as she approached the main house. When she went inside she discovered a dog and three cleaned males with their hair washed and slicked back, dressed in fresh clothes and sitting around the dining table set with plates, dinnerware, and a potful of beef and vegetables.

Suddenly she realized they were all looking at her expectantly. "Are you waiting for me?"

"We wanted to eat as a family," Sam announced, though his eyes kept lowering to half-mast and his head wilted to one side. "Ben let us wash up at the river."

Jimmy yawned. "I ain't never seen nobody take *that* long a bath. *Wimmen.*" Bowie snuffled in agreement.

"Thank you for cooking supper, Ben." She breathed in deeply. "And finishing the cinnamon rolls."

"Thank *you* for helping me in the field." The blue of his

eyes deepened with approval. "And for taking such a long bath."

Grateful that everyone was in a hurry to feed themselves and go to bed, Rachel pretended to concentrate on her meal and not the undisguised yearning she saw in Ben's eyes.

Later, when she tucked Sam in and brushed back Jim's hair from his forehead, she was not surprised to find Ben watching her at the doorway to the boys' room.

"Are you tired?" he whispered.

"Not at all," she answered truthfully, thrilled when he gently took her hand and led her outside.

The squeak of the front door as they exited made both turn to see if the noise had awakened the boys. Rachel held up one finger to signal they wait, silently counted to thirty, then nodded that all was as it should be.

Ben seated her in one of the rockers, and he took the other, tracing circles over the top of her hand with his thumb. Summer sounds filled the night. Cicadas buzzed in the cottonwoods. Frogs croaked their throaty love songs. Wind sighed through the prairie grass.

He leaned over and lightly brushed Rachel's cheeks, causing her heart to hammer in her throat. A glance at the moon proved a disappointment. No haze tonight.

"Today was wonderful, Rachel. Having you and the boys work alongside me. Eat at my table. Share my day." He interwove his fingers with hers and began to rock. "I feel . . . more satisfied than I've been in a long time."

"Me too." She took up his rhythm with her own chair and squeezed his fingers gently.

"You didn't mind the plowing?"

She heard his hesitance, sensed that her answer was important to him. "Not at all. It didn't seem like work. It felt good to watch you till your land and know I played a part in making something grow. It made me happy to watch you

teach the boys and see them discover how building something for themselves made that weariness worthwhile. It was
a good day, Ben. One of the best of my life. I seem to be
thanking you a lot lately . . . but thank you again.''

The rocking stopped.

As if one had asked and the other agreed, their mouths
met softly, testing, asking. His warm, wet tongue teased until
she could do nothing but answer its quest and sate her own
need to taste him. Ben stood, pulling her into the kiss, demanding a closer embrace. She had to touch him, to feel the
span of muscle she'd admired all day. Her fingers splayed
across his chest, traced the ridge of each shoulder, then
delved into the burnished thatch of golden hair at his collar.

Rachel felt herself unfolding, blossoming like the flower
his eyes reminded her of so often. Years of wanting to be
cherished melted away with each pass of his hands along her
back, with each caress that traced the curve of her hips. For
the first time in her life, she knew with certainty where she
belonged.

The squeak of the front door broke them apart. ''Can I
have some water?'' Sam asked, rubbing his eyes and yawn-
ing. ''I'm thirsty.''

Rachel wrapped an arm around the six-year-old. ''Of
course, sweetie.'' She urged him back to his room and started
to head for the kitchen, where she'd left a pitcher of water
just for this purpose. Ben reached out and stopped her, making her meet his gaze.

''Just get a goblet. I'll fetch a bucketful out of the springhouse. I need a bit of time to cool off anyway, and it'll be
fresher for him.''

''All right. But, Ben''—she paused, trying to make sense
of what she was about to say, hoping that it was the right
thing to do and not another one of her monumental blun-
ders—''this was a mistake. You're grieving. I'm . . . well,

I'm too needy for my own good. Let's not make more of this than it seems.'' *Please, don't make more of it unless you mean it,* she pleaded silently. ''Perhaps we need more time.''

''Perhaps,'' Ben laughed, but the laughter never reached his eyes, ''time is all I'll ever have to keep me company.''

✦ *21* ✦

IN THE THREE weeks that followed, Rachel set about changing Ben's house to provide more comfort for him and the boys. Down came the red brocade drapes, replaced by a pale green sheer that matched the foliage in the drawing room's cushions. She rolled up the red rugs and lugged them upstairs to be stored in one of the incomplete rooms, telling Ben that the house kept cooler with the lighter shade of curtains and the rugs put away. But the house was only a small part of the changes she made.

She discovered Ben ate the green vegetables on his plate first, grudgingly consuming the yellow ones so as not to waste food. He preferred to wear his blue chambray to work in at the store rather than the tartan or yellow gingham. Rachel made a point of laundering the chambray as soon as he pulled it off so it would always be hanging ready for use. But the most satisfying change she'd made was moving the upturned keg he kept outside on the porch into the boys' room. Ben liked to stretch his feet out on it when he read to his sons at night, but insisted that the old makeshift footstool would be an eyesore amid the other furniture.

Ben revealed pieces of himself to her daily, the love he had for his land, the dedication to his work, the sense of community that seldom allowed him to tell anyone no if he could be of help. Rachel discovered they were alike in many ways—both appreciated a clean house, neither were big eaters, each loved to tease. If there was any flaw in the man, she hadn't found it yet. In fact, Ben McGuire seemed almost too good to be true. Short of shortcomings. Too kind, too considerate, too *everything*. Even the boys had fallen under his spell of goodness and didn't bicker much anymore.

Strange as it sounded, the list of his perfections continued to grow until Rachel felt she would scream with frustration. He never complained. He made her laugh and patiently helped her correct her mistakes. Sometimes he dragged in so tired, he almost fell asleep at the table. Despite his exhaustion, he never failed to help Jim with whatever project the boy had, and always took time to teach Sam about the workings of their ranch.

How was she supposed to ignore everything she hoped for in a man? How could she ever live up to the standards he set for himself? Worse, how did she keep from loving such a man?

Tonight his halo was askew. Supper lay cold in its pot. The boys had gone to bed complaining that Ben wasn't there to read the *good part* of the book and now they'd have to wait till tomorrow. She'd read to them, but Sam said she didn't make all those different voices Ben did.

Quizzing Jimmy once again about exactly what his father had said when he sent the thirteen-year-old home gave no new insight as to why Ben might be so tardy.

Jimmy repeated the same thing he'd said earlier when arriving. "Ben said for me to tell you not to wait supper on him, he'll be late."

The rocker moved back and forth, back and forth, as Rachel peered into the night, watching for sight of him. Midnight came and went. She stood and stretched, went in and checked on the boys, then returned to her vigil. Wind moved the shadows, capturing her attention only long enough to determine her eyes were playing tricks on her.

"Raaachel!"

She rose at the sound of her name, sensing something wrong even before she saw who spoke it.

"Ohh, Raachel. I'm hooome!" He started giggling. "Or at leasht part of me ish."

The Appaloosa's tall form exited the tree-lined lane, moving slowly toward the house. With an absorbing glance, she strained to see Crockett's rider more closely. Rachel bolted off the porch and ran toward the figure slumped over the Appaloosa's shoulders. "Ben!"

Unmindful of shadows, she crossed the distance that separated them and flung herself against his leg, tugging at his limp body to pull him down into her arms. The stench of whiskey stopped her. She pulled away in disgust. "You're dead drunk!"

"Drunk? Yesh, madame, I think I might be. Don't know. Never been this way before. But I'm not quite dead." He attempted to lift his head. "Whoa, Crockett! Whoa, boy!" A groan erupted from Ben's throat and he clutched the Appaloosa tighter. "C-could you help me reach the barn, 'Chel? I don't feel so good."

"I most definitely will. I sure don't want the boys to wake up and see you like this." His halo was not only askew, but tarnishing by the second.

When they reached the barn, Ben's voice quavered, "W-will you guide Ol' Crock to that shtall over there?" His finger pointed, then swayed. "The one right over there." He closed one eye and opened another, trying to focus his finger in the right direction, but to no avail. "Jis put him in the one with all the hay."

"This one?"

"Yeah, but better shtand clear." Ben touched the horse and whispered a command. The Appaloosa reared. "Whoa, Crockett! Down, boy, down."

When the animal complied, Ben touched the horse with his other hand. "I seem to be getting my gee and haw mixed up for shome odd reason."

"It couldn't be the whiskey, could it?" Rachel couldn't resist.

"Probably shhow." When the Appaloosa knelt on its fore-legs, putting less distance between Ben and the hay, Ben's shoulders started bouncing up and down though his body never rose an inch off the horse. He looked like an engine chugging, but going nowhere as he chanted, "You can do this. You can do this. You can do this."

"Go!" Ben shouted, then rolled. His eyes flew open. His mouth gaped. Landing with a dull thud and a loud groan, he complained, "I thought I told you to kneel, Crock."

Filled with disgust, Rachel's elbows angled at her hips. "He did, but frankly I think it's you whose going to have to do quite a bit of that come Sunday morning."

The horse rose, bumping his nose against his master's left shoulder.

Ben's hand snaked out and stroked the Appaloosa's jaw. "Shhorry, Crock. Didn't mean to yell at you." His hand fell beside him as if suddenly drained of all energy. "Would you take him to another shtall? Don't wanna get shtepped on."

After Rachel put Crockett away, she took a closer look at Ben. Another odor mingled with the whiskey scent. Blood! Disgust faded to concern. He deserved to hurt himself if he didn't have better sense than to get liquored up like this. She bent next to him and started feeling for injuries.

"Shtop, that tickles." He chuckled.

Rachel smiled despite his drunkenness. It might prove in-teresting to know just exactly where he was ticklish. When she touched his left side, all mirth fled. Dried blood caked with sand stained her fingertips. "You've been shot!"

He pushed her hand away. "Shhot *at*. Nothing shher—shher—nothing to be consherned about. I fell."

Silence ensued. "Well, that explains it all!" she complained. "Care to tell me how you fell?"

"Oh, yeah. Crock's too tall for my own good. But I'm all right. Shee?" He pulled on his shirt, tenting it over his stomach. "Just a bit shaky, that's all. Don't know who took a rail to me though."

"Yes, you look perfectly fine, Ben McGuire," she admonished him. "Perfectly drunk is more like it."

"But I really did fall. Jis ashk Crock . . . he'll tell ya."

"I'd rather *you* tell me what happened."

Ben closed his eyes in remembrance. "I decided to pay Ophelia a call after I sent Jim home. You know, Ophelia's real nice, isn't she? I wish her and Nash would—"

"Yes, I do too, but could we get back to what happened to *you*?"

"Thaz jis it. I was telling Ophelia she jist better watch out, 'cause good men git tired of being so damned—oops, shhorry 'Chel—good. Nash won't always be such a paysh . . . such a . . . well, he'll get tired of waiting for her. Next thing I knew, Ophelia said she'd drink to that. So we did. Then we did again, and again, and . . . I forget how many agains."

"So, who shot you . . . the bartender?"

"Jake?" Ben looked at her as if she'd lost her wits. "He wouldn't shoot me. Besides, I left town waaay ahead of him. Whoever shot at me was in front of me and Crock. Good thing I twisted in my shaddle. Probably saved my life. I fell. Did I tell you that—?"

"At least three times."

"Threw out my hand to latch on to shomething, but couldn't. Next thing I knew, I was out."

Someone meant to kill him. Rachel's anger evaporated. "What time did you leave town?"

" 'Bout ten o'clock."

"That was almost three hours ago!"

"Shtumbled in the dark trying to find Crock. Whoever shot at me musta tried to catch him, but couldn't. Crock managed to find me after the shooter was gone."

Rachel mentally promised the Appaloosa an extra big helping of oats. She touched Ben where he rubbed his head, grateful to find only dried blood. "Whatever you did, it's not bleeding anymore."

"Aly calls me hardheaded all the time. Guessh I am." Ben mustered an exaggerated smile, then his lips thinned into a solid line of seriousness as his eyes looked suddenly vulnerable. He reached out to touch her cheek. "Gotta admit though, first time I evvver panicked in my life. I had to get back here." He patted her hand. "To make sure you and the boys were all right and he wasn't after you."

"We're safe," Rachel assured him, watching worry ease from his face. The man had panicked, a thing so foreign to his nature that it would have been unbelievable had his concern been for himself instead of his children. Yet he'd included her in his statement. A tenderness swept over her for his concern.

"I'll go check on the boys while you rest. Or better yet, let me help you to the house, and we'll both check on them."

He closed his eyes once more. "Don't want 'em to shee me like 'his. Let me lie here a bit longer. Still a bit dizzy. I'm prob'ly fretting for no reashon. Been long enough since the ambush, he ain't gonna make trouble for y'all."

She knew he was trying to reassure her, but a quick trip

to the house confirmed all was well and there was no cause for alarm. Rachel returned with her report.

"Good." Ben let out a long sigh and patted the hay beside him. "Come sit with me. We've got plans to make in the morning."

"What kind of plans?" Rachel sat next to him, propping her elbows on her knees and resting her chin on her arms.

"We've gotta find out who did this and why."

Unconsciously, she allowed her fingers to brush back the curl that dangled across his forehead. *Why do you think you have to be so good, Ben?* she asked silently, loving him more at that moment than any other. He was human after all. "Didn't you say it was dark and everything happened too fast to see who shot at you?"

His hand reached out and captured hers, bringing her fingers to his lips and pressing a kiss against each one. Rachel shivered with the tenderness of the gesture, her gaze riveted upon his blue eyes.

"Sometimes when things happen too fast," he whispered, his expression sobering, "you just have to let them happen and think later."

She wanted nothing more than to follow the sensual path he was leading her down, but his life was at stake and one of them needed to be sensible. A difficult choice when all she wanted to do was hold him. "And just how do you intend to determine who ambushed you?"

Ben propped himself on his elbows, but they buckled. On the third attempt, he managed to keep them stationary. "Whoever tried to shoot me will pay a call in the morning, and I'm gonna need about two dozen pots of coffee before he does."

"How can you be so sure he'll come?" Rachel helped him rise to a sitting position.

"Because the sidewinder will want to see if he just nicked

me or if he put me under. I wanta be prepared for him.''

"How do you know it's a *he*?" She picked some of the hay out of his hair.

Ben brushed a stalk from the folds of her skirt. "What makes you think he isn't?"

"I don't have any idea who it is, do you?" She realized how easily they touched each other and became suddenly self-conscious about it. Perhaps the whiskey made him bold. But then what was her excuse?

Ben rolled to one side, used the floor as leverage, then stood. When he held out a hand to help her up, she accepted the offer.

"I've got a fairly good idea who it might be."

"Well, why didn't you say so?" She gently pushed him, then reached out to steady him. She hadn't meant to push so hard.

"Owww! It hurts there." He exaggerated the pout of his lower lip.

She laughed. This big, fierce man who could commandeer a horse as huge as a barn was no more hurt than she was gullible. "You won't get sympathy from me, Ben McGuire."

"I don't want shymp-shympathy, 'Chel. I want—"

His uninhibited, whiskey-induced, passion-laden kiss nearly melted her bones to ash. With as much advance notice as he'd given when he kissed her, Ben ended the tender assault and shouted, "Yeeehaahh, I feel good!"

Rachel blinked. The only way she could describe what she felt was *well kissed*.

"Now I gotta catch me a skunk." Ben's eyes narrowed. "He's gonna find out just how bad ol' good Ben McGuire can be."

"You keep saying *he*," she stressed, willing her pulse to slow to its normal rhythm. "Is it someone you know?"

All playfulness faded from Ben's face. "I'm fairly certain of it. And if it is, then it's you he's after and not me."

"Look who's come to see us, Ben." Rachel swung the door open wide. "Mr. and Mrs. Whipple."

She stepped aside and waited as Matilda secured her parasol, then entered. Rachel extended her hand to the woman. "I don't believe we've met . . . officially."

They exchanged glances, and Rachel got the satisfaction of seeing her blush. Each knew the other was considering the gossip that had been spread about the deception.

"McGuire," the politician greeted, removing the top hat from his salt and pepper hair.

"Whipple." Ben did not extend his hand, but instead waved the couple to a seat on the davenport. "What are you two doing out here so bright and early?"

Matilda glanced at her husband, then began to speak. "We felt we'd been remiss in paying you a call. After all, you are now the father of two young sons, and"—she held a gloved hand in front of her mouth—"a tax-paying citizen of the community. We felt it was our duty, no, our privilege to see how you were coming along with your new family." She eyed Rachel. "Oh, and to see if you're settling into Valiant well too. Miss Sloan, is it?"

Don't look down your nose at me. Rachel's eyes narrowed. An impish thought crossed her mind, and she couldn't resist. "It's Sloan for now. I'm not sure what it will be tomorrow. Tharp, Sloan . . . Whipple's a nice name too."

Sterling Whipple tightened his cravat. Matilda's eyes rounded like saucers.

"Rachel, how about some coffee?" Ben leveled a look that warned she'd overstepped a boundary she shouldn't have.

She glared at him for sending her away. "I'll be right

back. Don't say *anything* important until I return.''

Rachel fretted over how long the coffee was taking to brew. Luckily the stove was still hot from cooking Jimmy breakfast that morning. She'd sent him early to open the store, in the event the culprit stopped by to see if Ben had opened up or if Jim worked alone. She sent a note with him for Alewine, asking the frontierswoman to take care of Samuel for them until the afternoon. Sam had been only too glad to ride shotgun beside Aly.

With an occasional peep around the door that closed off the kitchen from the cabin's drawing room, Rachel could tell the conversation was getting good. Widening the door, she watched, straining to hear every word.

Matilda pulled off one glove and fanned her face. ''I can't believe you would stoop to such levels, Sterling. If you didn't want me, you could have at least spared me the humiliation of putting up with all your skirt-chasing.''

Sterling jolted to his feet. ''I'm not guilty of this. Whatever Ben told you . . . he's lying.''

Ben stood. ''You best leave, Whipple, before I forget that your wife is in my presence.''

The politician sank on bended knee in front of Matilda, clasping her hand. ''Will you believe him over your own husband—''

Matilda jerked her hand away and rose. ''Do quit sniveling, Sterling. Of course I believe Mr. McGuire. When have you ever given me reason to trust you? Now, get up from there and let's go.'' She looked apologetically at Ben. ''Give my regrets to Miss Sloan.''

Damn the coffee! Rachel hurried into the room, pretending that she wasn't aware of what had transpired. ''The coffee's almost ready. Would you care for milk or sugar?''

''We won't be staying after all. Perhaps you'll pay me a visit soon.'' The sincerity of Matilda's invitation never reached her eyes until she added, "And bring that darling little boy. Samuel, is it? I don't have children of my own, you know. I should have lots more time on my hands in the near future to get to know him better." She moved away from the davenport and retrieved her parasol. "I'm not sure what all my husband has been up to since your arrival, Miss Sloan, but it seems he's been concerned that you . . . rather, Joanna Tharp . . . might reveal something to me that I should have been wise enough to see years ago."

Matilda glared at her husband. "No, let me take that back. I *was* wise enough to see it, but looked the other way for reasons I don't care to mention now. Needless to say, his actions have given Ben here undue stress. I hope he hasn't caused you any ill."

Whipple? Not unless he was the one who . . . ? Was it possible? Rachel tried to remember where she'd put the quill. She held up a finger. "Would you wait just a minute, Mrs. Whipple? I need to find something to write with."

Matilda looked puzzled. "Of course, but please call me Matilda. I would like to become friends."

Finding what she sought on the dresser in her assigned room, Rachel quickly returned and held out parchment and writing instrument to Sterling. "Write your name for me."

Sterling backed up, shaking his head. "It's time we leave, Matilda. This is getting us nowhere. We can discuss everything on our way home."

The politician's wife looked from Rachel to her husband, then at the paper. "Sign it, Sterling."

"I won't!"

"What's this all about?" Ben moved up alongside Rachel.

"Oh, he's such a well-known man." Rachel met the politician's obsidian gaze squarely, though she spoke to Ben. "Who knows what a little piece of handwriting could be worth to the right person? It reveals so much about a man, don't you think?'' She smiled knowingly at Whipple and felt a sense of satisfaction watching sweat bead his brow. ''You have given signatures before, haven't you?''

Whipple spun on his heel and nearly bolted from the room. Rachel watched the pair get into their buggy, but Matilda took the reins. From the way the politician's head shrunk deep into his frock coat, she was certain the man would suffer far more verbal punishment than anything she and Ben could dole out physically.

''Now, what was that really about?'' Ben took the writing material from her hands.

She told him about the threatening letters, and that she was certain Sterling Whipple had written them.

''Why didn't you tell me about them before? He could have attacked you during the night if he knew a way in.'' Ben unconciously massaged her shoulders.

''There were so many who obviously didn't like Joanna that I didn't know whom to trust,'' she admitted.

''Not even me?''

''I knew it wasn't you. You loved Joanna too much to make her leave.'' She turned. ''Now that I've answered your question, you answer mine. Why did Whipple write those letters? What was he so afraid she—*I* would tell?''

''That he and Joanna were lovers.''

Anger, hurt, betrayal darted across his expression, but Ben quickly masked the emotions. Rachel wondered what kind of love allowed him to continue loving Joanna after such disloyalty. Yet hadn't he said it best at the canyon . . . it was an obsession.

Ben toyed with the lace at her collar, rubbing his thumb and finger over its texture. She shivered clear to her toes, wondering how it would feel to have his fingers caress her skin in the same manner.

''If Matilda caught wind of what had been going on, she

would have cut off Daddy's funds. Sterling doesn't know how to earn an honest dollar and is too lazy to start learning now. And when you returned to town as Joanna, he wasn't sure of your motives for doing so. When you started avoiding me like the pox, he must have worried that he was part of that reason''—Ben seemed relieved to laugh—"because it sure wasn't to let me court you."

"Do you think he shot at you last night?"

Ben shook his head. "He doesn't have what it takes. Probably hired someone else."

"But why? What good would killing you do to keep me quiet?"

"If I'm dead, would you stay in Valiant?"

No, her heart spoke for her. Everything became clear now. The last place she would want to live was Valiant. Every blade of grass, every sidewalk, every ring of the church bell brought memories of Ben and his goodness. No, she wouldn't stay in Valiant, but not for the reasons Ben assumed. He believed she would have to seek employment elsewhere, find somewhere else to live. He had no idea Sterling's plan to force her out would have succeeded if he'd managed to murder Ben.

"Then his plan could have worked." Ben gently knuckled her chin higher. "But it didn't and now you're safe. We both are. Ready to put it all behind you?"

I've been ready for so long. Her eyes willed him to hear the yearning within her. But she had to be certain the obsession was over. "Does that mean you're also ready to put your love for Joanna away, Ben?"

"I never *loved* her." Ben searched her face for understanding. "I don't know anymore what I felt for her. But God knows it wasn't love, 'Chel. It wasn't love."

❖ 22 ❖

Rachel rode on the driver's box with Ben toward the east bank of Wild Horse Lake. The boys kept switching sides, so neither would have to sit by the other. Bowie finally tired of the game and curled up on top of the bale used to pad their backs during the wagon ride. Their Sunday afternoon was blessed with only a slight breeze, enough to sweep away summer heat but not enough to put a damper on the church's planned picnic.

It seemed everyone had come out to enjoy the early August day. Wagons, buggies, and surreys moved en masse across the countryside, converging on the makeshift camp that already bustled with activity. The aroma of roasting beef and turkey forced Rachel's attention away from the colorful ribbons that had been tied in the cottonwoods and from the tops of the wagons. She focused on the huge spits that held the meat and were constantly being turned by big-armed youths.

Someone struck up a mouth organ. Someone else a fiddle. A song popular from two years before, " 'Til We Meet Again," filled the countryside with its lively tune that drew young ladies toward the musician and the possibility of being asked to dance.

Everyone looked so happy, like one big family coming together for a reunion. A sense of foreboding forced Rachel to shift on the box. She didn't belong there. She was an outsider and always would be.

"There's nothing to worry about." Ben commanded the team to halt. He secured the brake, then reached over and patted her hand. "Just be yourself and you'll do fine. No one's said anything so far, have they?"

"No, because I've seen them only in church, where they're too God-fearing to say anything."

He helped her out of the wagon. When Ben set her on her feet, he touched the raven-colored curl at her cheek. "Don't worry so, 'Chel. They'll grow to love you. People just need time to see things differently, don't you think?"

He rubbed the curl between his forefinger and thumb, sending tingling sensations all the way to her scalp.

"Did I tell you how pretty you look today?"

"At least three times." She smiled, remembering when he'd repeated himself like that several nights before but not in such sober surroundings. "But I don't mind."

He must have remembered too, because he dropped the curl and rubbed his hand on his pants leg, looking slightly ill at ease. "I . . . uh . . . don't know if I ever apologized for the other night, but—"

"You did." Her smile broadened. "In fact, over and over again."

Ben rubbed a hand through his hair, his face flushing a light pink. "I meant when I was sober. Honest, 'Chel. I don't know what got into me. I'm not a man who abuses liquor."

She reached out and touched him, pretending to brush something from his shirt. "You don't have to tell me that, Ben. I've seen the kind of man you are." *Read it in your letters, long before I ever really knew you,* she wanted to add.

"Are you two gonna stand there all day and sweet-eye each other, or are you gonna join the fun?" Jim asked, jumping down from the wagon. He grabbed the basket Rachel had packed and headed toward the large row of tables laden with food.

"Wait for me, Jim!" Samuel belly-scooted over the end of the wagon, but his small legs dangled a good distance from the ground. "Said he'd teach me to skip them rocks if I made his bed this morning. Now I made it for nothing!"

Ben hurried to help him the rest of the way down. He plopped the slouch hat that looked more farm than church atop Sam's head and tickled him. "Go on and have a good time. Rachel and I will be along in a minute. Tell your brother that I know about the deal."

"And if you start feeling sick again, you come get me, you hear," Rachel called after him. Both she and Ben had spent the night walking the floor with the boy. Though he seemed much better this morning, the child still looked a bit frail. She hadn't the heart to tell him he had to miss the picnic, even though it would have given her the perfect excuse to stay home and not attend the gathering herself.

Ben handed Rachel the quilt and the parasol he'd brought home as a gift to her the day after his visit to the saloon. He'd said she needed one for the drive back and forth to church, but she'd suspected it was a token of apology. He carried the apple and cherry pies she'd baked for the occasion, and, she had to admit, the cinnamon coating made her own mouth water with anticipation.

As they approached the tables to add their offerings to the fare, Ophelia shouted at Ben, "Wait right there!" She excused herself from the group of men standing near the campfire triangled by three huge coffeepots.

"Well, it's good to see you are still with the living. I wasn't too sure how well you'd weather the storm the other night.'' Her gaze swept over Rachel now. ''Or how *you* might deal with the one that's sure to blow in with her here today.''

Ben placed the pies at the end of the table that held all the desserts. ''I recovered quite nicely, Ophelia. Learned quite a lesson too. And there's not going to be a storm today, I'll see to that.'' He glanced over at the group she'd left behind. ''You didn't flavor up the coffee, did you?''

Ophelia's fingers splayed over her ample bosom. ''Now, would I do such a thing?'' She chuckled, then let her hand drop to her side. ''I was tempted, mind you, but I'm trying to improve my ways.'' Her brows knit together. ''Do you know that almost every child in Valiant made money off me last month? If I asked one to put money in the offerings for me, I bet I asked at least two dozen. Not that I mind financing the little darlings, but I could've paid out a banknote for an entire orphanage with that kind of money. No, Mr. McGuire, the coffee's safe this Sunday. Decided to give my wickedness a day of rest.''

''Miracles do happen. We'll have to start calling you Saint Ophelia. Or better yet, Saint Finck!'' Alewine Jones chuckled as she sauntered up to the table and dipped her finger into the chocolate icing that puddled thickly at the bottom of a cake. She stuck the thieving digit into her mouth and sucked, her eyes rolling into her upper lids to disappear from view. ''Mmmmm-mmmm-hummmmm. That's the best dad-gummed cake I ever tasted in all my born—''

Rachel couldn't resist teasing her. ''It didn't look to me like you had any portion of the cake. Just the icing.''

''That's right!'' Ophelia complained, slapping at the fron-tierswoman's finger as it snaked out for another dollop. ''Now, get! You can wait just like all the other children. You'll spoil your meal.''

''Who elected you cake warden?'' Alewine complained,

but backed away from Ophelia's stern expression.

Rachel handed Ben her blanket and parasol, shook her head silently, and gave him an I'll-explain-later look. Making sure Ophelia could not see what she planned, she crossed her hands behind her and pretended to survey each of the food-laden bowls and plates. But she knew exactly where she would stop. Just in front of a platter of chocolate scones.

Grabbing one without drawing Ophelia's attention was harder than she expected. She touched the bowl of pudding beside the platter and nearly tipped it over. Readjusting the height of her aim, she felt along the tablecloth until she touched the platter's edge. The scone was soft and the icing slippery, causing her to flip the top into the palm of one hand.

Great! Now if Ophelia noticed, there would be no way to wipe the evidence from her hand. "Alewine, could I speak to you for a moment, please?" She kept backing away from the table, hoping she didn't stumble over the hem of her dress.

"After 'while, Rachel. I ain't finished arguing with 'Phele yet."

"Not after a while, Aly. Now. Right now." Rachel felt the icing ooze through her fingers. She'd have chocolate stains all the way down the back side of her dress.

"Bossy little Virginian, ain't she?" Alewine left Ben and Ophelia looking on in puzzlement.

When Alewine caught up, Rachel whispered, "Stand directly in front of me. No, not there. That isn't enough room. Yes, right there. Now, here." She handed Alewine what was left of the scone.

Alewine's bowed head rose from the crumbled mess in her hands. "I'm sure it'll taste mighty good, Rachel. But, woman, you need to learn to use some eggs in it. That'll hold it together."

Rachel's hands started to wring, but she resisted the impulse so Ben and Ophelia didn't catch sight of the chocolate on them. "I didn't cook it, for goodness' sake. I kind of . . . well, you know . . . I took it off one of those platters for you."

"You stole it for me?" Surprise etched Aly's features.

"Why don't you just announce it to the whole congregation?" Rachel tried to hush her. "This is a church picnic, remember?"

"That's about the second nicest thing anybody's ever done for me. And blamed if you ain't the one who done the nicest thing when you patched me up."

"How is your hip?"

"Good as new. You done a fine job of stitching. Ought to be a dressmaker."

"That's what I am back in Richmond."

"I figured all of that other talk was a lie." Alewine motioned toward the shore. "What say we stroll on over to the bank and let you wash up?" She stuffed the scone in her mouth all in one bite, looking like a squirrel with the mumps.

Rachel fell in step alongside Aly. "What do you mean, all that other talk?"

"Can't talk wif my mou' full."

"Is that the truth, or are you trying to keep from worrying me?" Rachel eyed her friend and saw Aly's expression change. The freighter was not a good liar. Once they reached the water, Rachel bent to wash her hands, giving Alewine the time to swallow her treat. When she stood, she could see Aly wrestling with her conscience.

"Just tell me. Quit trying to spare my feelings."

"Let's go sit up under that tree. This might take some telling. That shade'll keep you from blistering."

She'd left the parasol with Ben. "So what is all the talk?"

They sat. Alewine propped her back against the cottonwood's trunk. "Gwenella Duncan has it out that you're some kind of citified actress what came to make fools of Ben and us. And you somehow flamboozled Joanna Tharp into letting you use her house and her money. 'Course, Belle O'Connor set her straight. Told Gwenella she ought to be the one to talk, since she'd tried to flamboozle just about every eligible man in Valiant into believing she was still lily pure. *That* set a few tongues to wagging, I mean to tell ya.''

"But what about the others?" Rachel stared at the community of folks who gathered around the lake's edge looking like they were having a wonderful time simply being together. "I know I'll never be welcomed by some of the Tight Shoe Troupe, but that's not my concern. The city fathers and their families, Sheriff Edwards, Ophelia, Clementine, Nash Turner. Have they said anything about the way they feel about me?''

"Yep. Even had a town meeting over it."

Rachel moved away from the part of the trunk where she leaned and turned to face Alewine. "Wh-what kind of meeting? When?''

"The day Ben took you on as a housekeeper."

"Why wasn't I told about it? I would have been there to defend myself."

Alewine shrugged. "Weren't no need. It turned out all right. You're still here, ain'tcha?''

A glance at Samuel trying to play with the bigger boys as they skipped stones farther down the bank instigated Rachel's reply. "I'm still here because Ben needed someone to help care for the boys."

The buckskinned woman shook her head. "You're here 'cause Ben talked the council into lettin' you stay."

"They were going to make me leave?" Even though she expected them to be angry enough to tar and feather her, Rachel thought the townsfolk too kind to actually run her out of Valiant. "What did Ben say that convinced them otherwise?"

"He reminded them all that most of us came here for a new start. That all of us had a past that wouldn't necessarily polish up spotless if we took a good look back. He also told 'em that if we run somebody out of town every time they told a lie, the streets would be vacant by week's end."

"Brother Ethan's sermon today was deliberate, wasn't it? He'd been warning them to be kind to me at the picnic." Rachel recalled the discomfort that had invaded the congregation as the minister said, "Ye who are without sin, cast the first stone." "I don't want to *make* everyone like me. It isn't the same."

Alewine motioned toward the group. "Oh, there's always some who'll like you only because it's expected of them. But most don't think no worse of ya. Ben made it clear in the meeting why you done what you done. And you've sure been good to him and the boys. Ben's a lot happier'n we've seen him in years. And Jim, well, that boy would follow you to hell and back if you asked him."

"Jimmy?" This was a surprise to Rachel. "He never says anything. In fact, all he does is gripe and complain."

"That's 'cause it gets him attention. Jim ain't had much of that. It lets him know you care about him. But you can pat yourself on the back, Rachel. He's always asayin' Rachel said this, Rachel said that. Got plumb mad at me yesterday when I asked him if that's all you done was talk. I swear if he'd a'been two inches taller, his fist woulda connected with my jaw."

"He tried to hit you?" Rachel spotted the thirteen-year-old and Bowie playing tumbleweed with several of the other boys as they roll-raced down the grassy slope. A glance at each boy ignited an uncomfortable feeling within, making her stand. "Do you see Sam?"

"Didn't hurt me none," Alewine stood, dusting off the back of her buckskins as she answered Rachel's first question before focusing on the second. "Maybe the little critter's eating. He likes your fried chicken. Said he was going to get him a drumstick 'fore anyone else did. Probably under the table and you jist can't see him from here. Them checkered cloths likely got a patchwork of nibblers under 'em."

Something was wrong. Sam would have asked her permission. He was too polite to pilfer. "Will you go check with Ben and ask if he's seen him?"

"Sure. Then me and Jim'll look around for him."

As she hurried to the campsite, she searched the sea of faces. Sam wasn't among them. A look under the tables proved Alewine's prediction true, but he was not one of the nibblers.

Closing off her mind to the noise and the music, Rachel concentrated on Samuel's image and the last place she'd seen him. He'd been skipping stones with the bigger boys and Jimmy farther down the bank.

Terror consumed her as she broke into a run. She sidestepped Belle, only to knock Gwenella Duncan down. Rachel started to explain, but halted as she caught sight of the slouch hat floating on the surface. All she could do was plead, "I'm sorry. No time. Get Ben. Sam's in the lake."

Rachel dove into the sun-warmed water. Icy fingers of dread gripped her as she plunged deeper and deeper into the dark lake . . . groping, waiting to touch yet finding nothing. Nothing!

Her ears thrummed to near bursting. Her lungs burned for need of air, but still she searched. Groping . . . praying.

The need for oxygen drove her upward. She sucked in the precious air, then dove again, widening her search, willing herself to find him.

A hand touched her. She almost screamed from grief before she realized it was a man's hand—a living grip pulling her upward.

She started fighting whoever held her, struggling to break free, pounding him with her fist, kicking her feet. As she broke the surface, her anger rent the air. "Let me go! Sam's down there. I've got to find Sam."

"Stop, Rachel!"

Strong hands gripped her wrists. Just before she went under again, she realized it was Ben's voice she heard. He meant to stop her.

She quit fighting and surfaced, spitting out the gulp of water that had filled her mouth as she'd gone under unexpectedly. When she caught her breath, she blurted out, "Sam's down there! He was skipping rocks and . . . and he's down there."

Huge sobs racked her body as she clung to Ben, needing him for support, knowing that the boy could not have survived this long underwater. "He's dead." A soulful moan escaped her as reality sank in. "Sam's *dead*."

Townsfolk lined the shore like ducks on a pond, yelling words she couldn't decipher in her grief-stricken thoughts.

Ben held her and swam toward shore, crooning encouragement into her ear. "Maybe not, 'Chel. Maybe he's off playing somewhere. Jimmy said they'd argued and Sam said he was going to run away. Maybe he's not in the lake at all. But let's get you to shore and I'll look for him."

She could hear the desperation in his tone. Knew that he wanted to believe his words as much as she needed to. When they reached the bank, Nash and Nicodemus Turner pulled them out. The weight of her sodden skirt made standing difficult.

"Alewine found the boy asleep under the chuck wagon in the swingbed." The gambler offered Rachel his frock coat, but she refused. "He didn't even know the whole crowd was looking for him."

"Thank God." She fought the urge to cup her hands over her face and dissolve into tears. Instead, she lifted her skirt and ran as fast as she could to the chuck wagon. The crowd parted as if on cue and allowed them a clear path to the boy. Outdistancing Rachel by longer strides, Ben reached Sam first.

The six-year-old stood next to Alewine, hugging one buckskinned leg. His dark eyes widened and his face paled as every eye focused on him and the crowd closed in to view the unfolding drama.

"Am I in t-trouble?" his small voice quavered.

Ben bent on one knee and hugged the boy fiercely. "No, Sam. You just scared me out of my wits. Rachel too. Don't you know you're all I have left of your mother? I can't do without you, son."

The tears began to fall despite Rachel's effort to will them away. Everyone would think they sprang from the terror she'd experienced in believing Sam dead. Only she knew the truth. Sam's presence would be a constant reminder of that special time in Ben's life when he and Joanna must have truly loved each other, and they'd created a living portrait of that love. Rachel knew now that Joanna would forever haunt any life she might have planned with Ben.

As Ben allowed her to hold the child that had come to mean so much to her, Rachel cried in earnest. She couldn't resent Sam. He was exactly where he should be—in his father's home and under a loving roof. A roof that sheltered all that meant anything to her.

A roof that had suddenly become impossible for her to live under any longer.

❖ 23 ❖

"Here, Miss Sloan, let me give you my shawl." Alizabeth Bentley batted her lashes extravagantly. "You must be freezing."

"I'll have Stampede take me back to town and get a dress from my shop so you won't have to go home to change. I'm sure I'll have something there for Ben too." Clementine grabbed the engineer whose plate of food looked like it needed side rails to hold everything on it.

"Or borrow my buggy and go with her," Matilda Whipple encouraged, moving up to stand by Samuel and Rachel.

A dozen other voices offered help. When Rachel stared at each willing face, she was surprised to see that the kindnesses were being extended by some of those same people she was certain had wanted to run her out of town instead of toward it. What made the difference?

"Th-thank you" was all she could manage to answer under the outpouring of consideration.

"I think we best go on home," Ben suggested, taking Rachel's and Sam's hands and guiding them toward their wagon. Despite the crowd's protests, Ben shook his head. "Sam's a bit tired, and we should get out of these things before we get sick. Jim, son, why don't you take over the team? I'll sit in back with Rachel and Sam. It'll be warmer there.''

Jim's face looked as if it had turned to stone, but he did as Ben instructed. Bowie settled onto the seat beside him. Rachel shivered, partially from the gust of wind that chilled her skin, but more from the thought of being so close to Ben for the ride home.

''Here's your quilt.'' Alewine followed behind them and waited until they climbed into the back before she held out a drumstick to Sam. ''Thought you might get hungry on the ride back, boy.''

Sam darted away from Ben and hugged Alewine. ''Thanks, Aly. You're the best.''

''Awww, shoot.'' Alewine returned his hug, then realized everyone was watching. She quickly pulled away and told Sam to sit down, then hollered at Jim, ''Take 'em on home, James Donald. Your pa's teeth are achattering.''

The wagon lurched forward. Rachel grabbed hold of Samuel and drew him down into her lap. He leaned his head against her breasts and stretched his legs over Ben's lap. Ben spread the quilt over them and snuggled in tighter, while the townspeople closed ranks behind them and waved in unison.

Never had Rachel felt such a part of the community. How sad that she'd only just found a place to call her hometown. Tomorrow she would leave Valiant forever.

Perhaps tomorrow would alter Rachel's mood, Ben thought, closing the book he'd been reading to Samuel. The six-year-old had fought sleep all the way home. But once Ben changed into dry clothes and read Sam the next chapter of *Pirates, Beware!*, his newest son lost the battle to stay awake.

At first he'd thought her unusually quiet because of the scare Sam had given them. Then, as she deliberately avoided him for more than two hours, he wondered what else prompted her silence.

Ben dropped his feet from the footstool and stood. The upturned keg was just one of many changes Rachel had made to his home in the weeks she'd worked as his housekeeper. Changes that had angered him at first.

Though he understood her need to have her own home and sympathized with it, he'd planned his house exactly the way Joanna had wanted it. Down to the last detail. But as days passed, Ben began to notice Rachel's changes were of a masculine nature. What had once been fashionable and ornate was now comfortable and practical. The dozen kindnesses she committed every day had been solely to please him and his sons, not self-serving. Rachel hadn't changed his home into her own, but into *his*. To his taste. For his comfort.

An unselfish task. Something Joanna could never have done . . . no . . . *would* never have done.

The need to be with Rachel engulfed him. She had become part of his soul. When he walked out of the door each morning to go to work, he found himself wishing the day away even before it started. Every few minutes his gaze strayed to the clock on the store counter, wondering how much longer before he could hang the CLOSED sign. The ride home had become a race to see if he could beat the previous day's time. Yes, he wanted to be with her. Twenty-four hours a day. For the rest of his life.

He left the boys' room and knocked on Rachel's door. " 'Chel, can I talk to you a minute?"

No one answered. Perhaps she was purposefully not answering; she'd been so silent on the ride back. "I hoped we could talk. You've been kind of quiet since we left the picnic. You all right?"

He barely opened the door, waited for her to object, then

opened it wider when she didn't. Her room was empty. Her carpetbag and trunk had been pulled out from beneath the bed—as if she were preparing to leave.

Spying the piece of paper on top of the trunk, he stepped farther into the room and picked it up. As he scanned the words written on it, his heart felt as if Nash Turner had tied an anvil around it and dropped the anvil to the bottom of Wild Horse. The return ticket to Richmond. Ben put the ticket where he'd found it, then closed the door to her room.

Dual emotions battled within him, rage that she would leave him now when he'd only just come to understand how much he cared for her, and a deep sadness greater than his grief for Joanna. He loved Rachel. The reality of this new understanding swept over him, buffeting him like a strong wind. Ben braced one palm against the wall to steady himself. Rubbing his temple, he fought the urge to curse the unfairness of it all.

From the very beginning her actions had said she loved him, hadn't they? She'd cared enough to agree to Joanna's bargain. She'd cared enough to match him up with another woman. She'd even cared enough to become his housekeeper and help him when he needed her. But Rachel's real act of love came when she'd changed his home to his liking, worked beside him and the boys in the field, gave him back a sense of his own self-worth that wasn't gauged by someone else's needs and desires, but his own.

Yes, her actions said she loved him, yet she would leave him. Just as Joanna had.

Ben hurried through the drawing room and into the kitchen. When he didn't find her, he checked upstairs. Not there either. Certain she'd never leave without that precious carpetbag—she seemed offended every time he'd ever offered to carry it for her—he quickly dismissed the notion that she'd left without saying good-bye.

Realizing Jimmy was not inside the house either, he told himself the pair were probably off talking together. The boy entrusted Rachel with a lot he didn't tell his father. Ben didn't resent their closeness. In fact, he welcomed it. Both had similar backgrounds. Both needed someplace to call home. Both had been thrown away by their parents.

The silence holding Jimmy was anger. Ben knew his son too well. But Rachel's he assumed was trying to shake off the panic and dread Sam's disappearance had caused.

A search in the barn yielded nothing. All the horses were stabled, so they hadn't ridden off to talk. Finally a trip to the springhouse rewarded him with an answer. A red bandanna fluttered in the wind, tied to the door handle.

All his own fears washed away as Ben realized he may have overreacted. She had probably taken fresh clothes out of her trunk and laid the ticket on the dresser, planning to put it back later, when she returned. He'd worked himself into a frenzy for nothing.

"He loves Sam more!" Jimmy snapped. Bowie barked in agreement.

"Shhh, he'll hear you and wonder if something's wrong. Now, stop crying, Jim."

Surprised to hear both Jimmy's and Rachel's voices coming from inside the springhouse, Ben untied the bandanna and turned the knob, ready to find out what exactly was going on. But something made him barely open the door. He paused, waiting. Listening. Bowie barked.

"Shh, boy! Ben'll hear you."

Shh, boy. They'll hear me, Ben worried.

"You saw him at the lake." Jimmy's voice cracked. "All he could think about was where precious little Sammy was. He yelled at me! Said I shoulda been watching him."

"That was fear talking, Jim. Ben was afraid something had happened to Sam. Sometimes we react in anger, and it's really because we're too afraid to show our fear.''

"He'll never love me as much as he does Sam. I ain't his real blood. Besides, I stole from him.''

"Ben isn't the type of man to take away love once he's given it. There's room in his heart for both of you.''

"For all of you," Ben whispered, resisting the impulse to open the door and tell them both. To do so would invite disaster. They'd gone to elaborate means to talk privately. He wouldn't dishonor that.

"Can we walk for a while? The edge of this tub is biting into my legs. I wish there was somewhere else to sit. But I'm afraid to sit on the bank. It's too wet and Ben would notice the backs of our clothes if we did.''

"I need to stretch too," Rachel replied. "But let's stay in here, just in case he's finished reading to Sam. That bandanna will keep him away for a while if he sees it, but only to the point he starts worrying which of us is taking so long. Now tell me why you stole from Ben.''

"I was hungry. Hadn't eaten in two days when I got off the train. Planned on finding work as soon as I felt better, then I would've paid him back somehow. If I'd known how good he'd be to me . . . you know, how much I'd like him, I wouldn't have stolen from him at all.'' The boy's voice broke. "Do you r-reckon he'll ever forgive me, Rachel? I'd buy him a thousand pieces of jerky if he'd just forgive me.''

Silence ensued. Hearing the longing in his son's voice, it was all Ben could do not to reveal his presence. But he waited, wanting to hear if Rachel understood him as well as he hoped. Ben could almost hear her choosing words carefully.

"Let me tell you a story, Jim," she began, "about someone slightly older than yourself. She was almost fifteen at the time. We'll call her Kate. Kate had no home. She had parents, but couldn't live with them anymore. Lived on the streets most of the time because she tried desperately to be good and make a living. But everyplace that hired her gave her pauper's pay. She didn't belong to a prestigous family in town, wouldn't offer favors in exchange for better pay, and was so desperate just to survive, she didn't complain about what little wages she earned.''

"I've been there," Jim admitted. "On the streets of Salem. Went to bed hungry lots of nights."

Ben remembered too well the near-starving ragamuffin he'd taken into his home a year before. Only in the last four or five months had Jimmy put on weight and lost that gaunt grimness in his features.

"Kate had spied a certain house that filled her nights with dreams and hopes," Rachel continued. "She even got to go inside one Christmas when the wealthy family who owned it opened it to the community for a great Christmas ball. Of course, she didn't get to see the ballroom because she wasn't a true invited guest. But she was fortunate enough to be among those invited into the kitchen to warm herself from the winter eve and be served cookies and wassel. Everything smelled so wonderful, sparkled with cleanliness and neatness. Kate promised herself that one day she'd live in such a house. Maybe even that particular house."

Rachel exhaled a long breath. "Then she became acquainted with the young master of the house, quite by accident. He was not the best ice skater, and she was one of the few who didn't laugh at him when he fell. When she offered to help him up, he accepted her hand. From that point on for several months, they went everywhere together. He showed her a lifestyle she'd only dreamed existed. Though he never invited her to his home, he met her in a dozen places, mostly out-of-the-way inns, where they dined and talked and laughed and plotted their future together."

"Was Kate you?"

The boy's cleverness silenced her. Ben cheered Rachel on, knowing how difficult it was to admit her past.

"Yes, I was Kate. I took on a name for many years because I thought that if I did, I could make up a life better than the one I had." Sadness filled her tone. "It didn't work, but it was easier to pray for Kate than for me. I was always taught that it was selfish to ask for yourself, but wishes might come true if you asked for someone else."

"Did you marry that rich fella? Did you ever get to go home with him?"

"No, I've never been married. Oh, Daniel asked me once and I told him all right, then we both decided we'd wait. By the time I made up my mind that he was a decent enough man and would make a fine husband, he was already married to the army."

Daniel who? Jealousy rose within Ben.

"Was Daniel the skater?"

"No, he was a soldier I knew in Richmond. Just a friend, but a good one nonetheless."

Ben relaxed.

"Then what was the skater's name?"

Yes, what was his name? Ben silently echoed Jim's question.

"That's not important anymore. Though at the time it was a name that demanded respect in the community where I lived. The last night we were together, he actually took me inside that big, beautiful house—the one I'd admired for so long and wished were my own. I have to tell you, I was bedazzled, enchanted, and all those other words that make you feel someone or something has put you under a magical spell.

"But I learned that dreams sometimes become nightmares. He had listened to me talk all those times about how I wanted a big fancy this and fancy that. He'd used his home to lure me into his . . . his . . . well, into a situation I never want to be in again.''

Fury blazed through Ben as images filled his thoughts. He'd kill the man if he ever found out his name.

''He didn't hurt you, did he?''

Concern and a wisdom beyond his years filled Jimmy's voice, making Ben mourn for the pair's lost childhood.

''No, but I managed to get away before anything disastrous could happen. I ended up hurting myself because of my anger over it. You see, I waited until he and his family left their home for a trip north, then broke into the house and stayed a month without permission.''

''Did you get caught?''

''Yes. I had a hard time getting any work for a while. Nobody trusted me. But I punished myself far worse than the law ever could have.'' She paused and sighed deeply, as if she were expelling years of remorse. ''I never forgave myself for breaking into that house and using what wasn't mine. Up until then I had obeyed the law. I was poor, but I was honest poor. That month made a difference. It made me ashamed of myself for the first time in my life.''

''Ben wasn't the first person I stole from,'' Jimmy admitted. ''But he was the first who ever helped me after I stole from him.''

''Are you sorry you took his jerky?''

''Yes.''

''If Ben, Sam, or I had done something wrong, but we were really regretful and promised not to do it again, would you forgive us?''

''You and Ben. Sam, maybe.''

Ben bit back a chuckle.

''Would you expect us to forgive ourselves if we were truly sorry about what we'd done?''

''Well, sure.''

"Then forgive yourself, Jim. Forgive yourself for stealing from Ben, and expect everyone else to forgive you too."

"I want to believe that, but I'm not sure if Ben really does or if he's just saying he does 'cause that's the right thing to do."

"The right thing to do was to keep you from going to that boys' prison, wasn't it?"

"Yeah."

"But Ben not only gave you a place to work, but a home too, didn't he?"

"I guess he does mean it."

"He sure does. Remember that when you think he loves Sam more than he does you, just because Sam's his blood kin and you're not. Ben chose you as a son, he didn't just sire you. That should make you realize how much he loved you. You were his *choice*."

She cleared her throat. "And if it seems like he's paying more attention to Sam, then remember that a parent's time must be divided between children. That doesn't mean he loves either of you any more or less than the other. It's just that that particular child needs more attention from him in that given moment. Ohhh, my goodness. I—I should heed my own words, shouldn't I?"

"What's wrong? How come you're crying?"

Ben understood and wished he could hold Rachel in his arms now and comfort her.

"I'm not crying because I'm sad, Jim. These are tears of gladness. You've helped me do something I should have done a long time ago. You've made me realize that my parents didn't love me any less. They just fell on hard times and needed me to understand. Now, finally, I think I actually do."

Jim's voice drew closer to the door. "Maybe you ought to go home and tell your ma and pa they done all right by you. I will, that's for sure. Gonna make Ben glad he took a chance on me.''

The door opened. Ben sucked in a deep breath, knowing he'd been caught eavesdropping. Wondering if he'd be forgiven. Words of explanation escaped him.

• 24 •

THE THIRTEEN-YEAR-OLD stared up at him, his eyes shimmering with tears despite the boy's previous refusal to shed them. Ben's heart clenched at the need he saw etched in his son's face. With a will born of love, his arms opened in invitation. Jimmy flung himself into Ben's arms . . . and they both cried.

He sensed her standing at the door, felt her anger as she attempted to pass them. "Rachel, wait!" Ben let go of Jim and reached out to stop her. "We need to talk. Don't go."

Bowie barked, nipping at his boot.

"It's been a long day"—she stiffened at his touch and shooed the dog away—"and I'm tired from last night. Neither of us got much sleep, remember?"

She was right. Sam had kept them up all night. Rachel looked exhausted from lack of sleep and the misunderstanding at the lake. But he was tired too. Tired of people he loved always leaving him. "Get some rest, but we've got to talk in the morning."

"At first light," her voice echoed with a haunting sadness that filled her face as she stared up at him.

His fate seemed to look back at him from the depths of her emerald eyes, making Ben aware that the coming dawn would bring with it changes that would forever alter his life. "Stay with me." He drew her close.

"I must go." She pulled away.

"Jeewillikers, say good night, why don'tcha?" Jimmy complained. Bowie growled to add his opinion on the matter.

If that's all that was being said, it might not be so hard to watch her walk away, but Ben suspected she was marching out of his life forever. "Good night, 'Chel." *Stay.*

"Good night, Ben." *Good-bye,* the finality of her tone warned.

"You look like you lost your best hound dog." Jimmy bent and patted Bowie. The dog slobbered on his boot, wagging his tail at the attention given. "Awww, turkey puke! Why'd ya have to go and do that for, fella?"

"Because that's his way." Ben bent, his knees creaking as he balanced himself and scratched the mutt behind one ear. "He shows his affection in the only way he knows how."

Ben realized what he'd said and decided the dog could teach him a few things. He'd never told Jim how he felt about him, too afraid to show any affection because, God knew, he was no expert at it. There had been an underlying fear that if he got too close, he might scare Jim off the same way he had Joanna and now, Rachel. He'd planned his life for seven years and where had that gotten him? Alone and aware that his idea of love had been sorely mistaken. Maybe taking a chance was all that really mattered anymore.

The best way you know how, he reminded himself before plunging in. "About all those questions you asked Rachel earlier, Jim, she was right. Blood son or adopted, I love you and Sam the same."

Jim bent and balanced alongside him, scratching Bowie's other ear. "I love you too, Pa."

Pride blazed through Ben as Jimmy honored him with the

title the boy had never once offered him before. He had Rachel to thank for this, Rachel to thank for everything. She'd not only helped him get back his self-worth and made him see the lie he'd been living. But she'd gifted him with a son's love, as well.

She'd told the boy to trust him. To believe in him. Maybe that's exactly what he needed to do himself. Trust in himself. Believe that what he felt was real and not a substitute for what he had come to realize he'd never really wanted in the first place.

But loving Rachel scared the hell out him, and the possibility of losing her was even more frightening.

She wasn't a dream that beckoned to him from some distant horizon. She wasn't a goddess whose perfection he assigned no end and whose very presence he believed would set his whole world right, as he'd once believed Joanna might. Rachel was a living, breathing, flesh-and-blood woman. With a past and flaws. With a presence that demanded all of what Ben McGuire was, and not what she thought he should be.

It was time to put Joanna-the-dream aside and face the reality of Rachel.

Night promised no sleep. Time kept ticking away in Ben's thoughts. His life. His future. His opportunity to convince her to stay.

Pulling back the covers, Ben crept downstairs and lightly knocked on Rachel's door. No answer. Perhaps as tired as she was, she hadn't heard. He knocked again, slightly louder. Still nothing. A third knock and a whispered ''Rachel'' fared no better.

Certain she couldn't sleep through that much noise, he assumed she was awake but deliberately not responding.

Maybe if he talked to her enough, she'd listen. Maybe if he said the right words.

"Rachel, I accidentally saw the ticket on your trunk. I know you're going to leave us in the morning. I want you to know you don't have to. The boys and I . . . well . . . we'll miss you. You've really made a difference here."

He listened for movement but heard only silence. Though the door was not locked, he wouldn't go in unless she invited him. "I don't think I've told you how pleased I am with the house and the way you've got things arranged. I know you thought I was angry about it. And, I admit, at first I was. Since you wanted a home of your own so much, I thought you were rearranging it to suit yourself. But now I know different. You made it mine. Not Joanna's. I thank you for that."

He cleared his throat as he shifted position, trying to get comfortable but realizing the discomfort came from within, not without. Something held back the words he wanted to tell her, the words he'd once spoken to Joanna, only to have her leave him. He couldn't tell Rachel he loved her until he was certain, without question, she would never leave.

Instead, he offered her the one thing that might make her stay. The dream she'd cherished all her life. "Stay, Rachel. Stay as long as you like. You'll always have a home with me and the boys. Make this your home too."

The door to the boys' room creaked open. Samuel's head peeked around the edge, followed closely by Jimmy's above him, and Bowie's below.

"All that sounds real nice, Papa Ben." Sam yawned and rubbed one eye. "But Miss Rachel ain't in her room."

Jimmy put his hand over his brother's mouth. "Better close that trap or you'll be bug bait." Bowie licked his mouth and yawned, looking all too willing to join in. "Yeah,

Pa, we heard Rachel go outside about a half hour ago, after she got Bug Bait here a drink of water.''

"Thanks, boys. Go back to sleep. I'll see if she's all right.''

Sam yawned again. "Talk to her real good some more, Papa Ben. Tell her you and me and Jim and Bowie all want her to live with us forever and ever. Don't we, Jim?''

Jim ruffled Sam's hair, causing the six-year-old to bat his hand away. "That's about the smartest thing you ever said, Bug Bait. Might be a chance for you after all.''

"I ain't no Bug Bait.''

"All right, then . . . Turkey Puke.''

"Snake Snot.''

"Buffalo Booger. A green, slimy, wadded-up old buffa—''

"To bed with you!''

Ben rushed forward, pretending to chase them into the room. The pair giggled and dove under the covers. He tucked them in, tweaking each of the noses that made miniature mountains under the sheet. "Before you close those eyes, why don't you two say an extra prayer that I can convince Rachel to stay with us.''

"You will, Papa Ben.'' Sam sounded confident.

"She wants to, Pa.''

Ben armed himself with their faith. "I hope you're both right.''

The first place he looked was the springhouse, but no bandanna hung from the knob. Next he looked in the barn, but was met with only curious stares from Buchanan and Crockett. He found her sitting on a bale of hay in the corral, staring up at the moon.

"I wonder which lucky maiden is being kissed tonight,'' she whispered without turning to look at him.

He reached for Rachel, pulling her into his embrace. For a split second he thought she might protest, but her arms wrapped themselves around his neck and she molded her body to his. Something in her eyes mesmerized him, holding him almost as if in a trance. She looked up at him with the most tender expression he'd ever received.

God, how he wanted her.

Then his mouth was on hers in a kiss that scorched his very lifeblood. Her lips were soft, hot, demanding. Tremors in his stomach quaked outward until his entire body pulled her closer, wanting to absorb her into him. Her lips parted, whether in surprise or desire, he wasn't sure.

Ben deepened the kiss, his tongue hungrily tasting, savoring, tempting her with all she might leave behind. But she answered in kind, intensifying the need within him to show her no other woman would ever . . . had ever . . . made him feel this way.

"I want you, Ben," she rasped as she pulled her mouth away from his. "Make love to me under your hazy moon."

He forgot the possibility of her leaving. Worse, he didn't care. The only thing that mattered to his traitorous body was that she wanted him and he loved her.

Their bodies were so close, he could feel the rise and fall of her breasts. "I'll not take you in the hay, Rachel Sloan, but know this . . ." He studied her, certain that what he was about to say would forever change both their lives. "Once you come to my bed, it must be to stay."

She lay her head against his chest and clung to him. "Neither Joanna nor I could promise you forever, Ben. Only you can decide if tonight is enough."

✦ 25 ✦

W HEN HE LIFTED her into his arms, Rachel clung to the one reality in her mixed-up world. Making love to Ben was as inevitable as day giving way to night. As imminent as the changing seasons. As necessary as drawing in breath.

Inside the cabin, she demanded that he stop at the foot of the stairs and put her down so he wouldn't hurt himself carrying her up to his room.

"I've lifted far heavier things than you."

But she insisted, squirming until he loosened his hold and she slid from his arms. A wave of shyness enveloped her as she realized where the next few steps would lead.

"Second thoughts?"

It was said in such a low voice that she wasn't sure she heard him. Rachel shook her head. He gently pulled her against him, the passion in the blue of his eyes mesmerizing her, holding her more firmly in his embrace than his hands ever could. It seemed she ceased to breathe.

The fine hair on the back of her neck began to tingle. Sweet desire kindled deep within her abdomen and rippled in wave after heated wave through her bloodstream, making her world careen with the sheer want of him. Rachel's fingers moved up to trace the ridges of Ben's shoulders, marveling in the sensual shiver left in their wake. Triumph filled her thoughts. No matter what else he believed, no matter who else he loved, it was her touch that elicited such a response from him. *Her* touch.

Their gazes met in a long, searching look. Slowly, his hand cradled the back of her head and their lips touched in a tender kiss. Every kiss they'd shared before paled in comparison. He was every hunger that needed sating, every thirst she couldn't quench. The scent of hope.

His tongue played lightly on her bottom lip. Wanting to prolong each delicious sensation he created within her, she tried to wait, wanted to resist, but reason fled. Her own kiss became bolder, hotter, more demanding.

Tears filled her eyes. Blurred by emotion too potent to name, she didn't care what tomorrow would bring. She didn't care that the rest of her life would forever be gauged by the hours spent in Valiant with Ben. All she wanted, all she needed to be able to say good-bye . . . and survive . . . was the chance to see even the tiniest glimpse of forever in his arms.

"You're so beautiful, 'Chel. I want to touch you. Taste you."

While his gaze devoured her, Rachel shivered with an indescribable need. Deep and rich, his husky words held a touch of wonder. A thrill coursed through her. "And I you."

Though he allowed her to climb the stairs on her own, once there, he swept her up and carried her into his bedroom.

She watched in fascination as he undressed her one unhurried button at a time, slipping the clothing off and letting it fall around her like petals plucked from a flower. The whisper of goose bumps skimming across her skin rose more from the blatant desire staring back at her than from any chill permeating the room. In silent agreement they began the task of stripping away all that kept her from his closest touch.

Her fingers seemed inept, fumbling, revealing how nervous she was.

"Here, let me help you." His fingers covered hers, not replacing them, but adding certainty to tremulous effort. Soon they were standing face-to-face, body to body.

"You're so lovely," he whispered, reaching to trace a thumb from her bottom lip, down her neck, and into the valley between her breasts.

Trying hard not to look, she kept her attention on granite sinews nowhere near his thighs. But God help her, she couldn't resist temptation. "Will we . . . fit?"

He laughed joyously, pulling her toward him in a hug that promised so much more. When he began to nuzzle her neck, Rachel knew she was forever lost . . . forever his. But the hard proof of what they were about to do pressed wantonly against her, forcing her into a logic she wished only to push away.

"Ben"—she exhaled a ragged breath—"tell me you don't want me. Please tell me you'll never want anyone but—"

"It's *you* I want." His gaze deliberately, evocatively trailed every inch of her body to the tip of her toes and back up again, sweeping the uncertainty from her as if it were a single flame caught in the roar of a raging wildfire. She blinked, needing the moment away from his heated gaze.

"Come here." He lay down, opening his arms to welcome her into his embrace. Ben's hands enfolded her, caressing the curvature of her ribs as he turned her to lie beneath him.

" 'Chel"—his lips feathered along her arched neck as his hand cupped the underswell of one breast—"what made you really come to Valiant?"

Though she tried to concentrate on what he was asking, her mind was too sharply focused on the exquisite exploration of his hands. One slipped lower to stroke the curve of her hip and splay across the firmness of her abdomen, while the other played at the nape of her neck. She shifted, arching to meet the gentle but persistent press of thigh against thigh.

Ben's eyes glittered in the moonlight streaming in the opened window. " 'Chel, stay with me."

She shook her head, as if trying to clear away the alluring song humming through her senses. Her hands strained at his corded upper arms. "I'm not sure that's what's best—for either of us."

He loomed over her, demanding that their gazes meet . . . lock. "This *is* what's right for us. We've both felt it since the beginning. I just let Joanna get in the way."

Her eyes focused on the ceiling, the moonlight, anywhere but at Ben's face, until his fingers fanned themselves on either side of her head, and he bent to play his lips lightly over her mouth.

When he pulled away, his eyes searched deep into hers. Rachel knew he was allowing her an opportunity to change her mind, but her mind was set. She would have one night of heaven to hold back the hell of her days without him.

His fingers draped her hair in a raven-colored shawl about her shoulders. Under his intent regard her lashes closed and her breath exited in a ragged rhythm. Her lips pulsed with the beat of her heart, aching to be kissed.

"Rachel," he whispered, one knuckle gently curving under her chin to lift it, "forget there's a tomorrow that might take us away from each other. Make love to me as if there has never been or ever will be another moment like this."

When his lips sought the peak of one breast, her fingers threaded themselves into his hair. Wild excitement surged inside her. She would deny him nothing tonight. Would give herself with complete abandon. Yet deep within, Rachel knew the night was only a reprieve from the reality tomorrow would bring.

As his hands cupped her breasts and his tongue blanketed the sensitive pinnacles with kisses, reason fled. She wanted only his touch and the pleasure it brought her.

"Rachel, you're so beautiful."

His tongue flicked a line of disturbing kisses down the curve of her ribs. She quivered uncontrollably.

He murmured endearments, the warm rush of his breath fanning the flames his kisses had ignited within her. The inexplicable thread of tension that seemed to have bound her for years unraveled itself as his mouth resumed its tender kissing. Without warning he buried his face in the apex of her thighs, claiming it hotly with his tongue.

Surprised by the so-intimate touch, she gasped and arched. But her embarrassment quickly evaporated as his tongue skillfully kissed, nuzzled, teased her to the point that all shyness abandoned her, and her hands wound tighter through his thick hair to draw him closer.

An urgency filled Rachel. "Ben . . . please . . . I . . . want—"

He moved up over her. She parted her thighs, wrapping her legs around him to welcome him fully. He seemed to hesitate, but she arched toward him in need. When they joined as one, she stiffened momentarily. Pain radiated through her until his body moved in tempting, teasing, tantalizing strokes that turned the pain into pleasure and compelled her to match his rhythm.

His name rushed from her lips like a vow. "Ben . . ."

He whispered endearments, his sensuous strokes gradually accelerating.

Her body molded itself against his, wanting to feel the press of flesh against flesh, heart against heart, soul to soul. Fantasies of what could happen the rest of the night filled her thoughts as Ben taught her the delights she'd only dreamed his lovemaking would bring.

All at once she was gripping his forearms, her fingernails digging into his flesh. Something uncoiled inside her, taking her breath away with its incredible force. Ben held her against him, barely moving as he coaxed the full measure of the moment from her suddenly rigid body. Violent spasms convulsed her, leaving in their wake trembling, sated wonder.

He resumed his sensual strokes, rocking her, gathering her to him. An intense pleasure spiraled in waves from her very core. She felt him tense. Heard him moan. Heat enveloped heat, sweeping over her like a raging fire. His low voice crooned her name over and over.

Soft tears gathered in her eyes as her bones once more took form and shape. Never had anything touched her soul so deeply as Ben moving within her. She was forever changed. Unquestionably his. "It was more beautiful than I ever imagined . . . more—" Her voice broke as she sought a way to express what she felt.

"No words are necessary, 'Chel.'' He stroked her hair, threading his fingers through it as though the strands were silken cords of a beloved harp.

Her entire body blushed at the heated memory of the words he had spoken during their lovemaking.

He caught her in the small of her back, rolling her over with him so that she found herself astride him. An intense exhilaration swept over her as she promised to make the night last forever and hold the dawn at bay.

For Ben to discover all the levels of emotions aroused while holding Rachel in his arms, to appease the insatiable appetite for her touch, was as surprising as the realization that she'd freed him from whatever remnants of love he held for Joanna. He was in love with Rachel, undeniably . . . completely.

Suddenly he wanted to take back every second he'd lost

since she'd arrived. Wasted moments that could have been spent loving Rachel.

Through hooded eyes he studied the beauty of her softly sloped shoulders, the firm lift of her breasts and their rose-colored tips, the soft plane of her abdomen that would look even more beautiful rounded with his child. He watched her study him, her lips curving into a smile that made every muscle in his body harden.

"Again?" she whispered, her hair fanning his chest as she bent over him.

His mouth possessed hers in a kiss that was teeming with as yet unexpressed emotions, wanting her to know that their previous lovemaking had been inflamed by unbridled passion. But this time, this very special time, he wanted simply to make love to her. Carefully. Tenderly.

Her fingers trailed across his chest, teasing his nipples into hardened pebbles. A groan escaped him as her head slipped lower and her lips sucked the sensitive peak that strained to please her. Desire blazed through him.

Only when she sheathed him in her most intimate warmth did his gentle intentions falter. His eyes widened when her hands cupped the curve of his hips to draw him in deeper. Her lusty undulations infused such an intense heat, there was only one way to cool his ardor. He gripped her hips and met her thrust for thrust, sensing something almost desperate in her fervor. Sensing good-bye.

Rachel awoke to find herself wrapped in his arms, her leg threaded through his and her hand possessively laying across his hip. She stirred and glanced at Ben, finding him still asleep. Allowing her hand to play along the curve of his ribs, she saw his skin ripple beneath her touch.

At that instant she understood many things she'd wondered all her life—what kind of love made people kill for it, what kind of love made women stay with men who were not the best of husbands, what kind of love made a man patient enough to wait for it seven years. It all had something to do with the wonder of what she had just experienced with Ben.

Yet, through last night's whispered endearments, through all the ecstasy they shared, he'd never once said he loved her. A part of him still hung on to the dream that was Joanna.

And because Rachel finally understood what loving someone truly meant, she had to love Ben enough to let him go.

❖ 26 ❖

Rachel stared down at Ben as he slept, torn between wishing her summer in Valiant had never happened and cherishing even the briefest hours she'd spent in his arms. Leaving seemed more than she could endure, yet she knew she must. To stay without his love was to cheat him far worse than any bargain she and Joanna had made.

She brushed back the wisp of hair that hung over his brow, careful not to touch him again for fear of waking him.

Perhaps she was taking the coward's way out, leaving without saying good-bye, but she wasn't sure she could speak the words while he looked at her.

"Good-bye," she whispered, blinking back the tears that blurred the last image of him she would take with her. A glance at his room, the beloved blue chambray shirt lying atop the pile of clothes he'd shed in a fervor, the imprint of her head that remained upon the pillow next to his, brought silent farewells bidden from her eyes and her heart.

Every step leading her away from him and downstairs seemed a bridge burned forever. Rachel entered the boys' room and studied their sleeping faces, willing each treasured moment spent with them to a secret place within her heart.

"You are and will ever be my beloved sons," she whispered, unable to leave without pressing a kiss gently against each forehead. Had her parents felt this way when they parted—as if their souls were being ripped asunder? "I love you both with all my heart."

Rachel backed away, fearing her tears might spill and dampen their faces, awakening them.

"Woooff!" Bowie snuffled, raising his head to triangle the sheets he slept under.

Jimmy patted the dog that provided a living bunting board to separate the two boys, then rolled over and mumbled something incoherent.

Samuel yawned, his dark eyes opening slightly. "You going somewhere?"

A finger instantly rose to her lips as she hushed him. "Don't wake Jim and your father." Not wanting to lie to him, she searched for the right words to say, finally opting for a half-truth. "I'm going into town this morning."

His eyes widened further, but he obeyed her request to whisper. "You don't have to cry, Miss Rachel. Everybody likes you now. Some of 'em told me so. Said my mama was spice, but you're pure sugar."

Unconsciously brushing back a tear, Rachel smiled to ease the boy's concern. "Oh, I know that, Sam. I'm not crying for that reason."

"Then why are you?"

A thousand explanations raced to mind, but only one said it all. "Because I love you, Sam. I love you and Jimmy and Bowie. Most of all, I love Ben. Knowing that touches my heart and makes me cry. These are good tears."

"Are you going to take the train this morning?" Sam sat up and hung his feet over the bed. "I seen your ticket."

He knew. As did Ben. She would have to find another way out of Valiant. Rachel bent and met him eye to eye. "No, I'm not."

Relief softened the lines that furrowed his forehead. "Good. I don't want you to leave me, Miss Rachel. My mama left me. And Miz Narcissia and Mr. Thadeus went away too. I thought maybe I was doing something that made everybody not wanna be around me."

She crushed him to her as her heart clenched so hard she thought it might burst. His small arms wrapped around her neck as his head lay upon her shoulder. She breathed in the scent that was all boy, imprinting his touch to memory for the childless days to come.

Pulling back to stare into his eyes once more, she silently pleaded with him to understand, to forgive her. "Sam, it's not you everyone leaves behind. It's circumstances"—she searched for better words—"situations. Fear we—they—can't get rid of. They're afraid that if they stay, maybe they'll have to face themselves and won't like what they see."

Puzzlement filled his expression. "I don't understand."

"I don't much either," Rachel admitted, asking herself if she was offering this advice to the boy or to herself. "Now, you go on back to sleep."

"If you see Aly, will you tell her I said thanks for the chicken? It made me feel lots better."

She felt his brow and was glad to find it free of fever. "I'll make a point of telling her."

Alewine! Bless his heart! Sam had given her the perfect answer to her dilemma. Aly owed her a favor. Time to call it in.

"That's about the dadgumdernest nonsense I ever heard!" Alewine checked to make sure the cargo in the back of the freight wagon was secured. She jumped down from the wagon bed, raising dust as the soles of her boots connected with the hard-packed roadway.

"I ain't"—she pointed a finger at Rachel's face—"gonna

haul you to no Clarendon. No sirree, not me. You can jist ask somebody else. I ain't gonna sit here and watch my best friend look like a dog what lost his best bone. He's already spent too dadgummany years pining over that sister of sin you called a boss. Ben's only just now got hisself back any lick of sense he ever had. If you leave, he's gonna go plumb rickety again. And I ain't gonna be no part of it.''

"It's better this way, Aly." The words didn't even convince herself, how did she expect to persuade Alewine? "You . . . the whole town, for that matter . . . can make him believe I was a liar and a user from the very beginning.''

Alewine moved past her, checking the riggings of the six-horse team. "Won't work. The whole town thinks you're some kinda saint now 'cause of what you done at the lake.''

Rachel's thoughts raced back to the episode, trying to determine what she'd done that met with such approval. Understanding eluded her.

"You know. When you dove in and tried to save that boy?'' Aly stroked each horse, thanking them for the job they were about to do. When she finished encouraging the team, she returned her attention to Rachel. "People 'round here put a lotta stock in courage like that. Some of us think a body who's willing to put her own life in danger to save a child's is—well, all I can say is how I feel about it—I think you're pretty dadgummed good people. Valiant wants that kind of gal to call us home.'' She climbed into the driver's box and grabbed the reins, staring down at Rachel. "No, you won't get the townsfolk to bad-mouth you anymore for what happened. They're willing to give you a second chance now.''

"You leave me no choice.'' Rachel reached out and grabbed the reins. "You cannot go without me.''

Golden eyes narrowed as Alewine glanced first at Rachel's grip, then directly at her. "Rachel, we're friends and I'd like to stay that way. But I don't take kindly to anybody telling me what I am and I ain't gonna do. Now, you best let go of them reins and get on down to the depot. If you don't, I give you my word you'll wish you had of."

"That's just it, Aly. You *did* give me your word." Rachel let go of the reins and ran with the opportunity the freighter had given her. "And I'm calling it in."

"You're calling in what? I ain't never give you my word except when—" Realization dawned, causing Alewine to slap her thigh in exasperation. "Ain't gonna do it! That ain't no fair, Rachel Sloan. You done flamboozled me!"

The horses startled at their driver's tone and pranced nervously.

"Easy, boys. Eeeasy," Alewine crooned, calling each by name. She gripped the reins carefully, keeping her attention focused on the team while directing her anger at Rachel. "Don't make this mistake, Rachel. And don't force me to be the one to help you make it. Running away ain't much of an answer. And believe me, I've asked the question personally."

"You promised, Aly. You said if there was ever *anything* you could do to repay me. Now I'm asking . . . no, I'm demanding. Give me a ride out of Valiant." She handed her the train ticket. "Take this and have it refunded. It's worth more than your charge."

Rachel wished there were another way to leave, but she didn't have time to plead with anyone else, and Alewine was headed to Clarendon. When Ben woke up, he'd try to make her go back with him. But she couldn't return. The words she'd told Jimmy rose to haunt her. Ben *wasn't* the kind of man to take back his love once given. And she refused to be a substitute for Joanna in his life or in his bed. She loved him far too much.

Knowing Ben would assume she caught the train, she

could hitch a ride east with Alewine and be far enough away before the method of transportation she used and the route taken dawned on him. Alewine was her only hope.

Alewine jumped down from the wagon and sauntered over to where Rachel had hitched Crockett to a post outside the freight office.

"What are you doing?" Rachel asked warily. The woman was capable of anything.

"Tying off his reins so he can head home. Like Ben did on the night y'all were caught out in the rain." She completed the task, then gave the horse a swat on the rump and an order to go home.

"Does this mean you'll let me go with you?" Rachel stared at the angry set of Aly's chin. She looked mad enough to peel the hide off an armadillo.

"I gave you my word." Alewine walked past her and reseated herself. She thumbed backward. "Put that bag in the back. Good thing you're traveling light. Not much room for anything else back there. Got it packed tight."

"I left everything at Ben's," she said, taking out a handful of letters bound in ribbon, then stuffing the carpetbag in the small space between two sacks of flour. "Could we make one stop before we go?"

"Dadgum if you ain't the bossiest Virginian I ever met." She waited until Rachel took a seat beside her, then flicked the team into motion. "I'll stop one, and I mean one, place. You best get all your doings done. Ain't nothing between here and Clarendon but a bunch of mesquite and sage."

"Not for that reason!" Rachel blushed. "I need to drop these letters off at Ophelia's and ask her to give them to Ben."

"Those the ones he wrote Joanna?"

Rachel's fingers traced the ribbon that bound the letters. "No, these are letters I wrote him and never mailed," she said softly. "I pretended that I was Joanna and answered each one. It didn't seem right that she never responded to them. Since I was hired to be her substitute, I needed to do it in every way. At the time it seemed wise to practice her handwriting in case the need ever arose. So I kept myself busy on the journey out here by answering the letters. I've tried to throw them away at least a dozen times, but something told me not to. Now I know why. Ben should have them. If he believes she wrote them, perhaps he won't grieve so much."

The wagon swung in a wide arc toward the saloon. Anger no longer clouded Aly's face. "He'll grieve all right. But no amount of letters'll keep him warm in a world that can be a mighty cold and lonely place sometimes."

Rachel turned around on the driver's box and looked at Main Street and the feeling of home that engulfed her. She fought back tears as she closed her eyes to the sight for the last time.

Cold and lonely? That couldn't begin to describe the place where she was headed. Anywhere without Ben would become the outskirts of hell.

❖ 27 ❖

BEN SNUGGLED DEEP into the covers, his nostrils flaring at the scent that emanated from the bedding. A blend of fragrances that had become the way he thought of Rachel—part danger, incredible desire, and undeniably his destiny. Still sleepy from the long night they'd shared, he wanted nothing more than to shut his eyes and savor the memories evoked by their lovemaking. But the day beckoned and, with it, work.

He stared at the pillow adjacent to his own, splaying his palm over it and smoothing it as if it were Rachel's skin. Indented from the pressure of their ardent kisses, he smiled and remembered the joy he'd experienced discovering the many ways he loved her. Having her wake up next to him each morning would become a sight worth seeing. *Every* morning. For the rest of his and Rachel's lives.

Threading his hands beneath his head, he stared up at the ceiling and dreamed of those days to come and the nights that would precede them.

"Pa, wake up! Hurry!"

Jimmy's tone alerted him far more than the boy's words. His heart took on a rapid beat as he scrambled from the bed and quickly dressed.

The boy pounded on Ben's door. "She's gone, Pa. Rachel's gone. Sam and Bowie too."

Ben flung the door open. "Do you know if they all went together?"

"No." He brushed his hair out of his eyes. "Sam lit out of here on Crockett a few minutes ago. Bowie tried to stop him. Rachel must've taken Crock earlier, 'cause his reins were tied up like you showed me to do when I wanted to send him home without me. I yelled at him not to go without us, but Bug Bait wouldn't listen, Pa. He's gonna get hurt. Crock's too powerful for him."

"Saddle two horses. I'll look around for a minute and see if she left a note."

"Yessir." Jimmy spun on one heel and started out of the room. Then he turned around just as quickly and demanded, "Pa, don't let Rachel leave us. Me and Sam love her too much, and she needs us. You too."

"I won't, Jim. I promise you that."

Ben searched her room and discovered that she'd taken only her carpetbag. No note offered explanation. No indication of where she'd gone. No hope that they might be overreacting.

His mind raced through the haven of hours spent with Rachel in his arms. In spite of her deception, she'd become the only woman who had ever broken the wall he'd built around himself for protection. She was the only woman who had made him quit criticizing himself for what he wasn't, and be proud of who he was. She was the only woman he'd ever truly loved.

Just as Rachel had taught him his own self-worth, she needed to know that the obsession he had for Joanna would never compare to the true love that burned for Rachel in his heart.

* * *

A mile outside of Valiant, Ben and Jimmy caught up with Sam. Bowie's barking guided them in. Crockett was grazing and wouldn't move no matter how much the six-year-old prodded the horse's flanks with his boot heels.

Ben reined to a halt alongside him. "Having trouble there, son?"

The child crossed his hands over the saddle horn and let out a string of curse words that would have turned a blue norther pink.

"Where in this side of the territory did you hear such language, Samuel Benjamin Tharp!"

Jimmy made the mistake of snickering.

"I suppose you taught him that?" Ben glared at his oldest son.

"Did not. I made it up all by myself." Sam frowned at Ben, then realized who he'd argued with. A gulp started at his eyebrows, swept down his face, and bobbed his Adam's apple until it sunk to the base of his throat. "Uhhh . . . sorry, Papa Ben."

"You can save explanations for later. Right now we've got to find Rachel."

Ben plucked Sam from his saddle and settled the child in front of him. "Jim, you grab Crockett and bring him into town with you. Rachel can ride him home. Sam and I'll go on in and see if she's at the depot."

"The eight forty-five's never late. She'll leave before we get there."

"Maybe not, if we ride hard."

They made it with two minutes to spare. The engineer was none too pleased when Ben demanded that departure be held up while he and the boys checked every car for sign of Rachel.

Passengers stared in curiosity as he made his way down

the aisle, quickly surveying every female face. Though Ben checked thoroughly, Sam and Jim followed behind to make sure she wasn't overlooked or hadn't disguised herself. Bowie sniffed every hemline. Soon only one car remained.

Ben spied the politician sitting next to one of the windows, staring out as if he'd lost his last friend. Suspicion consumed Ben. Had Whipple anything to do with Rachel's disappearance?

"What are you doing here, Whipple?" he demanded. "Why the sudden interest in heading east?"

Obsidian eyes glared back at the dog. "Getting the hell out of this town, that's what."

Unable to resist the temptation to deepen his daggered words, Ben asked, "Matilda finally throw you out?"

Whipple straightened his cravat and cleared his throat, speaking loud enough for all to hear. "I'm leaving Valiant for an extended visit back East."

"Visit as long as you like." Ben didn't mince any words, glad Valiant would at last be rid of its least-favored citizen. Not wanting to waste any more time, he told Jim to go check with Aly and Ophelia. "See if Rachel left town another way."

"Aly's off to Clarendon this morning, remember? I'll ask if Miss Ophelia's seen her."

By the time they'd gone through the last car, Sam's face was crestfallen. Ben stepped off the train and helped the boy down. He hailed the engineer. "Sorry to keep you waiting, Stampede. She's not there."

As the engine built up steam, Sam yelled to be heard. "Why do you think she left us, Papa Ben? She liked it here. She told me so."

"Because"—Ben grappled for words as elusive as the smoke rising from the engine's stack—"I treated her just like someone else treated me . . . and it was wrong." He'd been so caught up in his own wants and needs that he'd forgotten to tell Rachel the one thing she desired, the one thing she most needed, to hear. That he loved her, and had never loved Joanna. To hell with whether or not she stayed. Rachel had a right to know how he felt about her, and he had a right to tell her.

"Then catch her and tell her you're sorry." Sam pulled on Ben's pants leg and stared up at him. "Like you make me and Jim do."

"I will if she comes home." Chasing her was the last thing he needed to do, Ben realized. "We need to open the store. It's getting late."

Rachel made him understand that moving to Richmond to court Joanna would have been shallow and weak. Staying in Valiant and accepting his own worth was the only way to make himself the kind of man Rachel Sloan would want. The kind of man who needed to learn that love couldn't be bought. The kind of man she might marry.

Finally understanding the difference, all he could do now was trust in the power of the love he had for Rachel, and the same he believed she held for him. He'd be there when she returned.

"But, Papa Ben, she'll go away forever and ever like Mama."

"No." Ben took his son by the hand. "Never like your mother." They walked past the boardinghouse and waved to Miss Abernathy. "Rachel *will* come back to us."

"You closed up already?" the woman asked, sweeping the dust from her porch. "Thought you were going to wait till September to sell out."

"I'm not selling, Miss Abernathy. In fact, I'm not ever leaving Valiant if I can help it. Come on by the store, and we'll extend that credit you asked for a while back."

"Sure to goodness?" Relief made her look years younger. "Everyone will be glad to hear it."

He glanced over at the saloon. "Speaking of which, Sam, would you run on over to Ophelia's and see what's keeping Jim? Tell her I need to talk to her. She'll be madder than a rattler if I don't tell her what's on my mind so she can get it spread around."

The boy took off at a run toward the batwing doors that gave entry to the Lazy Lady.

"Tell Banj to make you one of his hoecakes, and I'll settle up with him later!" he shouted. "In fact, make a whole panful and bring them over. I've got a feeling it's going to be a long day and lots longer before we have time to eat."

Passing several more townsfolk on the way to work, Ben informed them of the same opportunity he'd given Mrs. Abernathy. When he reached the mercantile, a mule skinner from Mobeetie waited atop his wagon.

"How do, Ben. Didja sleep in today?"

"No, just needed to open my eyes a little better before I got started, Dudley." Ben bit back a smile when the mule skinner scratched his head as if he could dig out a layer of understanding from beneath his hat brim. "How's business?"

"Not as good as yours looks."

Ben followed the direction of the man's gaze. When he turned around and looked behind him, the line of people waiting for the credit he'd promised to extend was backed up almost to the depot. This was not good. Ophelia was going to be one outscooped, outraged gossip when she learned about this!

"Why wasn't I told about this?" Ophelia shouldered her way through the crowd that led from the store's entrance to the counter behind which Ben stood.

"Now, 'Phele, I tried . . . honestly. But word of mouth

spreads quickly." *As you well know,* he thought, but decided not to tempt fate by speaking it.

"I'd like to talk to you somewhere private." She glared at everyone who pushed from behind. "That is, if there is such a place in here." She held up a group of letters tied with a ribbon. "You need to read these."

Ben glanced up from his ledgers. "What are they?"

"Answers to the letters you wrote Joanna."

She'd written? After all those years she'd actually written something more than a holiday greeting, a birthday message? Just enough to keep him hoping. How many nights had he tortured himself wondering why he continued to care, when she apparently hadn't? How many hours had he spent writing page after page, wondering if she even read them? How long had Ophelia kept them from him . . . and why?

Suddenly, it didn't matter what those letters said. It didn't matter that he'd never know how she really felt about his devotion to his dream. It mattered only that he was free of her and free of needing her confirmation about everything in his life.

"You keep them," he told Ophelia. "They'll probably make for some interesting discussions."

Ophelia tapped her cheek with the bundle. "Oh, they do, believe me. But the most interesting part is who wrote them."

She was baiting him. Her wolf-gray eyes had a predatory look about them. "All right, I'll bite. Who wrote them?"

"Rachel."

Ben snatched them from her hand as if they were the Holy Grail and she a heathen. "Take over for me, Ophelia. I need to go in the back."

Ophelia's brows rose so high, it looked as if they were flounces sewed at the bottom of the curls that dangled over her forehead. "What happened to please and thank you?"

"Please, Ophelia." He moved around the counter and tapped her nose affectionately. "And thank you for not lying about reading what isn't any of your business."

She straightened her shirtwaist and glanced at those customers next to her, lifting her chin haughtily. "My pleasure entirely."

Ben excused himself from the crowd and escaped into the curtained-off area where he kept animal feed, chickens, and other livestock that was often traded for goods.

He sat on top of one of the bags and untied the ribbon from around the collection of letters. After unfolding the three pages of parchment, he wondered if Ophelia had played a trick on him and for what purpose. The handwriting was Joanna's . . . or was it?

Upon closer examination, he realized the script was not Joanna Tharp's but someone who'd imitated her handwriting quite successfully. If he hadn't saved everything she'd ever written and studied it over and over throughout the years, this would have fooled him completely.

He read the letter slowly, wondering if the words themselves were her own or merely copied.

Dearest Ben,

I received your Christmas letter. I, too, feel overwhelmingly sad that I cannot be with you to enjoy the festivities and the caroling.

Ophelia sounds like someone who has a good heart, no matter how she tries to hide it. Paying for the entire church supper must have set her back a pretty penny, but giving each child a gold piece seems extremely generous.

The people of Valiant sound as if they know what home and family truly mean, and isn't that what Christmas is all about?

I wish I could cross these miles that separate us and

start all over. Wouldn't it be fun to pretend we were strangers, pretend we knew nothing of one another, and spend the time getting to know each other?

You're right, you know. It's really hard to see husbands and wives sharing adoring glances, holding hands, enveloped in the warmth of Christmas. A yearning fills me each time I spy a child's expression of wonder and know I'm missing a very special magic in my life. A magic stronger than Christmas, strong enough to wipe away the loneliness that seems even greater this time of year.

I began to wonder if everyone harbored some secret that couldn't be shared with me, until you expressed those same feelings in your letter.

Which makes me wonder if there are others like us. Do we choose this loneliness ourselves, or are we half a soul waiting to complete itself?

Now, see what I've done? I've revealed a side to myself you might not recognize. But I doubt you would recognize this Joanna Tharp I've become. I'm not the girl who left Valiant. I've changed, Ben. Changes that may be too big a gap for us to ever bridge together.

I read all about your many accomplishments and I imagine how proud everyone is to call you friend. But beneath it all I wonder how proud you are of yourself? Is what you do for yourself or for me? Are you happy with what you do, or is it merely a commitment you've made?

Just a piece of advice from an old friend. Take it or tear this up. Consider it a belated Christmas gift if you will. Live every moment as it happens. Don't wait for life, Ben. Fill your life with wonder.

May the New Year bring you great peace and that special someone you deserve.

Joanna

Ben folded the pages and slowly tied the ribbon as if he were sealing away the past. "It did bring me that someone, Rachel Sloan. It brought me you."

It was then he noticed the silence in the next room. Gone was the chatter of visiting neighbors, Ophelia's bossy commands, the heat of too many bodies pressed together.

He swept back the curtain that divided the feed storage from the main storeroom. Empty. Everyone had disappeared!

✦ 28 ✦

"ALY, STOP!"

"Again? I told you all that's out here is a bunch of sage and—"

"I'm going back. I need you to turn around."

"Woman, I done turned around twice already and you keep changing that switch-trail mind of yours. If I turn around this time, it better be for good. Got to get this here load delivered sometime before winter sets in."

"This is for good. I promise."

Though Alewine attempted to look angry, Rachel noticed the buckskinned woman's shoulders straightened, her face brightened with a smile, and she seemed pleased.

"What made you change your mind, Virginian?"

"Because I couldn't be like Joanna. I can't leave Ben wondering for years if I'll ever return. He deserves better than that. I don't know what he'll say, Aly, when I tell him how I feel about him, but I can't leave without doing so. And I have to know what he feels for me. I don't want to live my life not knowing. Guessing. Wishing. It won't be easy to listen if he doesn't say what I want to hear, but at least I won't put both of us through years of wondering what might have been."

She sat up straight, strengthening herself with purpose. "I won't take the coward's way out like Joanna did."

"The coward's way?" Aly averted her attention from the road and stared at Rachel. "You're more right than you can ever imagine."

Curiosity swept through Rachel. Aly seemed to be talking of more than Joanna. But just as Rachel was about to ask the frontierswoman to trust her and tell her what was on her mind, she heard a dog bark. The horizon suddenly swarmed with buggies, surreys, and wagons filled with people.

Jimmy rode Crockett, galloping alongside the gambler's horse. Bowie followed. The trio led the horde of townsfolk toward Aly's wagon. Ophelia rode a magnificent Arabian that stood at least sixteen hands high. White as snowflakes, the Arabian paled every other horse in comparison.

Gwenella Duncan and Alizabeth Bentley were among the group. Belle O'Connor waved from her father's wagon, setting off a chain of similar gestures from so many others that it seemed the whole countryside rippled with welcome.

Aly halted the team. Jimmy reined up alongside Rachel. He jerked down his hat and held it over his heart, while Nicodemus halted on the other side of the wagon, eliciting a glare from Alewine. The rest of the townsfolk formed a semicircle in front of the wagon, blocking their way.

A hush fell over the crowd. Anticipation scented the air. Rachel fidgeted on the driver's box, glancing at Aly to see how she felt about the circumstances. Rachel noticed the frontierswoman had eased the shotgun from under her feet and it now lay in her lap.

Aly's mouth slanted to one side as she warned, "Looks like a rope party to me. I'm good with a gun, but can't get a bead on all of 'em. It's been nice knowing you, gal."

"Put down that shooter," Ophelia demanded. "We aren't

out to hang nobody. You've been reading too many dime novels for your own good. What we are here for is to ask—''

Jimmy held his hand up to hush her. An ermine-colored brow arched, but the saloonkeeper conceded to the boy.

"Miss Rachel, please don't leave us." His voice started out as a squeak then grew bolder. "I never knew my ma. You're the only one I've ever really had, that I can remember." His voice trembled. "You mean a lot to me now, and I'd like you to stay. I—that is—we all want you to come back home with us." He motioned to the crowd. "I'll even try to get along with Sam better, if it'll make you come back."

A quick survey of the sea of faces failed to pinpoint the one face she'd hoped was there. Though disappointed, she refused to let his absence keep her from doing what she knew in her heart was right. Ben was a proud man. A trait she loved about him. He'd have to learn that she could be just as obstinate as he could. Rachel smiled. "Can I borrow somebody's horse? Aly has a load to deliver."

"You mean you'll stay?" Jimmy's face lit with hope as he dismounted. Bowie started barking and wagging his tail.

Rachel descended from the wagon, opening her arms to welcome the boy into her embrace. The hug that followed brought a joy she would look forward to no matter how old Jimmy became. "I will as long as I have unfinished business in Valiant."

"Use my horse, Miss Sloan. I'll give Alewine some company." Nicodemus Turner took the vacant place alongside Aly, dodging as the buckskinned woman swung a fist out to unseat him.

"Company ain't what you got in mind to give me, you petticoat-watching polecat!" she shouted. When the fist failed to connect, she yelled "Hyah!" startling the team into action. "Stand clear!"

The momentum sent the gambler tumbling backward over the driver's box. He landed atop the sacks of flour. Buggies and surreys jolted out of the way. The Tight Shoe Troupe shrieked. Bowie barked and chased everyone. Clementine and Ophelia laughed. Men cheered Nicodemus on as he regained his balance and started inching toward the hell-raising driver. Alewine glanced back over her shoulder and cursed. The team raced to the left, then right, then left again. Nicodemus looked like a pest Aly was trying to sling off.

Rachel stared after the furious freighter, wondering what possessed the pair.

"Now, that ought to be an interesting courtship, wouldn't you say?" Ophelia's yellow-gray eyes glinted with possibility. "Two of the biggest scoundrels this side of the Red River. I got a feeling they're gonna give me lots to talk about, don't you?"

Aly and Nicodemus Turner? Rachel watched the cantankerous couple disappear over the horizon. Who would have thought a rascal and a rogue were meant for each other?

But then, how much more unlikely was the hope that Ben might actually love her and was just too proud to say it?

"What's going on?" Rachel had to rein in the horse several buildings away from the general store. A line extended from Ben's business down as far as the livery. Her blood pumped faster. Fear rose in her throat, making her swallow back the metallic taste. "Is something wrong with Ben?"

Brother Ethan waved her forward. "Come on, child, we'll let you through. Everyone, she's here. Make way for Rachel and Jim."

Bewildered, Rachel glanced at the faces she passed and saw only smiles. They wouldn't be so happy, would they, if anything was wrong? "Ben's all right?"

The minister nodded. "He will be when he gets a look at you."

Ophelia used the backwash of consideration extended Rachel to make her way through the crowd as well. When someone complained or attempted to block her path, she gave the daredevil a tap with her cane.

The line seemed endless. As endless as the many reasons Rachel feared might prevent her and Ben from sharing their lives. But she couldn't leave Valiant without giving credence to those fears or ridding herself of them forever.

She spotted his blond head bent over the ledger, writing furiously. "Ben?" His name unconsciously rushed from her lips.

He looked up, moving around the counter. "Have you come home to stay?"

"We have a lot to talk about before I can do that." She crossed her arms as though they offered protection.

He gently grabbed her shoulders and held her at arm's length. "There's something you need to know first."

The crowd leaned in to listen. Ben pulled her closer, his breath fanning her earlobe. It seemed her whole world wobbled, and Rachel had to shift to the other foot to regain a sense of balance.

"We'll tell Jimmy later when Sam's not around," he whispered so no one but she could hear. "Joanna and I were never intimate, 'Chel, but I am Sam's father. She discovered the man she was spending her nights with was married and—"

"Whipple?" she interrupted, realizing she'd spoken the name aloud. It would explain why the politician feared her enough to write those letters.

"Yes." Ben confirmed her suspicion. "On the night she left Valiant, I swore I'd be a father to her child, whether or not she ever returned to me."

Rachel moved back and studied his beloved face. How very lucky she was to love such a good-hearted man. A man who would spare Joanna embarrassment even now. Her finger traced his lips lovingly as she whispered, "Ben, I need only one thing to make these children my own and Valiant the home I've longed for all my life."

He kissed first one finger, then another and another. To her surprise, his voice rang deep and rich so all could hear.

"I love you today, tomorrow, and every day of forever, Rachel Sloan."

"As I love you, Ben. From the first day I met you."

He pulled the letters from his pocket and smiled. "I think maybe a lot longer than that."

His kiss brought an inexplicable knowing that her search was over and, at last, she knew exactly where she belonged. *"Home,"* she sighed, the word echoing from her heart and exiting in the very breath she shared with him.

Four smaller arms encircled their waists, binding them as a family. Bowie slobbered on Rachel's hem, wagging his tail. Shouts of congratulation rang through the building, echoing out into the street. Blinking back tears, Rachel glanced down to see why Samuel tugged on Ben's shirt.

Obsidian eyes rounded with need. "Do you think you'll ever send us away, Papa Ben?"

"We want you and Rachel to raise us." Jimmy added his own plea to Sam's. "Both of you."

"I'll never let you go, sons." Ben's gaze swept over both boys and finally focused on Rachel. As he lowered his lips once more to seal their fate, he whispered, "You're all the keeping kind."

DeWanna Pace enjoys hearing from readers.
To her, you're all the keeping kind.

DeWanna Pace
c/o The Berkley Publishing Group
200 Madison Avenue
New York, New York 10016

Our Town

...where love is always right around the corner!

_**Harbor Lights** by Linda Kreisel

           0-515-11899-0/$5.99

On Maryland's Silchester Island...the perfect summer holiday sparks a perfect summer fling.

_**Humble Pie** by Deborah Lawrence

           0-515-11900-8/$5.99

In Moose Gulch, Montana...a waitress with a secret meets a stranger with a heart.

_**Candy Kiss** by Ginny Aiken

           0-515-11941-5/$5.99

In Everleigh, Pennsylvania...a sweet country girl finds the love of a city lawyer with kisses sweeter than candy.

_**Cedar Creek** by Willa Hix

           0-515-11958-X/$5.99

In Cedarburg, Wisconsin...a young widow falls in love with the local saloon owner, but she has promised her hand to a family friend—and she has to keep her word.

_**Sugar and Spice** by DeWanna Pace

           0-515-11970-9/$5.99

In Valiant, Texas...an eligible bachelor pines for his first love.

ROMANCE FROM THE HEART OF AMERICA
Homespun Romance

Homespun novels are touching, captivating romances from the heartland of America that combine the laughter and tears of family life with the tender warmth of true love.

_FOR PETE'S SAKE 0-515-11863-X/$5.99
by Debra Cowan

_HOME AGAIN 0-515-11881-8/$5.99
by Linda Shertzer

_A CHERISHED REWARD 0-515-11897-4/$5.99
by Rachelle Nelson

_TUMBLEWEED HEART 0-515-11944-X/$5.99
by Tess Farraday

_TOWN SOCIAL 0-515-11971-7/$5.99
by Trana Mae Simmons

_LADY'S CHOICE 0-515-11959-8/$5.99
by Karen Lockwood

_HOME TO STAY 0-515-11986-5/$5.99
by Linda Shertzer

Coming in December 1996